MY SUMMER
OF
KATHY

MY SUMMER OF OF KATHY

Sometimes a little catastrophe

can make you grow

R.C. DAVIS

Copyright © 2025 R.C. Davis

All right reserved

ISBN-979-8-9927155-0-7

My Summer Of Kathy is a work of fiction. Although its form is that of a memoir; it is not one. Any resemblance to actual events or persons, living or dead, is purely coincidental. 1973, however, was very real, and so was the beloved music of the time. It was the wish of the story's protagonist to bring it to you, so you too may search it out and perhaps experience some of the best musical artists of the time. Please keep in mind, though, most of the opinions expressed are those of the characters and should not be confused with the authors.

.

Dedication

This story is dedicated to all of the real Kathy's in my life who were willing to give me the time of day, teaching me the ways of the world without the slightest inkling that they were.

Chapter 1

<u>Good Vibrations</u>

It was the second Saturday of May, 1973. I was glad the weekend had finally gotten here, but I knew it wasn't going to be a normal one. I could just feel it. Some kind of a weird vibe had been eating at me since the second I opened my eyes. Something was going to happen and there was nothing I could do about it. It had me wishing I were psychic, least that way I could see what was coming. With summer vacation only two weeks off, I was in a really good mood and didn't want anything to wreck it.

I promised Ernie B that I'd show up to do a little work down in his lawnmower shop. The weird vibe stuck with me the whole time I was there. My morning rolled into four long hours of aggravation. I secretly changed the radio station on his greasy, white Motorola and found the Beach Boys singing, 'Good Vibrations' The old guy never seemed to notice it wasn't Perry Como belting out 'Papa Loves Mambo' and was I glad for that. Ol' Ernie complained about everything, the protesters that didn't like the Vietnam war, the cost of gasoline going from thirty-five to forty-five cents, the town council, but worst of all—my hair. The good side of that was, he always let me sass back, and he never really got mad.

"Why don't you get that cut? Hell, I'll pay for it myself if you'll just go up and see ol' Starkey. He'll do a decent job. You get your hair caught in a machine and… well… it'll rip it right off!"

"Don't worry about it, I'll be careful."

"You? Careful? Yeah, right. Hey, Cos, you know something, people around here just don't wear their hair that long."

"Ah hell, Ernie, I think you're just jealous cause you can't get yours to grow. You know… the first president of America had long hair, and so did that Ben Franklin guy."

"Yeah, well, they're all dead now. Probably from getting their hair ripped off."

My family had been in Iowa for nearly five years. I've known Ernie B for maybe two of those. It was long enough for me to sort out when he was teasing and when he wasn't. I played the 'ignoring game' and we got along just fine. The problem was, Ernie B might just have been right. I wanted to make sure that losing my hair wasn't what that weird vibe was all about. When he wasn't looking, I put it in a ponytail and shoved it under the collar of my official 'Ernie B's Lawnmower Shop' work shirt.

What people need to understand about my hair is, it's like a symbol of freedom to me. Ever since I was five years old, my da forced me to get my head shaved at least once a week and trying to get out of it had always given him the reason that he was looking for to beat the crap out of me. Those thrashings only got worse over time because I refused to scream or cry. That's what he really wanted; to hear me howl. After a while I learned to take it no matter how much it hurt.

The long hair idea started last year in March. It was just after my fifteenth birthday that my older sister, Fiana, bet me her new Pink Floyd album that I wouldn't go against our da and grow it as long as hers. Getting it down to the middle of my back was going to be difficult, though, but I took her up on it, anyway. The problem with that was, just when I thought I was winning, my da up and disappeared. He just never came home from work one day. The rumor had it he'd run off with some woman on his milk route. To make it worse, he grabbed Fiana, and my little sister, Shauna, after school, and took them too.

I missed my sisters something terrible, but I kept myself busy with school, fishing, and hanging out with the guys. I worked really hard at trying not to think about it. My ma, on the other hand, thought about it all the time. That's all she ever did. It finally got her put in the mental institution. I was sent to live with my aunt and uncle on their farm, which was totally not my thing. I wasn't into getting up at four o'clock in the morning to milk cows or having to sit my arse in an outhouse. I was overjoyed the day ma came home. But that didn't last long.

In less than a week, I realized she wasn't the same ma I used to know. I didn't want to be at home anymore because I couldn't talk to her. She was always going on about how much she missed my da. If she sorted that she'd got my attention, she'd start in bawling her eyes out. That made things a little too uncomfortable for me. My nose would start to numb up as the first sign that I wasn't too far behind her. So, I'd get the hell out of there. There was no way I was going to give in to that. It just wasn't manly.

When I got done at Ernie B's, I came home to change out of my work clothes. After getting into my Levi's and sandals, I scrubbed my hands nearly raw, trying to get the grease off. Then I put on my favorite shirt and buttoned it up on the way out the door. I liked to leave the tails untucked and of course, but my ma had to nag me about it. Since ignoring people was becoming somewhat of a thing with me, I just gave her the Ernie B treatment. I let the screen door slam loud enough to let her know I didn't care what she thought. Stopping on the stoop out front, I rolled up my sleeves and checked out the street. Not much was going on, but it was a small town after all. Seeing some activity up on Main Street, I jumped off the stoop, missing all three steps, and dashed half block to the corner.

My ma and I lived in the old post office. It sat on Fourth Street, which started way down at the railroad tracks, and going past our place, it ran for another eight blocks, straight up to the high school's front door. Main Street ran for about the same distance from up the hill at highway 13, all the way east to the railroad bridge where the tracks curved north.

It was where the two crossed at the center of Clarksburg that I hung out with my friends. Everyone called it the town square. If a guy were smart and wanted to know what was going on around town, that's where they'd spend at least a few minutes of their day.

Steve and Brian were already there having a contest to see who could spit the farthest. I joined in because I was the champion of this little game. The winner would be whoever got their missile to land directly beneath the blinking red light that hung above the center of the intersection. It was a good distance out, so not an easy thing to do.

The sidewalk was raised about a foot above the street on our side which made it the perfect launching pad.

That vibe I'd woken up with was still with me and seemed to be getting stronger. It made me nervous, and I wished whatever it was trying to tell me would just happen so I'd be free of it. Ten minutes later, a pop truck came around the corner down by the bank. The driver must have forgotten to shut a side door and about half a ton of bottled pop crashed out onto the street, wooden crates, and all.

They had to call out the volunteer fire department to wash the glass and soda into the storm sewer. Right after that, someone's car caught fire down Main Street in front of Hale's Hardware. As we stood there watching them dump enough water on it to fill a swimming pool, something my ma said, years back, started running through my brain.

We had been together at our old place out in the country and a car had crashed out front on Highway 13. The sheriff and the ambulance showed up, making all kinds of racket, and not five minutes later, our horse had an epileptic fit, damn near tearing its stall to pieces. My ma said, "Ya know, lad, these things usually happen in threes," and sure enough, not even ten minutes later, my dog, Lee-Pooh, started giving birth to a litter of pups.

Now, I've always wondered if she meant things that were supposed to be good, bad, or, exciting. Because to me, sometimes it was hard to tell the difference. I figured she must have meant exciting. So, since that vibe was hanging on to me like a bloodsucking tick, I found myself wishing the third thing would get around to happening so I could just be done with it.

About eight minutes later, a brand new 1973 Ford Pinto rolled up Main Street from the river bridge. It stood out from the older cars like a single wildflower in a big field of grass. Everything seemed to go into slow motion for me and Brian threw me a weird look when I mumbled, "Got to be it."

The little Ford was a shiny lime green, and there were two girls in the front seat. They looked so much alike they could have been twins. When they got closer, I could see the one driving was a little bit older. So, probably just sisters.

They were having one hell of an argument, but they hushed right up when the car stopped for the intersection. The driver lowered her face down and looked straight at me over the tops of her sunglasses. Our eyes met through that window and it was like I was put under a spell or something. All I saw—was her.

Then she did a strange thing. Tossing her sunglasses on the dashboard, she hit the gas and started driving in a clockwise circle around the intersection. She didn't seem to care about any other cars and every time she passed me, she'd poke her head out, giggle, and holler, "Hi!"

Horns were honking, people were yelling at her and swearing. Every time one of them tried to sneak through that intersection, they had to slam on their brakes because she'd be coming back around. The younger girl was cracking up. One minute she'd be hiding her face in her hands, and the next, she'd be throwing head back and laughing so hard that I could see her face was turning red.

After the third time by, Steve walked over, grinned at me with his huge teeth, and said, "What the hell she doing, Cos? That stupid bitch, she's going to get somebody killed."

Now, you have to understand Steve. He's a moron. Everybody knew he was a moron. Even he knew he was a moron, and if you called him that, he'd just say, "Well... that's just the way I am, ain't nothing I can do about it." I figured he thought that being a moron was okay and because he now had an established identity (something Fiana was always going on about), he didn't want anyone to take it away. We all finally accepted it, as such, and got along just fine.

Another thing about Steve was, he always smelled bad, like he needed a bath. I wanted to tell him he should probably wash his blue jeans once in a while because they were turning green, but I didn't. Steve lived on a farm, so it was kind of expected. He also had the face of a neanderthal with wild, bushy hair. I think the whole school gave him a lot of crap for that. Sometimes I felt sorry for him. I didn't dare say so because Brian, and my other friend, Harry, would start calling me a wuss. A word I had never heard of before I came to Clarksburg. I guess, it's supposed to be a weakling, or something.

"She's checking us out. Oh, fuck me. One of us is going to get laid tonight," Brian said loud enough for everybody on the square to hear.

"Maybe all of us," Steve yelled, snorting, and laughing in a way that always made me think of a donkey.

I wanted to tell him to shut up and do the math. But I got distracted when his comb got caught in his dark, frizzy mop. He jerked it loose and ended up pulling out a patch of hair. We both stood staring at it for a few seconds before we locked eyes, but then he went back to spiffing himself up like it never happened.

Spiffing. It was something he and Brian did when they thought girls had noticed us. I had first-hand knowledge that last-minute spiffing was a waste of time. I had already learned my lesson. One time, a girl noticed me way back in the sixth grade. I wrote her a poem on a little piece of paper and then went to spiffing myself up just after slipping it to her under the desk, kind of like one of those notes we weren't supposed be passing.

My whole world just kind of fell apart after that. She held it up for the whole class to see, saying, "Look, everybody, Cos wrote me a poem." They nearly laughed me out of the room. It took me a long time to get over that. So, spiffing myself up was not something I did. Well… least not in public, anyway.

I watched Brian spitting on his hands and combing his hair back with his fingers. This always grossed me out. I figured if any girl ever saw him doing that, he was screwed; and not the way he wanted to be. There was no way that a girl was going to hang around with a boy who had spit in his hair.

He had a thing for James Dean, and even though his hair was the same color and combed the same way—his face was way too chubby. But that didn't stop him. He always wore the same old red jacket with the collar turned up, a white tee shirt, and kept the cuffs of his Levi's stuck inside a pair of black motorcycle boots. One time he even stole his older brother's uniform dress hat from the army, and turned it into a '50s style motorcycle cap. That was actually a Brando thing, but I didn't want to burst his bubble by telling him. He wore that around for about a week until he couldn't take the teasing anymore.

His favorite thing was to watch, 'Rebel Without a Cause' on the Sunday matinee. He was sure to invite me down to watch it with him whenever it came around. I gave in once, but that was the last time. Afterward, I did everything possible to avoid it. It was when I joked with him and said, "You're just going to have to be a rebel without a Cos, and go watch it by yourself," that he got mad. About a week went by before he stopped ignoring me and we went back to being pals again.

Anyway, when that Pinto finished its fourth lap, that girl stopped right there in the street facing west in the east bound lane. I got my final, "Hi!" and then she just sat there looking at me like I was her favorite food. Her foot must have slipped off the clutch and the little Ford jumped forward, causing her to have to slam on the brakes. The engine sputtered to a stop and backfired. She never took her eyes off me the whole time, staring like I've seen some women look at jewelry. To top off the moment, she said to the other girl, "Get the fuck out! I'll pick you up later."

The younger girl got out and slammed the door so hard, it popped back open. She laughed and yelled, "Piece of crap." Then running off across the street, she clomped up the stairs that led to a place called the Trulla Lodge. It was above Phil's Royal Blue Grocery and took up the whole second floor.

We didn't know much about that place. It was still kind of a mystery. We spent a lot of time making up stuff about it, though. Then we'd try to convince each other that it was fact. Rumor had it that's where old men went to preform secret rituals. Now, a young girl was going up there. All I could think of, was—human sacrifice. I mean, that would require a beautiful virgin, and even though I knew that younger girl fulfilled the beautiful part; I had to assume the other.

"Averell, you slut. I'm gonna get you for that," the driver screamed, and then, even without blinking an eye, she turned back to me and changed into a completely different person. She flipped her hair (something Fiana told me girls do when they're interested), and said so sweetly that it made my teeth hurt, "Why don't you jump in? I'll give you a ride in my new car."

Brian headed toward her, pushing me out of his way, then leaning on the windowsill, he did his best James Dean. In a matter of seconds, Steve was right behind, looking over Brian's shoulder and grinning with those big teeth.

"Which one of us do you mean?" Brian asked, looking back at me, sneering.

"Not you, dummy," she snapped.

He jumped back, almost knocking Steve down. His smirk melted away like a snow cone dropped on a hot summer sidewalk and sticking his hands in his pockets be backed off and just glared. Now, honestly, I was glad. He was trying to steal my chance. What she said to him was pure justice, but then she had to go and dump salt in an open wound by pointing at me and saying, "That cute, little, long-haired boy, there."

At first, I didn't like that. Mostly because I was only five foot-one, and it bugged me when people called me little. But I decided to make her the exception. Brian's face got all red and he looked like he wanted to kill someone. Too bad!

Brian knew the rules. It was every man for himself in this game. I couldn't waste time worrying about his feelings right now. Besides, it seemed like he always got the girl. He'd already had three girlfriends to my zero since the eighth grade. So, I figured, my turn had finally come around.

I watched Steve go to the passenger side of the Pinto like he was going to jump in. I ran over there and bumped him out of the way, before climbing into the front seat. I didn't want to do an Averell, so I pulled the door shut real easy like, getting it to latch the first time without all the drama.

"Got it," I said proudly and threw her a grin.

"Of course, silly, it's a girl car. All you have to do is be nice to her."

She said the last part in a sexy kind of voice, and it gave me a chill. But it was the good kind of chill, not like I was catching the flu or anything. I could smell her now, all bubble bath and patchouli perfume. It felt like one of those times when you finally get to try something that you've been dying to try, but weren't allowed.

As soon as she started the car and put it in gear, Brian yelled out, "You selfish bastard, McDhai! That's right, just leave your best pals stranded on the corner, you…"

I didn't hear the rest because the girl floored the gas pedal, switching back to the right lane just in time to avoid hitting the Rowett's VW bus head-on. We had actually come close enough that I had to fight to keep from screaming and covering my eyes. That would have meant that I was afraid, and I surely didn't want her to know.

"What the hell's his problem? Your friend, I mean. He pissed about something?"

"Oh, Brian? He's always pissed about something. He's just a mad bastard, and maybe, just a little jealous."

I looked back over my shoulder, realizing then that I was too far away to see them. I imagined that after sitting down and lighting up the last of their cigarettes, they started in cussing me. That would be followed by them trying to outdo each other with stories of the evil Irish lad who had come to terrorize the peaceful little town of Clarksburg, Iowa.

Chapter 2

We hadn't even gone a block when she said, "You talk funny."

"Like I haven't heard that before. I think I've had to fight every kid in my class when I first came here because of that. But I learned pretty much to talk like... ummm... you-all, do. That way, people won't make fun of me."

"Well, don't worry, I'm not going to make fun of you. Sooo... where are you from?"

"Oh, uhhh... Ireland. My uncle met a woman from Iowa and married her. He started a dairy farm here and then sent for my da to come help. That was about five years ago, though."

"Really? That's so cool! What part of Ireland?"

"Uhhh... you know... I'm here now, and... I'd rather not talk about it." Turning away, I looked out the window at the river as we passed over the bridge.

"That's all right, I'll get it out of you sooner or later," she said and patted my leg. It startled me and about put me through the roof. A hot flash came over me and I have to admit, I glared at her. It got hard to breathe, and I saw she had noticed. Giggling, she pulled her hand away.

"You okay? You're not scared of me, are you?"

I shrugged and made myself grin. You see, it's not that I didn't like her hand there, it had more to do with the fact that, that had never happened to me before. I mean, someone as beautiful as she, actually touching me, especially since I didn't even know her name yet. She smiled this lovely smile and then put her eyes back on the road. That gave me a chance to look her over while we raced up the hill toward the highway.

Her hair was thin and straight, probably just a wee bit longer than mine, ending about halfway down her back. She parted it in the middle, and it was what my ma had always called, 'strawberry blond' It was trimmed straight across the bottom, so I figured she must love her hair as much as I did mine. She had this button nose like my sister, Shannon, but her face was kind of oval shaped. The girl was simply gorgeous.

I wondered if maybe her ancestors had been Swedish or something because her skin was so light, it was milky. The kind that would burn easily on a hot summer day and peel like a snake afterwards. Freckles ran up over her nose from cheek to cheek and her teeth were perfect. When she grinned at me, her light green eyes twinkled like she was looking for trouble.

She wore men's bell-bottomed Levi's like mine, and a blue summer top that had tiny yellow flowers all over it. It had string for straps and that left her shoulders completely bare, letting me see she had even more freckles. A piece of elastic kept it tucked tightly up underneath her smallish boobs and from there, it hung loose to her waist.

I don't think she had an ounce of fat on her body. I couldn't see her feet, but I figured she was barefoot because her sandals were laying on myside of the floor. 'Birkenstock' had been stamped across the sides, so I knew they were expensive. I figured she had money, or at least, her da did.

That girl blew the stop sign where Main Street ended at highway13, almost getting us rammed by a speeding dump truck. The driver laid on the horn as he slammed on the brakes and I about pissed my jeans. Then she had to go and let out a loud whoop, and I think a couple drops did squeeze by. She tossed me a look and said, 'Isn't this fun?' Pushing myself deeper into the seat, I was hoping that she hadn't noticed the impressions of my fingers had left in her dashboard.

Looking my way, she threw back her head and laughed before putting her eyes back on the road; where I thought they should be. The way she was acting, I figured she might be a little crazy. But it was the fun kind of crazy, not the, 'I'll stab you with an ice pick, if you make fun of me' kind of crazy.

I had no idea where we were going until she slid the little Ford into the entrance of Pine Cone Ridge, our county park, spraying gravel everywhere. The dust clouds rolled up behind us as we raced down the road, our hair whipping about because of the open windows. After going about half a mile in, she turned into a parking area next to a bunch of picnic benches. Pulling up underneath the trees, she shut off the Pinto without even taking it out of gear. It bucked a bit and backfired, again. She grinned and patting the steering wheel, she said, "Whoa, girl." Switching the key back on and turning up the radio, Skylark's big hit, 'Wildflower' floated out of the speakers.

The sun was at the treetops on the hill behind us. It reflected off the metal roof of a pavilion up there and shone in through the back window. The light made the inside of the car glow and the girl's hair turned gold from the light. She went to brushing it out with her fingers, smiling at me in a way that made my heart flutter. It was so unreal, like in a magical sort of way. I gulped and wondered to myself what might be coming next.

"Come on," she said and opened her door.

That girl seemed like she had to unfold herself to get out of the car. It wasn't that her legs were too long, it was just that—she was long everywhere. I reckoned she was a foot taller than myself. When she stood up outside the car, her jeans slid down her hips a bit, taking her paisley underwear with them. I glimpsed a good part of her backside before she spun around, saying "Hey! You didn't see that." Giggling, she pulled up her jeans and pushed the door shut with her foot. Then she leaned on the windowsill, grinning in at me the way she had back at the town square.

I felt kind trapped, and a scene from a Tweety bird cartoon popped into my head. Tweety had been sitting inside his cage, trembling, as Sylvester the cat stared at him through the bars. Then he bared his teeth at that wee bird and rivers of slobber ran out of his mouth.

Pushing that out of my head, I fumbled to open my door as she walked away to the front of the car and half leaned, half sat, on the hood. She was checking out the fingernails on her left hand and after nibbling at one, she switched to the right. I walked around the front fender on my side of the car and I saw she was watching me out of the corner of her eye. Smirking to herself, she flipped her hair again.

I have to admit that I couldn't take my eyes off her. I was feeling something I had never felt before and it felt pretty damn good. The word 'delightful' even though not a word I used too often, came to mind. I now knew exactly what it meant.

Trying to sort out whether I should go and sit beside her, or just stand there, staring like an idiot, she decided for me by saying, "Come here."

Now, it wasn't like she was telling me what to do, but she wasn't asking, either. I didn't like being ordered around, but I couldn't see where that was going to be a problem—not with her. I walked over and faced her, stepping in just close enough to touch, I grinned and shoved my hands in my pockets. I had to tip my head back to look up into her eyes, and when I did, I saw that same look Fiana got when she was staring up at her poster of David Bowie. Reaching out with both hands, she rubbed them slowly up and down my upper arms, and smiling, she said, "What's your name?"

"Ummm… Cos."

"Cos? That's a funny name. Like… Cosby?"

"More like, Cosantoir. Cosantoir McDhai. So, C-O-S."

"Say, what?"

"Oh, it's an Irish thing. You know? Like… my father's, father's, father's name, kind of thing? Something that parents like to do. You know? Name their kids after other relatives. It's a pain, so… can we change the subject? I mean, that's why they call me, Cos, and not my full name. So, just—Cos."

"Just cause? Like… a just cause, or… just because," she said and giggled.

My face got hot, and must have turned red because she said, "Ahhh, you're blushing. Poor thing."

Before I could deny being a poor thing, she said, "I'm sorry… I'm Kathy. Kathy Henton. Maybe you've heard of me? Ummm… us. I mean… my family. Ummm… lives up in Coogan. Well, actually, kind of on the edge of it. We have a little ranch up there, anyway. You know where I'm talking about, right?"

"I do," I answered, as if it were the one thing, I could bet my life on.

"Oh, sorry. Duh! Of course, you'd know."

Kathy giggled again and looked away toward the river behind me. Then, in a matter of seconds, she brought her eyes right back to mine and stopped grinning. She got this real serious look on her face and putting her hands flat against my chest, she rubbed them up and down. Fiddling with a button on the front of my shirt, she looked back and forth between it and my face.

"You smell good," she said, her eyes searching mine.

"Uhhh… thanks?"

"I love your curly brown hair, it's so long. You know, it's almost as long as mine."

"Uhhh… thanks again?"

"Cos?" she said, dropping her chin to her chest.

"Himself," I said, hoping this was going somewhere.

"Did anyone ever tell you that you look a lot like a young Paul McCartney—but with longer, curlier hair?"

"Is that a good thing?"

"Good for me. Ummm… Cos?"

"Ummm… yeah?"

"Kiss me."

That wasn't at all what I thought was coming. She might as well have hit me over the head with a 2x4. I just froze. My whole body went numb, my knees got weak, and I thought I would fall over backwards. She wasn't asking if I'd kiss her—she was telling me too. I really needed to lean on something before I fell down. The car was the best bet, but she was in the way. So, I wobbled in place with only one word coming out of my mouth, "What?"

"Kiss me, please?"

She wasn't going to wait for me to sort it. Grabbing the front of my shirt with both hands, she pulled me in, and I didn't try to stop her. It wasn't like any other kiss I'd ever had before this day. One I knew I'd never forget. Even though I had woken up with that weird vibe, I didn't think it would lead me to where I'd be kissing a tall, beautiful, strawberry-blonde haired girl by the time evening rolled around. But here I was, standing in the park, my arms wrapped around this beautiful body—and never wanting to let go. I wished all my friends could see me right now. That way, when I got done, I could turn, look at them, and go, "Hah!" right in their faces.

Kathy finally pulled her lips away and looked into my eyes. I saw excitement there, like she'd found something that she hadn't expected. When our lips came together again, she opened her mouth and her tongue wrapped itself around mine. My heart started pounding so hard I thought it was going to burst out of my chest.

Now, the only time any other tongue had ever been in there, besides mine, had been my dog's. Lee-pooh had been trying to get at the beef jerky I was eating while I was laying on the lawn out behind my apartment. The gross factor with that was pretty high. There was no telling where Lee-pooh's tongue had been minutes before finding its way into my mouth.

But with Kathy, it was a whole different story. I suspected her tongue hadn't been used to taste all kinds of disgusting things that she had come across in her day. So, as for the gross factor—it was non-existent. Had I known it would feel like it did, I might have been trying a whole lot harder to get a girlfriend, sooner.

Now, the downside of kissing Kathy was the whole standing on the toes bit. I kept falling back every time they started to hurt. When she realized what was happening, she picked me up and swinging me around, sat me down on the hood of her car. I was a little shocked. She had lifted my entire 105 pounds as if it were nothing. It's not like I hadn't ever been manhandled before, just, never by a girl. Then again, I had never had a girl before, so I didn't know what to expect. Anyway, what she did solved the whole kissing problem. It made me look like I was the weaker sex; but I could live with that.

The kissing continued as music from the radio filled the park. The sun had gone behind the hill, but the sky still glowed. The frogs and crickets started in, and fireflies soon filled the air. My fantasy was coming true, something I had only read about in books or seen in films.

When we came up for air, Kathy wiped off her lips and sighing, asked a question that I figured we could have gotten along without.

"Oh man! How old are you?"

"Uhhh… sixteen."

"Oh, my word! Where did you learn to kiss like that?"

My face got hot again. I looked down at her bare feet and noticed that the second toe on each foot, was longer than the rest. It must have been a thing with her because when she realized I was looking, she curled them down, hiding them beneath the bells of her jeans. She then lifted my chin with a finger and looked straight into my face.

"You have the nicest, brown eyes," she whispered.

I gave her a little smile, hoping she really didn't care about the kissing question or about my age. She must've found what she was looking for in my face, because she pulled her finger away and wrapped her arms around me. Laying a cheek on the top of my head, she said, "Well, damn, here I am, freshly eighteen years old with a sixteen-year-old boyfriend."

She hugged me real tight and hummed along with a song on the radio, kind of weaving us back and forth to the music. I kept the side of my face pressed up against her chest, happy to be there. Not knowing what to do with my hands, I let them stray to her waist. But they refused to stay there and eventually made their way down to her hips.

I lightly ran my fingers over them, taking in their roundness. She could've stood to put on a few more pounds, but when it came to being with a skinny girl, versus no girl, I'd take skinny every time.

Kathy's jeans had dropped well below the waistline again, and I figured it must be a common occurrence. I soon realized I was running one of my fingers back and forth inside the elastic band of her underwear. I wondered if I was being too bold, but she didn't seem to mind. There came a strange feeling in my belly—an unfamiliar kind of happy.

It wasn't because I was touching girls' underwear, though. More like because I was touching girls' underwear that were still on the girl. I mean, I had lived with sisters. Helping with laundry was never out of the question. No way was my ma going to let me get out of folding their unmentionables along with everything else. So, I had no choice.

It took a couple of minutes for what Kathy said to sink in, and I blurted out, "Boyfriend?"

"Of course, silly. Nobody that kisses as good as you, is going get away from me. So now, you have to be my boyfriend. Ummm… is that a problem?" she said and laughed.

"No problem, a-tall."

But now, I couldn't get it out of my head. Boyfriend. I was finally a boyfriend. Which meant—I had a girlfriend. This discovery made me think about that one guy who was searching for that cup, I think it was the Grail, or something like that. We learned about that way back in the seventh grade.

These knights had been searching the entire world for it. It was the very thing that was supposed to change their whole lives. I kind of felt they were on the wrong path, though. If they wanted to change their lives, they should have been searching for a woman—instead of dishes. Like me, they might have been a whole lot happier.

Anyway, Kathy went back to hugging me, and I, to rubbing her hips. After a while, something started to bug me. Like a bad thought was trying to weasel its way into my head and push all the good things out. Her question, *"Is that a problem?"* kept coming back. There had been a seriousness behind her joking. Even though she was trying to sound funny, I knew she meant it. If I said the wrong thing, I might lose her as fast as I'd found her.

I imagined myself hoofing it back to town as the little green car zoomed away, leaving me in the dust. So, along with all the new feelings I was having, I realized I had to get serious now. Which meant being true to Kathy. My search had come to an end. I had found my grail. Now, there could be no other girls but her.

It was all too weird, though. This sort of thing just didn't happen to me. If this was that third thing that was coming along, then what I believed about the 'Three Things Rule' had to be true. Exciting—not bad. I mean, what could be bad about this? I decided not to care about that anymore and I pushed it back into that part of my brain where I stored all that crap.

I was where I'd always wanted to be since I was about thirteen. Something I had always dreamt about when I wasn't doing much of anything else. It was the subject on the lips of every boy in my school—every day, all day. We were all in agreement that it was the best thing in the world to have a girlfriend and to have the right to brag about it. The feeling was wonderful, and it seemed like I was drunk, or high—or something. So, if this was *'Falling in Love'* then there was no reason, ever again, to wonder why people did it.

"Damn! What time is it?" Kathy said, startling me. Peeling my hands off her hips, she bent down to look at the big wristwatch that hung from the rear-view mirror.

"Ah shit! We got to go. I have to go back and get Averell."

I didn't argue. Sliding off the hood, I ran back around the car, both of us flopping into our seats at the same time. Kathy started the engine and slamming the stick shift into reverse, she spun two complete donuts going backwards. Coming out onto the road, she shoved it into first, and running through the gears, we raced to the entrance.

"Who is this Averell person, anyway?"

"Aw, she's my little sister. She's only fifteen now, but she'll be sixteen in a week. She had to get fitted for a stupid dress this afternoon because she's now eligible to be in the Sunrise Girls. You know… that stupid, fucking, girl's social club sponsored by the Trulla Lodge."

"There are fucking girls in it? You mean girls that…"

"Nooo! That's not what I meant," she said, sounding annoyed.

"Just teasing. Naw, I don't know nothing about it."

She got this worried look on her face and said, "Hey, why are you asking? Don't you get any ideas, mister! You're MY boyfriend now."

Kathy was looking at me, frowning, and the Pinto almost back-ended an old lady in a black Lincoln. Whipping the Ford around the bigger car, she acted like it never happened. The expression on her face told me she was a wee bit angry. I was trying to think of a way to make her smile again. So, I laughed and grinned at her, then raised my eyebrows and shrugged trying to make it seem like no big deal. It didn't help. So, I said, "Don't worry, I'm not interested in your scrawny little sister. Besides, her arse sticks out, and she has those freaky, pale-blue eyes that make me nervous."

"Her what sticks out? Her arse?"

"Ummm, well… yeah."

She laughed so hard, she lost control of the car. It bounced up the curb, bashing ol' lady Edgely's mailbox. The old crone was out sweeping the front steps of her big ol' mansion and I heard her scream out, "Freeeaks!"

That wasn't the first time I'd been called that, just never by an old lady. I started to say something, but Kathy blurted out, "Oops! Oh shit! Got to get out of here before she calls the cops."

Laughing like crazy, she hit the gas, and turned down an alley. I held on to anything I could, seriously thinking about putting on the seatbelt. Gravel pinged off the bottom and overgrown bushes slapped and scratched at the car as we shot through. Looking over at me, Kathy said in a serious voice, "I like you, Cos, you're funny, and lately… it seems I need a whole lot of funny."

I grinned large. No one had ever told me that before. It made me feel important. When my face started to hurt from all the grinning, I figured it might be a good time to stop or risk looking creepy.

The alley we were going down, ran behind my place. I thought about pointing it out to her, but changed my mind because I didn't want her to know I was poor. It would be best to keep that to myself. So, unless she asked, I wasn't going to say anything.

We zoomed past the rear parking lot of the new post office, just down from the old one, and at the end of the alleyway, she threw the car into a right-hand drift. The tires squealed when they hit the asphalt, slamming me up against the door.

"Whoa! Let's do that again!"

"Some other time, huh?" she said. "I've really got to get going."

"Okay, some other time, but… you have to promise."

"I promise. Cross my heart and hope to shovel pig shit."

"What?"

"Nothing—just a farmer joke," she said, and laughed.

"You're not joking about the other, though… right? I mean… you'll be back?"

"Of course! Don't worry, silly boy. You'll see me again."

She blew the stop sign at the corner by Ernie B's and took a left. We headed back up 4th Street in front of my place and rolled up to the square. Averell was there, talking to the guys on the corner. Kathy slammed on the brakes, stopping the Pinto right in the middle of the street. I started to jump out, but she hollered, "Hey!" and grabbing my arm, she towed me back inside. Twisting my face around with her free hand, she kissed me, long and hard. Our audience began to whoop and holler and then Averell yelled out, "Kathy Lillian Henton! You, booger!" It made me think Kathy done that just so everybody would see us, and maybe, piss a few people off. I didn't know for sure.

I grinned at them right along with Kathy and getting out, I stood beside the car as Kathy went around to the front of the Pinto to check for damage from the mailbox. I heard Averell say goodbye to Brian and Steve, and I watched over the top of the car as she walked toward me.

The guys were checking out her backside, and I heard Brian say, "Want some fries with that shake?" He then elbowed Steve, who started in with his embarrassing donkey laugh.

Kathy heard what Brian said to Steve and flipped them both off, saying to Averell at the same time, "Get in the damn car, stupid."

"I am… bitchy, beanpole girl. What's your problem, anyway? You got your period or something? Why don't, YOU, get in the car?"

"Did you get your ugly dress?"

"Yeah, sooo… what's it to you? You don't care about that stuff anymore."

"Just get in the car!" Kathy yelled as she folded herself back into the Pinto.

"OKAY!" Averell said.

I stepped out of her way so she could open the car door, and she made kissing noises at me before falling backward into her seat. She gave me an exaggerated wink as she swung her legs inside. Kathy hit the gas, and the door shut by itself. The tires smoked, and the car slid sideways a tiny bit. I jumped back to keep from getting hit, and the Pinto raced away across the square. Kathy's hand came out in a wave, followed by Averell leaning out her window, yelling, "Goodbye, cute, little, long haired boy!"

Throwing me a kiss, she slid back inside just seconds before getting her head smashed against a parked truck. The little Ford screeched to a halt, the motor dying. I heard Kathy yelling at Averell as the starter kicked in and the engine roared back to life. The rubber smoked a second time, and I suspected that Kathy was hard on tires, something I assumed her da was not real happy about.

When I got over to the corner, Brian mocked in my face, "Goodbye cute, little, long-haired boy," before punching Steve in the shoulder and walking away.

"Ooow! You, turd!"

Brian turned around and shuffled backwards. Bringing his hand up in front of his face, he gave us the bird. Pushing it in an out for effect a couple of times, he turned away and went inside the Blue Front tavern. I looked back at Steve and asked, "What's his problem?" He didn't answer and just stood there rubbing his shoulder, giving me a dumb look. So, I moved over and leaned against the telephone pole, looking up the street in the direction Kathy had gone. I was wishing I were still with her and thinking back on that moment when our lips first touched.

"Wow, did you see the ass on that girl? It was perfect."

"On, who?" I said, and turning to look at him, he picked his nose for my viewing pleasure. I wanted to slap his hand away and cuss him out like my ma did me, but I decided against it. It wouldn't help— nothing could help Steve.

"You know? That Aver… Aver… what's her name…? The shorter one?"

"You mean, Averell?"

"Yeah, yeah, that one."

I turned away, trying to take myself back in time to that moment when Kathy called me her boyfriend. I was almost there when Steve said, "Well? Did you get any?"

"Moron," I said and punched his other shoulder.

"Ah! Stop punching me! You're all a bunch of pricks, you know that?"

Walking away toward the river bridge, I was glad Steve didn't follow. I needed time to think. I felt weird. It was like I'd stepped through a door into space. I was floating. It was at that moment I realized nothing would ever be the same, again. All I wanted now was to be with Kathy. It left me wondering how soon she'd be back. Hoping that it would be tomorrow.

Chapter 3

<u>Tired Of Waiting</u>

A week went by and I didn't see Kathy once. I started to feel like it had all been a dream. But I wasn't going to give up that easily. Steve and Brian weren't helping. Sitting on the corner with Steve, one day, he tried to convince me that Kathy and Averell were only messing with me.

"Well, you know, Cos, there are these girls who just drive around picking up strange guys. Then, after they get them all hot and bothered, they dump them on the side of the road and speed away, laughing. You understand, right? Like it's a big joke or something."

"I kind of doubt it. That doesn't make any sense. I think you're just wishing that would happen to you."

"It don't have to make sense! Not if they're doing it for the hell of it."

"Well… Averell wasn't making out with anybody."

"How do you know? You weren't here. Maybe she was up there making out with some old guy? Maybe she likes old guys?"

"You've got to be kidding me? Are you some kind of a nitwit? Wait… don't answer that. Okay, so listen, she had to go get measured for a dress, simple as that. I'm thinking they had to be here, in Clarksburg, for that reason. Kathy needed to kill some time while she waited. Then she saw me, I rocked her world, and… the rest is history."

"Yeah, right, because you're such a he-man. Cos! It's been a whole week, and you haven't heard shit. And what friggin dress are you talking about, anyway?"

The dress thing blew his theory. I decided that was a good time to get away from him. I had come up with this brilliant idea to go around town and ask people if they had ever heard of the Henton's. So, I left him sitting there and he never asked where I was going. I mean, he looked at me, but it was like he wasn't seeing me. I figured he must've drifted off into another dimension. That was something he did a lot of. I sometimes wondered if he had brain damage.

Besides talking to people, I figured there was a good chance I'd find the Henton's name in the phonebook. So, I walked up the street to the telephone booth. The directory was still in one piece, so I was able to come across her last name in the 'H's' The problem with that was—I didn't know her da's first name. There were a ton of Henton's in there. So, it was of no help.

Falling back on my first plan to question the town folk, I figured I'd start over at the library with Mrs. Inabinett. Then I'd work my way down to the bank to talk to Mr. Barns, and then Wally Whitcomb at the insurance office, next door. If no one could tell me anything, I'd go over and chat it up with Bobby Burns, the soda jerk at Nordon's drugstore. Then maybe ol' man Slade at the body shop (he kind of scared me, though). I'd finish up at the Royal Blue with Phil the butcher, and his granny, whose job it was to checkout your groceries.

After a couple hours of going around talking to all those people, the only good stuff came from Grandma Schneider over at the grocery store. She must have been about a hundred years old and pretty damn cranky most of the time. It was hard to be around her. Grabbing a piece of bubble gum so it wouldn't seem like I was hanging out, I laid two pennies on the counter. She ignored me and kept right on reading her magazine.

I wasn't sure what I should call her to get her attention. I had a choice of Grandma Schneider, just Grandma, or Mrs. Schneider. Because everyone I knew in Clarksburg called her Grandma Schneider, I figured I'd start there.

"Grandma Schneider? Ummm… do you know if there are any Henton's that live around here, or, uhhh… maybe up in Coogan?"

Hers eyes slowly came up to meet mine and she gave me a mean look. I thought she was going to chew me out. But she didn't yell at me or tell me not to call her grandma, instead, she just answered my question. Simple as that.

"Yep, there's some Henton's up Coogan way. Cattle farmers if I remember correctly. He's got himself four young'uns, I think. Two girls and two boys. I'm figuring they're mostly grown now. The wife's nice, a real sweet woman. But she's not blood kin. The rest of them Henton's... well, all that man's relatives live down in the southern part of the county. If I recall, Westerberg. I kind of wish those Henton's there in Coogan, would move down there, too. That guy was on the county board for a while. He's a real A-hole."

The way she finished it kind of scared me because she got loud, and the last part came out like a growl. Her face looked like a gargoyle, or maybe, something scarier. I edged toward the door, figuring I'd heard enough. Then she had to go and ask me, "Why do you want to know? You planning on doing us all a favor by going up there and murdering them in their beds? Maybe ol' Truman Capote could write a book about you, too. Maybe call it, In Cold Blood Number 2-the Henton Murders. What do you think?"

"Uhhh... What? No! I wouldn't do that."

"Ah, shucks. So... why, then?"

"Well, I met a girl named Kathy, and she said she was a Henton from up Coogan way."

"Hmmm... why a well-off girl like her, would have anything to do with a welfare case like you, is beyond me."

She made big, scary eyes at me as she leaned forward on her stool. I wished that I had never asked. The '*Freak*' thing came to mind, and it made me feel bad. It felt like it was me, or my ma's fault that we were poor.

"Ummm... okay, thanks. Got to go."

"Oh! And by the way, don't you come in here bothering me when I'm reading my Cosmo, just because you want a piece of gum. You hear me?"

I didn't say anymore and left the store thinking, 'Man! What a grouch!'

She must have read my mind, because just before the door shut, there came a, "Smart ass, longhair."

I wondered if talking to people wasn't such a brilliant idea after all. All my trouble to solve the mystery only made me feel worse. So, I quit. At least I found out that there were actual Henton's up in

Coogan. The odds were in my favor that Kathy hadn't given me a fake name. It blew Steve's theory to smithereens. There was still hope.

It was on the next Monday, the last week of school, a group of us were out hanging around Jimmy Soor's car at lunch time. It was this huge, yellow Buick wagon with fake wood panels on the sides. He was only allowed to drive it to and from school. That left me a little confused. I mean, it was only five blocks from his house, and it was one, big, ugly car. It must have been a status thing, like Fiana used to say. Just having it, made you cool.

Jimmy always parked about a block down from the high school with a clear shot up to the front door. That way if Principal Trotman should come out, it gave us time to make the cigarettes go away. Jimmy had somehow gotten WLS out of Chicago on his radio and the Kinks were singing, '*Tired Of Waiting*' I was thinking that maybe, that Ray Davies, the lead singer, had been in a similar situation once because that song was all about me.

So, there was Jimmy, who was something of a loner, and always smoked in the front seat by himself. Harry Fulton, one of the local troublemakers who'd been held back a couple years, and of course, Steve and Brian.

There was also this one guy, Mike Trabnelicek, who we just called Mike T since none of us wanted to tackle his last name. Also, because there were two other Mikes in our class besides him, and that made it even harder when you wanted to holler out, 'Hey, Mike' to only one of them. So, we used the first initial in their last names and not only did that work well, but it was kind of cool.

Mike T was one of the popular kids. He was always getting a lot of crap for hanging out with us. He told me once that he'd rather hang out with me and my friends than go to football practice. His black hair looked almost like some kind of a helmet, and his face reminded me of one of those porcelain dolls they sell in the toy section down at Nordon's.

His eyes were also kind of weird because one was brown and the other light blue. It bugged the crap out of me when he stared. He was also one of the '*Motorheads*' Guys who really loved cars and probably had some project going on at home in their garage. Mike's project was fixing up an old '57 Chevy. He kept us hoping that we would get to ride around in it someday.

Mike almost always brought the smokes, since his da was some kind of Marlboro man. It was the macho cigarette to have. Our second choice was Winston, followed by the Kool's that Harry sometimes brought. I could only get Pall Malls because that was what my ma started smoking after she got back from the institution. But the guys said they were a woman's cigarette. So, unless we were desperate, they weren't going to be caught with one of those hanging out of their mouths. I figured, what the hell, more for me. Tobacco is tobacco, right?

I was leaning against the Buick on the curbside, trying to blow smoke rings and listening to Harry complain about having to still be in the twelfth grade. I was feeling sorry for myself, thinking that Kathy had decided I was too young for her, after all, and was never coming back. Mike was standing around, laughing like crazy at Brian, who was giving Steve a wedgie. It was something we all agreed was pretty brave since the rest of us would never even think to touch Steve's underwear, let alone grabbing a handful and trying to pull it up Steve's crack. Brian all of a sudden like let go of Steve's underwear like something had caught his eye. Stepping out into the street, he yelled loud enough for the whole school to hear, "Hey Cos, look who's coming!"

I looked in the direction he was pointing and about a block away, I saw the green Pinto do a slow roll around a corner. It picked up speed, coming our way. I started grinning so big that people might have thought I'd lost my mind. I dropped my cigarette into the sand and scuffed it out with my sandal. A roll of Peppermint Lifesavers suddenly appeared in Harry's hand and he pushed them in my direction. He was always watching out for me. Kind of like the big brother I never had.

Taking one, I shoved it in my mouth, thinking Kathy couldn't have come at a better time. Now, everyone was going see us together and put an end to the rumor. That was cooler than having a stinking ol' car. For some reason everybody backed up onto the sidewalk as the little Ford screeched to a stop. I was looking across the top of the wagon at Kathy, and she gave me this big, excited smile like she couldn't believe her luck.

"Hey Cos! Want to go for a ride?" she said in a really sexy voice.

"Soy-ten-ly" I answered, doing my best impression of Curly from the Three Stooges.

Turning back to Harry, I sneered. He whipped his bright, blonde hair back and blew smoke into my eyes through his weird little nose. I wanted to make fun of it, but I remembered a time when a guy called it a 'Tinker Bell' nose. Harry found out and rumor had it that, that guy spent a night in the hospital.

Giving Harry a playful shove, I strutted around him to the street. He followed me, and leaning down, he checked Kathy out through the car window. Before she could say anything, he walked away. Flicking me in the earlobe on his way by, he said, "Youuu… lucky fucker."

"Fucker is right," I heard Brian say, but I pretended that I didn't.

We pulled away with everyone whistling and howling like wolves. Kathy was still smiling pretty big, so I figured she was really happy to see me.

"Who was that?"

"Oh, that's Harry. He's like my big brother."

"Looks too old to be in school."

"Ummm… yeah. He got held back a couple times."

"So, is he just dumb or…"

"No, he's not dumb. He's… well… kind of a troublemaker."

"Oh, okay," she said, making a face like she didn't want to push it. I didn't want to talk about that, anyway. If she came down too hard on Harry, I'd have to defend him and I'm sure that would put Kathy and I at odds. Besides, Harry didn't have anything to do with us. Harry wasn't a problem at the moment, not like Brian, and I certainly didn't want to make him one.

All I wanted was to concentrate on Kathy. She wore the same style of jeans as before, but today, she had on a yellow blouse with little blue flowers. A small braid ran from each side of her forehead, coming together at a huge, leather, butterfly barrette at the back. She must have lost the little wooden stick that you were supposed to stick through it because now, there was a small, artist's paintbrush stuck in there, instead. All I could think of was how lovely she looked.

I knew she was doing the hippy thing, trying to impress me. I was starting to think that she was kind of a rebel. It seemed that she was doing everything possible to break away from her boring, rich girl life. That meant not doing anything that she was supposed to do. Breaking the rules was a big part of that whole thing. I figured her being eighteen gave her the right to do almost anything she wanted.

I pretended to ignore her, waiting for her to talk first. So, I dug around in her music cassettes, looking for something that could replace the talk-show on the radio. After about four blocks of that, she whipped the car over to the side. Pushing the gearshift into neutral, she whipped around in her seat, and said, "Oh, my gosh! It's been like, forever. I've been missing that kiss, sooo much!"

I didn't even get a chance to say anything. She grabbed me, dragged me across the center console, and we kissed for what seemed like forever. Right in the middle of it, a car horn blared in our ears. I thought Kathy had accidentally honked the Pinto's horn with her elbow, but it was too loud. We pulled apart and saw it was an old couple in a beat-up Dodge Dart. They were parked so close that the guy's wife could've reached out and tapped Kathy on the shoulder, or worse yet, heard the noise she made trying to suck the tongue out of my mouth.

The old guy looked at us through thick glasses and said, "Mind if I get into my driveway, missy?" I looked to the right and realized that when Kathy had pulled over, she must not have been paying attention. I watched her turn beet red, and putting the Ford in gear, she floored it, fishtailing away from the old couple.

"Shit, I hope that guy doesn't know my ol' man. That's all I need right now is for him to go blabbing."

"Why is that a problem? You can't have friends?"

"Oh, I can have friends, ones that my parents would approve of. They seem to have forgotten that I'd turned eighteen. It's a big hassle. All my dad has to do is take this car away from me and I'm stuck at home until I can get a ride. Then, I'd have to suck up to him to get it back. This was supposed to be my brother's car, but he moved to California. He didn't want to drive a Pinto. So, it became mine. Because, well… I didn't care. Any ol' car will do. Anything that can get me out of there. Hell, I'd take a stupid tractor if I had too."

"I think you'll be alright. That guy looked like he was practically blind anyway, and we can always hope that he has that old person's disease. The one where you can't remember crap? Then he won't remember who to talk to at the next lodge meeting. He might even talk to the wrong father and some other daughter will get in trouble."

"You trying to cheer me up?" she said.

Giggling, she reached over and pushed the hair out of my face.

"Of course. So, don't worry about it. We're together now, and that's all that matters, right?"

"Thanks, you're too sweet, but I… oh, forget it. I'm just being paranoid."

"It will be okay. Let's just try to have some fun, huh?"

"Okay," she said, but the worry was still in her face.

We spent the rest of the day driving around, talking and getting familiar with each other. Every once in a while, she'd lean over and want to kiss me. I knew when it was coming because she'd look at me out of the corner of her eye and pucker. I would meet her half way, pulling back as quick as I could, because I was afraid the next thing we'd be kissing was a telephone pole.

Her mood got better, and she quit worrying about the old people. That made me happy because I was really having a good time. I didn't want anything to bum me out. She talked a lot about her family. Her father was not only a cattle farmer, but also worked for the federal government. His name was Seymour. I really wanted to make fun of it, but I didn't have a lot of room to talk. Her ma's name was Annette, and there were two older brothers, like Grandma Schneider said. One of them was in graduate school, and the other one who was living out west and getting married soon. And of course, there was Averell.

Kathy's folks were highly respected people at the lodge and were not only members, but also helped run it. If Coogan had a lodge, we'd never have seen them down here in Clarksburg. That was the only reason they came into town. Well, other than the fact that Clarksburg had the county fairgrounds. If you were seriously into farm animals, you couldn't avoid that place. Steve talked about it all the time, almost as much as he did girls.

Kathy told me she wanted to be an artist and become a famous painter. When she wasn't helping with chores or hanging out, she'd stay in her room, painting. I told her how much I wanted to be a writer, which she thought was pretty cool. I explained how Creative Writing, along with Literature, were my favorite classes. Also, how hard it was for me right now because of my screwed-up family life.

She went right to complaining about her screwed up family life and didn't even bother to ask why mine was so messed up. It seemed to help calm her down, though, her ranting about her da, mostly. So, I let her chatter on. It all sounded good to me until she got to the part about how if her da ever caught us together, there'd be trouble. That's really when my worry started. She had to go and make it worse by adding, if he ever did catch us, it would be best if I got out of there as quick as possible. I was thinking to ask why, but felt like I already knew. Also, if we started talking about that very thing, it would most certainly drag me down. That's not the kind of day I wanted.

I got to thinking about how being afraid of getting caught, just might be the thing that made it exciting for her. I mean, sometimes I caused trouble just for the hell of it, not caring what might happen afterwards. It reminded me of a tee shirt I had once. It showed a stork on the front with a frog half way down its throat. The frog's arms were still sticking out of the beak and it had a tight grip on the stork's neck. Underneath it read, '*Last Act of Defiance!*'

So, the way I figured it, I must be Kathy's last act of defiance before going off to college. That was the name of the game she was playing. Sure, it was dangerous for me. But I was willing to play 'catch-me-if-you-can' just to keep what I had. Maybe not a smart thing, but I wasn't afraid. Nothing could be as bad as what I used to get from my da. Harry told me once that because of that very thing, I now had skills. I suspect he'd know—his da was worse than anyone da I had ever met.

"I am so tired of their crap!" she screamed at the windshield. "Oops! Sorry, I don't know where that came from!"

"I do, but it's okay. I think I know how you feel."

"Yeah, well, it just never seems to end. Kathy do this. Kathy stop doing that. Kathy, Kathy, Kathy… ahhhhhh!"

"So, what about Averell? Do they give her the same crap?"

"No, and that's part of the problem! She's the perfect little angel. Sometimes I want to strangle her."

"My sister, Shauna, she's... oh, forget it."

I stopped because I realized if I started talking about my family, I would accidently spill the beans about not owning anything but the clothes on my back. Right now, she still didn't know anything about my life, or at least, I didn't think she did. I felt that's how she wanted it to be, though. If she already knew, she probably didn't want me to know that she did. So, except to ask where I'd come from, there had been no other questions.

She was looking at me like she wanted me to finish what I'd been saying. Realizing that I was going to do the very thing I was trying to avoid, I changed the subject.

"So... you're off to university in August? Which one?"

"Oh, ummm... Drake. They offer some really good Art classes and it's my mom's Alma Mater."

"Alma what-er?"

"The school that you graduated from."

"Oh, yeah, okay, I get it. So, like, if I graduate from Clarksburg high, then that would be mine?"

"Well, kind of. It applies more to colleges and universities. You know what, sometimes, you're just too cute."

"What do you mean?"

"When you act like you don't know things."

"No, honestly. I..."

She pulled the car over to the curb, this time making sure she wasn't blocking a driveway. Turning in her seat, she reached out and clamped my face in her hands. Pulling me to her, she kissed me gently on the lips. Then looking into my eyes for a few seconds, she said softly, "Too cute..." and then she hugged me.

So, we had nearly two months to get acquainted, and that didn't mean I couldn't ever go down to the university. It was not like it had to end between us the day she left. It would be easy to hitchhike to Drake. I brought that up, but she said, "All I want is to be with you right now and enjoy these moments. We'll worry about all that other crap later. We still have lots of time."

The rest of the week ran pretty much the same. Every day at noon, she'd come to town and pick me up at the school. I'd skip out and not return for the rest of the day. My literature class was in the morning, so I didn't have to cut that one. I really didn't think they'd miss me in any of the others, and the guys wouldn't say squat if Trotman asked. Kathy had to put in at least half a day doing chores and could skip out after she helped her ma make lunch.

On Wednesday, it rained. So, we didn't get out of the car. We went for long rides out into the countryside trying to find roads she had never driven before, or visit towns unknown to her. When we came back into Clarksburg after the last tour, she seemed antsy. It was like she wanted me to suggest something else to do. But I was happy doing what we were doing. I just wanted to be with her, no matter where we went.

At one point she suddenly turned off the river road and raced down the hill to the boat ramp and—toward the water. I figured she'd had enough and was going to commit suicide, killing me too. I closed my eyes and waited to die. She slammed on the brakes at the last second, and we slid on the wet concrete, the car stopping with its front wheels in the river.

"What the…!"

"Thought we were going for a swim, huh? Sorry, just a joke. Got your blood flowing, I'll bet?" Not sure if Pinto's can float, or not. Silly me!

"Well, yeah! I about crapped my pants."

"Oh! Can't have that. So… kiss me instead. Quick, before you calm down."

I did, still thinking that it was kind of weird. Afterwards, I sorted out why. Kissing was better when you're all worked up and it made me wonder how she had found that out. We stayed there for a couple hours, making out and cuddling as the rain beat on the roof. We figured nobody would be going boating in that downpour, anyway.

The next two days were free of rain, so we drove down to the sandpits. 'The Pits' were these huge ponds out in the woods on the edge of town. They were all that was left behind after some guy dug about a billion tons of sand out of the ground so he could make cement. It was the favorite place for the local folks to hang out. The county Conservation Department had stocked every pond with fish, so it was a good spot to go and toss in a line, swim, and even camp.

On top of that, it was an even better place to throw a party late at night.

If you walked far enough back into the woods from where the road ended, you could raise some serious hell. The sheriff's deputies didn't like to get out of their cars much and certainly didn't want to get their clean uniforms dirty. So, they didn't bother us. I even overheard our town marshal say to the grocer one day, "Ah damn, Phil, nobody's gonna bother those kids down there. Hell, you can't even hear' um when they are… least not in town, anyways. As long as nobody dies or drowns, well… they'll be doing it for years. And you know as well as I do, kids will be kids."

On Friday Kathy and I lay in the grass by one of the bigger ponds. She had an old quilt that she kept in the back seat for that reason. Mostly because she didn't like the ants. She was soon lying with the back of her head on my chest. She started telling me all about her sucky family life, and how she couldn't wait for August to get here. I had no problem waiting for what seemed like our final moment together. So, I didn't want to talk about that. For her, it meant leaving Coogan to start a whole, new life. But for me—she was my whole new life.

I was lying there, listening to her voice, realizing that when she took the time to talk slow and soft, it relaxed me. Most of the time she was talking fast and loud. I figured it was because when she was at home that maybe it was the only way she could get a word in. After a while, I started to doze off. She startled me by jumping up and putting her hands on her hips, she said, "We should go skinny dipping."

"What? Oh… I don't think so."

"Why? You got your period or something?"

Getting down on her knees, she started poking me in the ribs with a finger.

"Come on, Cos. Come on. I won't laugh or anything. Come on! COME ON!"

"Sorry, I uhhh… can't swim."

"Ahhh crap! That sucks! Well… I am going in, anyway."

She got up and walked toward the pond. I rolled over onto my side and getting up on an elbow, I chewed on a grass stem, waiting. You see, I didn't believe she'd really do it. So, I got ready to give her some crap when she chickened out. She fooled me.

Skipping over to the edge of the pond, she looked it over, and stuck a toe in the water. I heard her say, "Ahhh, just right." Then she surprised the crap out of me by pulling off her shirt and dropping her blue jeans. I went into a state of shock. There she stood in all he glory, naked as one can get, giving me a clear shot of her backside as she grinned over her shoulder.

After a minute, she turned completely around, one arm across her chest and the other hand pressed against her crotch. There wasn't any sign of paisley underwear this time and it left me to wonder if she had planned this whole thing right from the beginning.

She stopped smiling, and her face got all pouty. I could tell she wanted me to join her so badly it must have hurt. But what I said was true, I didn't know how to swim. That's why I freaked out the day she charged the boat ramp. I was hoping it wouldn't make her mad, but the pictures in my mind of me floating face down or being dragged ashore and zipped up in a body bag, kind of overruled everything. Because I stayed clear of swimming pools and only took showers, I must have lost touch with how much afraid of water I truly was. I almost drown in Loch Major back in Ireland when I was about five years old. That's stuck with me ever since. I think people call it a phobia. I told my guidance counselor in school about it and he started joking with me, telling me I had Hydrophobia. But I wasn't fooled because I was a hundred percent positive I didn't have rabies.

"Sorry! I'd loved to join you, but... I swim like a rock!" I called out.

She stared at the ground for a moment and then she looked out the top of her eyes at me. I could tell she was disappointed. That seemed to only last all of a minute, and then she stuck her tongue out at me, flipped her hair, spun around, and ran into the shallow water. When she got to where the deep part started, she dove in and swam away from the small patch of sand that made up the beach.

Kathy had me between a rock and a hard place. Here I was, afraid of water, but here there was this gorgeous, naked, girl begging me to come into the water with her. It was supposed to be a romantic moment. I know that's what she wanted, and honestly, so did I.

I was blowing it.

I should have been more excited than I was, or maybe the word I'm looking for is, 'aroused' I knew the time for sex would come and I was pretty positive I was ready. It's just—I hadn't counted on there being water involved. It was scaring the excitement right out of me. I should have been chomping at the bit to get with her, and here I was, on the verge of freaking out.

The guys and I were always going on about sex, and we bragged a lot. Harry was probably the most experienced and if he talked about it, we listened. Then there was Steve, with no experience—period. What he knew was limited to magazines. Now and then he would bring them to school and stash them in his locker. I'd see him sitting at the top of the bleachers, way back in a corner of the gym when there wasn't anybody else in there, looking at one of those magazines. He'd holler at me to come and sit with him. The problem was, if I did, I'd have to put up with, "Oh man! What a rack!" and "Wow! Look at that ass!"

He'd share pages full of big-boobed women, not one of them looking like anyone I would ever meet on the street, especially in Clarksburg. They didn't seem real to me. Steve told me it was because they were all models, and it was their job to get naked. So, it was okay. I had to think about that for a while because I wasn't so sure that it was. I mean, I played along whenever the subject came up, but only to a point. If the guys got too gross or maybe started bad mouthing some girl that I knew, I'd make up some excuse and be off. I had sisters, and all I could think of is, what if one of them was being talked about in the way these guys were talking. It just made me feel bad.

Because Kathy had stripped down in front of me, I figured she must trust me. So, it was something that had to stay between us. No matter how much the guys worked on me to give it up, I had to keep my pie hole shut out of respect for Kathy.

Now, I was in a situation that was real—not a story, or a picture in a magazine. Like some kind of a fool, I was letting the fear of water stand in my way. I decided I was going to have to gather all my strength and force myself to go over there and get in that pond.

I was watching Kathy swim around like it she was here by herself. Then she went to treading water and making the mean face. I gave her a little wave that was supposed to say that I was embarrassed, and she hollered, "Come on, Cos. Come in. I'm getting kind of lonely in here. You can always stay by the shore… please?"

"Well… okay, but if I drown, don't tell my ma. Just drag my body over into the woods, cover me up with some leaves, and let the animals have me. She'd be better off thinking I'd run away."

"Oh, don't talk like that. You'll be okay. I'll save you if you start to drown."

I got to my feet and she whooped like she did that first day in the car and dropped out of sight under the water. I could see her swimming in a circle just under the surface. She was pretty graceful and reminded me of a mermaid—without the big fishtail, of course.

When I got to the sand, her head popped up again and pushing the wet hair out of her eyes, she said, "So, you're coming in? Do you want me to close my eyes? I can close my eyes at first, least until you get in?"

"It's okay, don't worry about it."

I stripped off my shirt and after kicking off my sandals, I stood there looking out across the pond. I could see she was waiting for the big moment when my Levi's would hit the sand. It turned into an awkward moment of silence. I didn't always wear underwear, especially on washday and today was one of those days. If I did drop my jeans, it would be the first time I was ever naked in public. I realized I was shaking a wee bit and felt like I was going to chicken out, and then—I did.

Forcing myself to walk about six feet into the shallows, I stopped, laughed, and said, "Okay, I'm in, now what?"

She didn't think it was funny. Even at that distance I could see something change. It was in her eyes. A crazy, mean kind of look. She was going to stop being nice to me. I was going to see a side of Kathy I hadn't seen before.

Coming up out of the deep part, she stomped toward me, splashing loudly with every step. I wanted to believe she was only pretending to be mad, but she wasn't smiling. I saw, instead, she was gritting her teeth. It was like she was on a mission to get what she wanted—or else. Then she jumped on me, throwing her arms and legs around my body. I was too short for that, and I fell backwards with a splash.

She lay on top of me, her lips pressed tight to mine and then our heads went under water. That's when I really did freak out. She must have realized I was losing it and getting off of me, she stood up, turned around, and dived back in the deep part.

Sitting almost waist deep in the shallows, I shook the water out of my hair and watched Kathy swim around with her head just above the surface. She'd look at me every once in a while, grin and make big eyes, like, '*What? I didn't do anything*' I got a feeling that she was waiting for the right moment to come back for more.

"*Wuss!*" rolled through my head in Brian's voice. I didn't want to be that. My da had done his best to make me a man—the man he thought I should be. Then there were others, the bullying by the tough farmer boys at school, the phys. ed coach, and then some old fishermen I knew, who I hung out with once in a while down on the river. There was some version of a man I was supposed to be and I guess—I wasn't it. Fiana told me that being too masculine was a bad thing, but how could so many people be wrong? That bothered me, but what worried me most was—I think Kathy might be one of those.

Getting to my feet, I could see where the sand kind of sloped away into nothing but dark water stretching all the way across to the other side. I believed certain death waited out there and I got a chill. If this pond was as deep as I've seen some quarry holes, then I was surely pushing my luck.

I smiled at Kathy and that seemed to set her off again. In one smooth turn, she swam right up to my feet. I said, "Kathy, wait, listen…" She didn't, instead she tried to grab my ankles. I fell back again and tried to scoot away. She wasn't going to give me a break. This was a game to her and she wanted to win.

"Your pants are all wet now, you might as well take them off."

The tone of her voice was scary calm and putting her feet down, she stood on the sand slope looking like she was studying me. I got up and said, "Are you sure that's what you want? For me to drop trou?" I wanted to sound confident but I was just stalling and we both knew it.

"Well… yeah."

"You should know, I've never been naked in front of anyone before."

I don't know why I said that. If she wasn't going to back off because I could die from drowning, why would me not wanting to be naked in public make one wee bit of a difference?

Her eyes were moving up and down my body, like she now had a plan. "So... no one? I've always gone skinny dipping with my brothers and sister down in the big creek behind our place. Nothing to be ashamed of, you know? Everybody looks the same under their clothes. It's pretty much limited to four things, and once you've seen them all, that's it. There's nothing else. So, you just... kind of have to get over it."

There it was—get tough, or go away.

She was moving closer as she talked, taking slow, short steps like she didn't think I'd notice.

"So, ummm... yeah... I've never... not even my family," I said.

"I'm sure when you were a baby?"

"I didn't care back then. Now that I'm older, well, I guess..."

"It's only me here, Cos. You can be naked in front of me, I won't make fun of you."

"You say that now, but..."

"Cos!" she yelled like she wasn't going to put up with my crap anymore. I kind of froze, thinking this wasn't the Kathy I thought I knew. I wanted to negotiate some kind of deal, like maybe we could get out of the water and go lay on the blanket. She was still moving, and began to slowly reach out toward me like her hands were invisible and I wouldn't see them. Slipping her fingers into the waistband of my jeans, she latched ahold and said, "Gotcha!" Laughing in a wicked way, she started to pull.

"Kathy, listen... maybe we can go lay on the blanket or something?"

"Naw, I think you're way too afraid of water, and the only way you're going to get over it, is by being in it."

It was the, *'The only way you're going to learn is to just jump right in'* theory. This was a side of Kathy I didn't know, but maybe should have expected. The 'I'm going to have my way, regardless' Kathy, or maybe the, 'I am way too crazy from horniness right now to care'

Kathy. I had ruined her plans. I figured she was all set to have sex and today was the day. My statement about the blanket gave me a plan: Lure her back to shore. Get her out of the pond.

Kathy grinned and tugged even harder at my blue jeans. I pulled in the opposite direction twice as hard and the button at my fly let go. She lost her grip and I spun around and started for the beach. She was quick and must have slipped a finger through a belt loop at the back. I kept pulling as hard as I could, my feet sinking into the sandy bottom. I started to pivot to the left, then to the right, and back again. After a few times of that, I finally got centered and pulled as hard as I possibly could. It felt like she had set her feet and they were now sliding over the bottom as I towed her closer to the little beach. She was giggling and whooping, "Yippee, ride 'em cowgirl." I had maybe eight feet to go before I would have her on land. The picture in my head of me dragging a naked girl up out of the water struck me funny and I let out a short laugh.

Big mistake.

"Oh, so you're having fun, now?" Kathy said. "Good, I don't like spoilsports." I looked back over my shoulder and frowned at her. I wanted to negotiate some more but I didn't dare stop pulling, or she'd have me right back where we started. She was a lot stronger than I ever thought she would be, but it only made sense because she was a country girl and was used to hard work. I truly felt out of my league at that moment. Kathy liked to play rough and I supposed if we were going to stay together, I would have to do the same. But… I didn't want to. That went against what I had imagined having a girlfriend was supposed to be. I vowed to myself that I would sort it when things calmed down.

My zipper was slowly working its way down, and I figured my jeans were going to give up real quick. But we were just a few feet from the beach, now. If I lost my trousers, least it would be on dry land.

It was about then that the beltloop ripped off with a pop and in a splashing stumble to my left, I rammed my head into a good-sized tree sticking up out of the shore. The water was about a foot and a half deep there and the last thing I heard was Kathy's loud, "Oh, crap!" before I fell face first into it.

I don't think I was under for more than a few seconds before hands grabbed me under my armpits and picked me up. Then I was being dragged, and soon, I could feel the warm sand on my back with Kathy's voice in my ears.

"Cos! Cos, wake up!" she said, shaking me.

When my eyelids popped open, I saw she was on her knees, her face right in mine. Her long wet hair was dripping, and her eyes had changed from that feisty mermaid, to those of a scared, little girl. Turning my head, I spit out some pond water and tried to smile.

"Oh my… I thought you were dead. I thought I'd killed you."

"Dead? Ah no, just took a wee trip, is all," I said. "I don't think I was even knocked out, or… was I?"

"I'm not sure, but…"

I realized that my Levi's were now down around my ankles now and I sat up with a start. I was totally exposed to Kathy and the rest of the world. During the time that I was towing Kathy back to shore, I had, unexpectedly, become aroused. I was now rock hard, and there was no hiding it. It was weird that it happened that way, and I have to admit, I was stunned.

"Wow, you're kind of big for a little guy," she said, sounding spellbound. I looked at her face, and she was looking right at it. I could feel myself blushing. So, as quick as I could, I lifted my backside off the sand and pulled up my jeans. Yanking the zipper to the top, I buttoned them. I wasn't sure what to say to Kathy's comment, so I just sat looking at my hands that were now hiding the bulge in my jeans. I must have looked pitiful, or something, because she suddenly threw her arms around me, put the side of her face against mine, and said, "I'm sorry."

I didn't say anything and just hugged her back, but my heart wasn't in it. I felt too weird for having accidentally shared something that I hadn't planned to. It was like when you realize your fly is open while you're at school and up in front of the class reading something. You don't know if you should zip up right there, or just pretend you didn't notice and get on with it even though the whole damn room is laughing.

We stayed that way for a while, just hugging. She finally sat back on her calves to check me out and we just stared into each other's faces. Even though she had tried to drown me, I wanted to make her feel better about it now that she was sorry. So, I ran a finger over the bump on the top of my head and finding no blood, I showed it to her.

"See, no blood."

She smiled and sighed. I thought it weird that she didn't seem at all concerned that somebody else might come along and see a naked girl sitting next to a soaking wet, long-haired kid. I looked straight into her eyes and said, "I'm alright, lass."

Taking a long breath, she let it out slowly, and standing up, she helped me to my feet. We picked up our clothes and went back to the quilt. After getting dressed, we sat down and drank from our cans of warm coke in silence.

"You okay?" she asked again.

"Fine as frog's hair… but I want to know…are you?"

"I want to apologize. Sometimes I get a little crazy and things get out of hand. Some people don't like me because of that. But I really shouldn't care… I just can't help it."

"Like I said, girl… it's okay. It's happened to me before where I've done the same. I'm surprised that my sisters are still alive because of some of the crap I've pulled."

I was lying; I had never gotten that crazy. I was still trying to mend this thing, though. Afraid things might be ending between us before they even got started.

"Yeah, I almost killed Averell a couple of times... I mean… by accident. We don't get along that great, but I'd feel terrible if she died."

"No one is dying here today, darling."

"Darling…" she mumbled to herself, almost like she had a hard time believing that she was one. She smiled over at me like she was in pain. I fell back on the quilt and lay there watching the sky like the whole situation was no big deal. I went to trying to sort out ways to make her happy again. She lay down on her side, staring at me. Pulling up her knees, she moved closer and put her forehead against my arm.

I almost didn't hear it when she said, "I'm so glad I have you."

"Same here," I said, and reaching over, I moved a pile of wet hair out of her face. She smiled without looking at me, but I saw a tear roll down. I knew things were still not right with her. I sat back up and so did she. She had the saddest face I'd ever seen. I started to think that something else might be wrong. Something that she was keeping secret. I mean, she was actually crying. I was confused.

I sat up and Kathy suddenly threw her arms around me again and kissing me softly on my cheek, she looked me square in the face. A little sob came out of her lips just before she said, "Hold me, please… for a little while?" She put her chin on my shoulder, and I did as she asked.

We sat there for the longest time with just the birds singing and the breeze blowing through the trees. There was the smell of the pond in her hair, along with a wee bit of patchouli. Every once in a while, she'd sniffle. Then squeezing me hard, she'd kiss my cheek, again. That was when I realized I too liked being held. It was probably good for the both of us.

I mean, there was a lot of hugging going on these days. No one had hugged me this much in years. My ma had hugged me when I was a wee baby, but there hasn't been much of that, since. Now that I had it again, I was afraid I might lose it. I liked the hugging. I mean, the kissing was nice and got me pretty excited, but the hugging made me feel, well… loved. What if I got used to all the lovey-dovey and then it went away? Who could I hug, or who'd hug me, after that? I might get desperate and go around hugging people all over the place. Some people would probably punch me for it, or start calling me a wuss. That was the problem with my da, I should have been able to hug him. I wondered what would happen if I started hugging my ma, or, my aunt, the next time I saw her in town for groceries. But honestly, I only wanted to hug Kathy. We were familiar now. I could throw my arms around her right out of the blue, and she'd let me. With all these things running through my brain, I got a wee bit nervous. But then a little voice that sounded a lot like Fiana, pushed its way through, saying, '*If you don't stop worrying, you're going to end up like ma!*' So, I made it a point to listen to the sister in my head and stopped

Kathy soon let go of me and wiping at her eyes, she got this look like she had an idea. Opening her big shoulder bag that looked like it was made out of some one's sofa, she pulled out a hair brush.

"May I?" she asked.

It took a moment for me to realize that she wanted to brush my hair. I thought it was kind of weird, but I let her do it without saying anything. If it made her happy, fine. My first serious step in being a good boyfriend.

I turned myself around and sat there humming an old Irish song called 'Grace' while she went to work. For some reason, this song had popped into my head. I didn't dare sing the words, though. It was about a man, who was talking to his girl, about how he was going to die in the morning. So, I suspected that wouldn't go over very well, being just a minute before, Kathy thought that she had killed me.

"I do this with Averell, sometimes. It calms me down," she said, pulling the brush through my hair.

"Fine with me. Nobody's ever done that for me, before, but there always a first time, right?"

"Thanks," she said in a whisper, and I went back to humming, looking off into the woods as she stroked away.

I offered to do hers afterwards, but she said, "No, but thanks. It's just… no one brushes my hair except for me, or Ruthie at the beauty salon. I'm sorry."

She smiled like she was embarrassed and went to brushing her own hair. I just watched, figuring she probably was doing a better job than I would have, anyway.

When the sun dropped behind the trees and we were in the shadows, I knew it was time to go. The birds and Cicadas had given way to crickets and frogs and the fireflies soon appeared. Kathy was usually on her way by this time of the day, doing her best to show up at home for supper.

"Shouldn't we be off, girl?"

"I suppose—not that I want to. I'd rather stay with you, but… yeah, dinner with the Henton's, awaits."

"You could always invite me up? Surprise the crap out of them. I bet Averell would get a kick out of that."

"That would be a great joke, yeah… but I'm afraid it would be the last one."

All of a sudden, she laughed really loud, adding "Maybe we should do that on my last weekend at home? That would make it more fun. But I don't think much eating would get done. Okay, we got to go."

She stashed her brush back in her bag. I got up, gathered the coke cans, and took them to a nearby bin chained to a rusty fence post. Rolling the quilt into a ball, she came over and taking my hand she swung it back and forth as we walked to the car. Every once in a while she'd look down at me with an embarrassed kind of grin. I figured that was because this was the first time she had cried in front of me, or maybe because she wouldn't let me brush her hair. I wanted to tell her that everything was okay, but I think she saw it in my face when I smiled back. That is, when my now, 'light and fluffy hair' wasn't blowing into my mouth.

Heading back to town in the Pinto, she didn't have much to say. We agreed that she could drop me at this place called the Dairy Dreem. It was an ice cream and burger shop where a lot of kids hung out. If she left me there, she could make a straight shot down the highway. Crossing the trestle bridge at the river, she could head up over the hill to Coogan. I didn't mind if she had to leave me there. I had enough change in my pocket to get something to eat. Then I could head downtown afterwards and meet the guys on the corner.

We pulled into the empty lot and I saw through the big windows that there were a bunch of kids hanging around inside that weren't of driving age. After she stopped the car, we kissed for the longest time. When she pulled her lips from mine, she looked into my face for what seemed like forever. It always made me wonder what she saw there. Letting out a long sigh, she closed her eyes and pushed her forehead against mine.

"Okay, got to go," she whispered, and without saying anything more, I climbed out. Turning the car around, she raced away, honking her horn as I turned to face the applause of all the little kids who had gathered at the glass.

Chapter 4

Kathy decided not to come down to Clarksburg on the first day of June. It was her graduation night, and she had to prepare. She also told me that it would be best if I didn't come up there, saying something about how it was a family affair and how all that ceremonial crap was just for show and not worth my time. She said that particular part of her life had nothing to do with us. Nobody in Coogan should ever be given a chance to stick their nose in our business. I was her little secret. Only Averell knew. Kathy must have sworn her to secrecy with a bribe, or maybe—the threat of a big snake in her bed.

With school being out, we had to make plans to meet, or I'd have to sit up on the corner all day and take my chances. The Dairy Dreem sat right at the entrance to Clarksburg where Main Street started at Highway 13. So, I added one of their big red tables that sat just outside, to my list of places to hang out. That's where she always started her search when she came looking for me.

But Clarksburg wasn't so big that she couldn't just drive around and stumble on me. As long as I stayed out in the open, we were fine. Then, as usual, we'd take off to someplace to sit, talk and tease. But mostly, to make out.

I'd hang out in all the usual places, waiting and hoping. She had told me not to do that, though. But that didn't make any sense. There was no other choice but to wait, and while I was, I had to do something. So, hoping was the thing I did most. The two just seemed to go together. Maybe what she meant was that I should just go about my day as I normally did. I supposed what she didn't know was, I didn't like any part of my life that didn't have her in it. Being together was the only thing that really mattered to me. That day at the pond was behind us now and I hadn't seen that side of Kathy since. I figured she was trying her best not to show it. I was all for that.

The month of June sailed right by. I was enjoying myself so much that time didn't seem to exist. Also, there was a lot more happiness than I was used to—and it was changing me. It felt like we had known each other all our lives. Being nice was becoming a big part of me, all because of the attention (plus the hugging) I was getting.

The last day of the month fell on a Saturday. Kathy was supposed to be touring the campus at Drake. So, I was on my own. At this point in our relationship that didn't bother me much because she had come around just about every day. Of course, she had to make up a lot of excuses to her folks why she couldn't be home doing chores or cleaning their house.

There was work for me down at Ernie B's that Saturday morning. So, I went to the lawnmower shop. I'd secretly changed the radio station after being there a minute or two and when '*Hot Fun In The Summertime*' came rolling out of the little speaker, the old guy didn't seem to notice. He had been in a teasing mood and was poking at me the whole time I was there. I just poked back. When I left, I was feeling pretty good, mostly because I could give Ernie no end of crap without it being a problem. I was actually mouthing off to an adult and wasn't being threatened with death. As long as I didn't step over the line, we could do that all day. Sometimes I wondered if I was like a son to Ernie. He'd never say it, but sometimes it showed. He had a wife in the little house out behind his shop, but I never met her because she never came outside. They didn't have any kids, so I suspected they had a pretty quiet life.

After work, I went up to the Blue Front. Since the guys weren't on the corner, I figured they were inside the tavern. The windows of that place were enormous. The bottom halves were covered in dark blue paint with 'ARNIE'S BLUE FRONT' painted just above that in big, fancy gold letters with red trim. Brian and I got a game of pool going, and occasionally I'd stop to peek out he 'O' in FRONT. There was a chance that a little green Pinto might roll up to the square, telling me it was time to go. The picture in my head was of me flinging down the cue and flying out the door, presenting myself to Kathy in all my glory. But that never happened.

Steve was in a booth, twirling some of his hair, just zoning out. A bunch of old farmers were sitting at the bar, talking about tagging pigs and the price of heating oil. Harry was following me around the pool table trying to corner me so he could ask questions about girls that I knew. He was kind of shy in that department. But that didn't make him any less hard up. I think that maybe he was hoping I could help him out. It gave me an inkling of how hard it was for all those Matchmakers I'd left behind in Ireland. But they got money for their trouble, and I didn't feel right about charging Harry for information.

"Hey, Cos, does Kathy's sister, ummm… what's her face?"

"Averell?"

"What?"

"Averell… her sister?"

"Okay, so Averell… what kind of name is that, anyway?"

"A normal kind of name, I guess… so… what?"

"Does she have a boyfriend?" Harry raised his eyebrows a bunch of times in a row and grinned.

"I don't think so, why? Oh no… don't even think about it. She's just turned sixteen and you're not her type."

"So, what is her type?"

"Well, it's not you." I said, teasing him.

"How do you know?" Brian asked, moving around the table toward us, bumping the bottom of his cue on the floor as he came. Up until that point, Harry and I had been joking with each other. But Brian's tone told me he wanted to start a fight.

"I just know that her folks are snobs, and besides, Harry's almost three years older than Averell."

"Well, Kathy's two years older than you."

Harry backed away. Going to the booth where Steve was curled up, picking his nose, he sat down on the end and just watched us move around the pool table as we played.

If Brian stepped into any argument that Harry was involved in, Harry always backed out. It just meant that he didn't care enough about the subject to argue—not that that he was afraid of Brian. Harry just didn't like him well enough to let it look like they were both on the same side. Harry told me once that he didn't like how Brian could 'Lose his shit' over nothing. Then afterwards, have some kind of tantrum right in front of everybody. On top of that, he was always starting an argument just for the sake of it. Harry got enough of that at home.

Harry didn't argue—Harry hit. Most of the time, you didn't see it coming. It was just bam, and you were on the floor. The few times that Brian got into his face; Harry just dropped him. Brian was too stubborn to sort it out, and I figured there'd be a few more times coming before he learned his lesson. Besides, Harry and I were the better friends for the very same reason. We both agreed that arguing was pointless. The thing is, I couldn't go around punching people like Harry did. He knew how to knock you out with one blow. Me, I'd have to hit you four or five times to do any real damage.

So, it was at this moment that I realized my mistake. I was trying to protect Averell as if she was my own little sister, Shauna. Brian was going to use that against me.

"So, what's your problem lately, Cos? You starting to think you're better than us?"

"I'm not, why'd you think that? I am hanging out with you right now, aren't I?"

"Yeah well, not as much. You don't seem to care about us anymore since that Kathy showed up."

"Well, okay, so… I have a girlfriend now. So… I can't always be with youse."

"Youse," Steve mumbled and snickered. Harry turned and gave him an evil stare. Then faster than lightning, he hammer-fisted Steve's knee.

"Owww! Harry! You prick! What the…?"

"Shut the fuck up, moron, or I'm going to pound you into this booth, got it?"

"Gosh! Ok, fine," Steve said, trying to avoid Harry's eyes as he rubbed at his knee.

Harry got up and moving to the bar, he ordered a coke. Arnie brought the soda, and I heard him whisper to Harry that we had better calm down or we were going to get kicked out. Then looking at the lot of us, he said, "This is a tavern, not a goddamned kindergarten! So… straighten up!"

"See what you're doing, Cos? You've got everybody fighting. Now we're going to get kicked out," Brian blurted.

"Don't blame me for this! You're the one who started the crap."

"How did I start this? You're the one who got a girlfriend. All of us were perfectly happy, just hanging around together, until that girl showed up."

"No… I mean right now. We were doing ok until you stuck your big nose in Harry's and my business.

"Bullshit," Brian yelled and stomped back around the table, to take his shot.

"Tis!" I said.

"One more time, and you're all out of here!" Arnie hollered from behind the bar as he washed a glass. All the old farmers who were sitting there, turned, and looked at us. I got a feeling that they'd all be willing to help toss us out into the street if Arnie asked.

"Fine with me, Arnie," I said, and leaning my cue against the wall, I walked out.

"Ah, Cos…" I heard Harry say as the door closed.

Walking across the street, I sat on the corner. Leaning back against the pole, I lit up one of my ma's Pall Malls. Harry was watching me through the 'O' sometimes turning his head toward the bar like he was talking to Arnie.

There was something going on here that I didn't understand. Brian getting a little jealous because I had a girlfriend, was expected. Also, because Kathy had chosen me over him was something that was never mentioned; but was probably fueling the fire. But the way he'd been acting lately told me it was probably something else.

My ma said he had stopped at the apartment during the week when I was away. That was something he had never done before. He punched the door frame really hard when she told him I wasn't there and that scared her. She told him to leave.

Now, what you have to understand is, my ma still didn't know about Kathy. But I knew she suspected there was someone. She said she noticed changes in me. I thought that was kind of strange because

I didn't think she noticed much of anything that was going on outside of her head.

A few days ago, she said, "What's wid ya lad? Ya fall in love or somedin?" Then she mentioned she saw I was spending more time in front of the mirror and wasting a lot of water by showering every day. Now, Brian was coming around asking for me. He had probably called Harry or Steve's house, first to see if I was with them. If I wasn't, I must have been with Kathy.

Then a strange thought came to me. I started to wonder if Brian was queer. It's possible that one guy can love another guy without being homosexual, though. Because, well, boys love their da's, grandda's, and brothers. So, they must be able to love someone who is like a brother, but isn't related by blood.

That made me think about Brian's younger brother, Bart. He had died in a car accident over two years ago. I remember when it happened. Things got a little strange afterwards. Brian's older brother Ben, came home from the army for a few days, and there were a lot of people hanging around their apartment, downstairs. We didn't see Brian for a long time after that. When he finally did show up, he was kind of like a zombie.

After about a month, he came back around to almost being normal. But the more I was with him, the more I thought that he hadn't gotten over it. He kind of blamed his ma because she was the one driving at the time, and she had survived. One time he even said he wished it were her, not Bart. So, I think that is why he's always so mad.

Once, when we were on the corner, Steve asked him a question about Bart. Brian just blew-up and started swearing at Steve. Then he surprised us by crying right there on the street. He was really loud. People were stopping to stare, leaving me not sure what to say or do. Then Steve had to go and laugh at him. But instead of knocking Steve out, like he should have, Brian just ran away.

We watched him jump into the horseweeds between Slade's Auto Body and Whitcomb's Insurance office. There was nothing back there but a little, 'L' shaped open space between the buildings. It ran to the back of the body shop where it opened up into the parking lot behind the Royal Blue. There were more weeds blocking that end and because horseweeds grow really tall, if you stayed down, no one could see you in there. We had boxes and stuff set up in there to sit on. It's the place where we went to hide on Halloween after we smashed pumpkins or set off firecrackers.

I couldn't sort out why Brian cried that day, but I decided to just let it go. Mostly because people were always saying, "Just let it go, Cos. Just let it go." Brian was always trying to be tough and was usually the one to come down on me for not being tough enough to suit him. I think he got a lot of crap from his older brother, though, and maybe his da before he ran off to Vegas to try to get rich. Mr. Tribble never came home.

Now, I got to thinking, what if Brian was using me to fill Bart's shoes? That wasn't such a bad thing. It was kind of like hugging Kathy when she's feeling bad. If I just let Brian pretend I was Bart and let him treat me like I was, then he could feel better, too.

I needed to talk to him about this, but I didn't think he'd let me without freaking out. I had to try, though. He'd get over it like he did all the other times and I don't think I could go on like this much longer. Putting out my cigarette, I got up to go back to the tavern just as a car came around the corner way up by the school. It roared like a fighter jet down toward the square, leaving me to wonder what kind of trouble might be coming now

Chapter 5

<u>Highway Star</u>

It was a '57 Chevy, painted candy apple red. It didn't have any front fenders and someone had used rope to tie the headlights right onto the grill. There weren't any mufflers to speak of, or they might have been the Cherry Bomb brand. The ones that pissed off Marshal Tylor because they were noisy, but still legal. As loud as they were, the music pouring out of the windows was louder. 'Highway Star' by Deep Purple filled the square and rattled the windows of the buildings.

The car stopped at the intersection and the driver revved it up. He must have popped the clutch because the tires started to spin, and the rubber smoked. As it came across the square, it spun backwards. Then sliding sideways toward me, I jumped back up on the curb, hacking like crazy with the hot smoke burning my nose and lungs. For a second, I thought it might be Kathy. I imagined her da had taken away the Pinto and she had stolen a car so she could escape. But it was only Mike T. He slammed on the brakes and leaning out the window, he yelled, "Hey Cos! What's happening!"

"This your car, Mike? You finally got it finished?"

"Yeah, I still have to put the fenders on, though. The headlights don't work, they're just for show. But I can drive it until dark. I figured this getup would keep Marshal Tylor happy."

"Brilliant! So… where you off to?"

"Oh, I got sick of all that football practice. So, I left before they got done. That way I could drive around a while before dark. Want to go for a ride? Still got over an hour or more before the suns down."

"Soytenly," I said, and jumping off the curb, I got into the passenger seat.

Mike revved up the engine and that was about the time I saw Brian coming out of the tavern door. He yelled something at me, but I couldn't hear him over the car. Mike's foot slipped off the clutch, and he burned rubber for half a block as we raced back up toward the high school. I twisted in my seat just in time to watch Brian throw up his hands and have a tantrum right there on the corner. I turned away because I didn't want to see that.

I suddenly felt sad. He must have had the same idea as me and was coming out to talk. Now we'd have to wait until later to sort things out. I thought of asking Mike to go back and pick him up, but I didn't want to talk with Brian in front of him.

"Hey man, put your seatbelt on, this car is hot, sooo… you might need it!"

I looked over at him and got this weird feeling that getting into his car might have been a bad idea. He wasn't the same kid when he was behind the wheel. It reminded me of that, Dr. Jekyll, and Mr. Hyde story we had in Literature class. Mike was now a daredevil, stuntman, racecar driver. But I didn't want to be so uncool as to ask him to stop and let me out. My thoughts strayed back Kathy at the pond that day for some reason. I hadn't thought about that for a long time. I started to ponder that and then realizing I was, I cut it off and diverted my attention to the seat belt.

It wasn't the normal kind—more like a jet pilot's harness. Taking a quick peek into the backseat, I saw a couple tanks laying there marked, 'Danger-Nitrous Oxide'. There was also a medium sized, cardboard box wrapped in plastic that had 'Jaycee's Best Accumulator' printed on the side. That made me even more afraid.

"What the hell is that?"

"Don't worry about it, just put on your belt. It's behind your back and underneath your ass. Damn it, you're sitting on it! Get up!"

"Relax, will you."

Throwing him a dirty look, I pulled the top part over my head and the other half up between my legs. I snapped them together at my chest and now there was this huge red button at my chest like that I was supposed to hit if I wanted to get out.

"Cool, huh?"

"Uhhh… yeah, cool… I guess."

"You okay? You look kind of scared. Not chicken, are you?"

"Ummm… no, I'm okay," I said, probably still looking chicken.

He clicked his tongue and winked at me. Whipping the car left to avoid driving up the walk to the high school steps, we raced down past the junior high and elementary buildings. I looked over at the speedometer and saw the needle was right at seventy miles an hour. We passed the football field where a bunch of guys were out practicing; even though it was baseball season. Mike laid on the horn and kept it going until we got to the highway. Sliding into a U-turn at the stop sign, we raced back. This time all the guys on the field went to jumping up and down, waving their arms. Mike gave them a slow, cool wave, letting them know he was—the Highway Star.

To my relief that was the end of the race car driving. From that point on, we idled around town, taking every possible side street and alleyway. I was sure he wanted everyone to know he was out with his Chevy. I figured he was going to drive by every kid's house that he was friends with, hoping the rumble of the mufflers would bring them to the windows.

Soon the Marlboro's came out, and he offered me one. After lighting up, he rolled the radio's volume to high as we rolled slowly down Main Street, through the square, and across the river bridge.

We were smoking and listing to a band called Golden Earring, whose new hit *'Radar Love'* was booming from the speakers. That made Mike excited since it was a song, about a guy, driving a car, who was going to see a girl.

"You still seeing that girl, what's her name, ummm…? Katie?"

"Kathy. Yeah, why?"

"Oh, just wondering how that was going?"

"It's going super."

"You guys doing it?"

"Doing what?"

"You know, ummm… screwing? Have you screwed her?"

"Well… that's my feking business now, isn't it?"

Even though we both laughed, he understood I meant: 'Shut up or die!' I also suspect that is not what he thought I was going to say. He was expecting me to brag like I've heard other guys doing in the back of the class, in the locker room, or at lunch. Something I would never do. I stayed quiet when guys at school were bragging about stuff they did with their girlfriends. Since there was a girl in my life now that wasn't my sister, I figured it wouldn't be fair to talk about her like she was a piece of meat.

Fiana ragged on me about it all the time because she was a feminist. She followed that Jane Fonda person, and that other woman, Gloria something or other. When I was younger, she'd punch me if I laughed at my da's jokes about women. She'd threatened to mop the floor with my face if I ever talked like that. One time she even broke a framed picture over our da's head because he was beating up on her and ma.

I have to say, Fiana was pretty brave. She had to run away for a couple days after she hit da, but that was just the smart thing to do. She needed to give our da a chance to cool off. It was way back in '69 when she was my age and we had just moved into our country house. It was also around that time when she took me aside and tried to explain all about feminism and equal rights. I didn't get it all, but a lot of what she said made sense. It was because I wanted to be loyal to her that I did as she asked. Kind of like now, with Kathy. I mean, Fiana was my sister, and she was always looking out for me. There were times she helped me out of some tight spots. I kind of owed her. The guys wouldn't understand that stuff. So, I had to be careful. Which, brings me to: Chuck Griffin.

He was a friend of Mike T's. They played football together. He wasn't much taller than me, but he was, *"Stocky as a farmer!"* as my aunt was fond of saying. All the jocks pretty much tried to wear their hair the same, dress alike, and join the Country Club as soon as they could. Some were just born into it because their families were already members when they popped out of their ma at the hospital. Chuck was the only jock that wore glasses. But no one dare make fun him for it. Well—except for me and the guys.

Anyway, I had a friend whose name was Tammy. She made the mistake of going out with Chuck on a date. Things got really bad for her afterwards. Tammy was one of the first girls to make friends with me. She even wiped the blood off my lip with a tissue after Victor Barnes punched me in the mouth on the first day of fifth grade.

Tammy and I could talk about anything. When we were together, she always sat right up against me or had her arm over my shoulders. We stayed that way through jr. high and if I showed up for a school dance or ballgame, she'd be right there to hang out with me. I imagined at the time that she would become my first serious girlfriend.

She was short for her age, even shorter than me. She had blackish-brown hair, cut in what the girls called a 'shag', and a really cute, round face with dark eyes. Kids sometimes made short jokes about her, calling her 'munchkin' and things like that. But never if I was close enough to grab them.

The day after her and Chuck had their date, he bragged around the school how he had gotten into her pants. In less than twenty-four hours, it became everybody's business. Then there were not only short jokes, but slut and whore jokes. So, I got pretty busy making the other kids understand how I felt about it and not caring who they were on the popular scale.

Peggy Bowman, the most popular, but the meanest girl in our class, outright called her a tramp to her face. We had been in the art room at the time. When Tammy started to cry, I let Peggy know how I felt about herself and her opinion. Picking up a jar of paintbrush water, I baptized her on the spot. It soaked her pretty good, and she called me a few choice names before she ran out into the hallway. I had never heard her swear before that day. A lot of the other kids must not have either, because they all laughed like crazy. The art teacher did too, even though he tried to hide it.

I almost got into a fistfight with Chuck when he showed up at our afternoon cigarette break. The guys had to get between us, with Harry threatening to lay Chuck out if he didn't leave. I spent a lot of time in Principal Trotman's office that month. But I figured it was worth it for Tammy's sake.

One day, about five months ago, Tammy asked me to stay inside and eat with her in the lunchroom. I gave in because she wanted me to, but school food sucked. So, unless I had too, I didn't go in there. She told me that her family was moving to Omaha in July, and she wouldn't be back to school in August. My nose started to numb up, and I tried to hide how upset I was about it. It must have showed, though because she hugged me right there in front of everybody. I didn't believe the reason she was leaving Clarksburg was because of Chuck, but I sure wanted it to be. I needed someone to blame and he was the most likely (and deserving) candidate.

Mike T now had us across the bridge and down the river road at the south end of town. We were cruising along, and he had his head turned just enough, so he could look at me with his one pale blue eye. I wanted to make fun of it by asking him to shut that one and only stare at me with his brown eye. But I knew that wouldn't go over so well. He was sensitive about that and besides, I was practicing trying to be nice to people.

We hadn't talked to each other since he asked his question, and I supposed Mike was deciding if he should kick me out of his car or let me stay. I held my cigarette in my lips, with the smoke rolling up, giving him my best Clint Eastwood look. It was my version of the one from that '*Hang Em High*' movie. You know the one? Where Clint is squinting and looking mean all the time? Mike quit watching me then and brought his attention back to the road. After about a minute or so, the smoke started to hurt my eyes. I put the cigarette out in the ashtray and went to looking into the windows of the passing houses.

Now, I can't give Mike T a lot of credit for being smart because it didn't take long for him to start in again. The very same thing that Brian did that always upset Harry. He didn't know when to quit. I supposed it was stubbornness because they were so used to getting their way. I was having a tough time trying to sort out if that was a good thing or not. I figured being that way with their folks was how they got their way. But with guys like Harry, all it did was get you knocked out.

"So… doesn't she have a sister?"

"Who?"

"This, Kathy."

"She does and her name is Averell. Why? Do you want to date her too? Seems like everybody else wants to date her. So… why not you."

"Really? She doesn't have a boyfriend?"

"No, but she's sixteen now, so she might soon. Her parents are strict though, but they probably wouldn't mind if she hung out with a guy like you. I could always ask. I'd make sure you had your car in one piece though, and I wouldn't pull up in front of their big ol' mansion, revving up your engine."

"Would you ask for me? I mean… that would be great!"

"I suppose."

Now, I wasn't being honest. I just wanted things to calm down between us. If he thought I was mad at him, he'd always be nervous around me. If I was willing to do him a favor, he'd feel that everything was all right. I didn't have the heart to make him feel bad for too long.

"Wow! Man! That would be great!" he hollered, flipping his cigarette butt out the window.

Grinning that stupid grin of his, he checked his face and hair in the mirror. Then fumbling more cigarettes out of his shirt pocket, he gave me another one and then lit it for me with the cars lighter. I figured if I hung around with Mike T too much, I'd turn into a chain smoker. I decided at that moment I wasn't going to accept every damned offer of tobacco that came my way. I would be dead of cancer before I even turned twenty-one if this kept up. In fact, it was Mike who got me started smoking in the first place. Then along came Brian and Steve. But Harry had been smoking since he was twelve.

Mike changed the subject from girls, to talking about the Chevy. It was one tough decision after another for him. To go with Fat 50's, or Mega Deluxe 60 sized tires? Slicks or tread? A nitrogen booster versus an overdrive unit—whatever that was. He had a whole list of things to make it 'high performance' as he put it. I wondered where the money came from, thinking my ma and I could live pretty decently on what Mike T spent on his car. I would never become a Motorhead.

We soon turned north, going up Snob Hill through the rich folk's neighborhood, and came back around by the highway. Mike T drove through the Dairy Dreem parking lot so we could see who might be inside. He suddenly slammed on the brakes and stopping the Chevy right in front of the big windows, he revved up the engine. I could see the glass vibrating and a few people inside covering their ears. A bunch of jr. high kids, came over to stare at us. They were pumping their arms up and down, like they wanted him to do a few more revs. So, of course, he did. I just sat there looking at the glove box, feeling like a fool.

Shelagh Bennett walked up to the glass wearing a red apron that had two big, white capital D's on the front. She had a broom in one hand, and I figured she was using sweeping as an excuse to come out from behind the counter. That way she could get a closer look at us. I could see she was staring right at me. She smiled big, bringing her free hand up real slow, like she wasn't sure if she should wave or not. Mike waved for me, and Shelagh dropped her hand real quick and started pushing her broom around the floor. She'd only been working there for about two weeks. Somebody told she was related to the owner.

Mike finally took his foot off the brake, and we coasted out the exit and rolled back down Main Street toward the river bridge.

"Did you see Shelagh Bennett? She works there now. She's hot for your bod, man! She told me so one day when I was in there with the football team. She can't date yet, but said when she turns sixteen, she's going to ask you out."

"What? Are you kidding? Well… it's too late for that now, isn't it? I mean, I'm going steady with Kathy. I don't plan on breaking up anytime soon."

He made a face like he didn't care and continued, "I asked her if she'd go out with me, but… she only said, maybe. She told me she doesn't like jocks. So, I guess that meant me. I told her that you and I are really good friends and that we hang out together… a lot. I think that made a difference. But I don't know for sure. You don't mind, do you?"

"I suppose not, but let's see… you want to date Averell, and you want to date Shelagh. So… who don't you want to date?"

"Well… uhhh… I don't want to date that girl everyone calls Lewis. That really fat girl in Mr. Rodinger's history class! Man! She's a giant."

"Okay, but you know, she's a nice girl. I've talked with her about homework stuff and she's smart. And you know what else? She's not fat. She's just… well… big and tall. Besides, I don't think Lewis would go out with you, anyway."

"What? Why not?"

"What does it matter?"

"Well, because I'm a cool guy."

"Come on Mike, like I said, she's a smart girl. Why would that matter to her?"

"I don't know. Everybody wants to be cool, I guess or… be with somebody who is, right?"

"So, maybe I should tell her you want to go out with her?"

"What? No! Don't do that. I mean… that's crazy."

"It doesn't matter—you're never going to get laid, anyway."

"WHAT?"

"Just kidding."

"You're still going to ask Averell, right? I mean, to see if she'll go out with me?"

"I will, so… shut up about that now."

"Oh, good! That would be so cool. You are so cool."

"Yeah," I said and sat there, puffing on my Marlboro, supposing I was pretty important to him right then, but still wishing I could get out of that damn harness.

After about our twelfth trip down every street in Clarksburg, Mike decided he had to go home. We were only three blocks down from the high school on 4th Street when he asked me if I could walk back to the tavern. It was dark by this time and he was afraid of getting in trouble for not having headlights that actually worked. I felt he was being kind of a jerk, but I understood about getting into trouble. I didn't argue. I walked those eight blocks twice every school day. So, five of them, one way, wasn't going to kill me.

It was a nice night out. The moon was coming up, and the stars were popping out everywhere. A cool breeze was blowing through the trees and that was one thing I really liked about Clarksburg, it had a ton of trees, big and tall ones, lining just about every street. I liked trees. There was also a good chance most of them had been there way back before there was a town. I don't think there was one place in Clarksburg where you could stand without being around trees. It wasn't like this in my town back in Ireland. So, I kind of fell in love with them.

Sadly, another thing you have to understand about my town back in Ireland was—you had to be careful where you walked. How you wore your hat. What color your shirt was, and what football team you fancied. In Iowa, I'd gotten used to not having to worry about any of that. At least, until this particular evening.

It was because of those big trees that I didn't see the car parked a block behind me. Least not until it whipped out and its headlights flashed across me. I suppose I wasn't paying much attention because I was thinking about other things. Happier things.

Chapter 6

Hair

I felt the hair rise on the back of my neck when I heard, "Hey freak, whatcha doing?"

It was Chuck rolling along beside me in someones car. I figured he felt he had something to settle with me. Keeping my eyes forward, I gave him the Ernie B treatment, hoping he'd leave me alone. From the corner of my eye, I recognized the orange Plymouth Duster as one of the cars that had been parked at that football practice.

"He looks like a cute little girl, doesn't he?"

That was Tommy 'The Weasel' Fiesel. He was this tall skinny guy who was the kicker for the team. A real loud-mouth who was good at running away after he opened it.

"Hey freak, why don't you get a haircut?"

I gave in and looked over at them, trying to see who might be in there. Chuck was on my side in front with Weasel at the wheel. There were two others in the back, but I couldn't see their faces. I wasn't afraid, but if all four jumped on me at the same time, I was in big trouble.

They were talking among themselves, but I couldn't hear what they saying because of the country & western music pouring out of the windows. What I did hear was a line from the song, saying something about not letting your hair grow long and shaggy. I felt one of those bad chills.

"Hey freak! You going to say something, or am I going to have to get out of this car and pound it out of you?" That was Chuck again. Everybody else was laughing and then the guys in the back seat yelled, "Do it, Chuck, do it."

I kept walking, looking at them sometimes, still counting the blocks back to the square. I only had three more to go, but as stupid as it was, I thought about stopping and taking Chuck on. So, I did, and facing them, I watched the car roll to a stop with everybody piling out.

"What's with you, boyo? Can't do this alone?" I yelled at Chuck.

He came at me, but stopped short of the sidewalk. That's when I saw the other two from the backseat. Kevin and Bobby Schupp. They were big guys who played as tackles on the team. The thing is, even though they played good American football, they weren't real brave off the field. They needed to have a leader to follow. Somebody once told me they were 'easy going'. They wouldn't start the crap, but they'd most certainly join in. Now, they were with their quarterback, so they had to look tough.

I suspected the four of them would surround me and start pushing me back and forth between them, punching or slapping me. That's the way it always went. I decided to do the smart thing now that they were out of the car—I ran.

They all jumped back in the Duster and I was almost a half a block away before I heard the car move. Now, if they had chased me on foot, they would have caught me for sure. Mostly because I smoked regularly and they didn't. The only time I ever ran was when we were out playing 'catch me if you can' with Marshal Tylor.

They had no choice but to keep following me until I passed out or they were able to cut me off. When Weasel finally sorted it out to use the car to block my path, he whipped it into the short driveway at Slade's. Pushing the bumper right up against the big, wooden garage door, he blocked the sidewalk. I didn't want to slow down, but I knew changing directions meant that I'd have too. If I ran around behind the car, Chuck may jump out and grab me. I wanted to keep his door between the two of us. I pictured myself jumping completely over the hood like I thought I was some kind of broad jump champion. But no, that wasn't going to work. The front tire was turned out, so I used it as a step and jumping onto the hood, I ran across, caving the steel as I went. Jumping off the other side, I hit the ground running.

I was pretty proud of that move, but that lasted all of five seconds. Weasel was already out of the Duster, yelling, "Damn it! My car!"

and in no time at all, he had a hold on the back of my shirt. This stopped me dead in my tracks as all the buttons on the front popped off. I thought to slip out of it and run away bare chested, except there came this loud grunt and he let me go. Looking back over my shoulder, I sorted that Bobby must have tripped coming out of the car. He fell on top of Weasel and they crashed down onto the sidewalk with Weasel screaming out, "Ahhh! My nose!" followed by, "Get your fat ass off me, Bobby!"

"You idiots! He's going to get away!" Chuck yelled.

He was right because that's just what happened. Even though my lungs felt like they were on fire, having escaped Weasel's grip gave me a boost of energy. I ran like crazy for the corner with only half a block to go. By the time I got there, the Duster was already racing up to the square. Realizing at the last second, it would better if I got inside the tavern, I cut across the street.

Of course, I was thinking Weasel wouldn't run the stop sign, but— nope. The Duster screeched to a halt, the bumper inches from my legs. Stupid mistake on my part. Even though they wanted to hurt me— they didn't want to kill me. I supposed they were thinking that prison would ruin their football careers.

I made it to the opposite corner, just as the tavern door swung open. The guys tumbled out onto the walkway, along with Arnie, holding his infamous Louisville Slugger. I stopped there and turned around to face my enemies. The equal numbers made me brave. The Duster hadn't moved from the spot where it had stopped.

It looked like they were going to climb out, least until Harry and the others lined up beside me with Arnie behind, standing on the steps, tapping that ball bat against an open palm. The car doors clicked shut as Weasel revved up the engine. Popping the clutch, the wide rear tires smoked as the car zoomed away down the street.

Arnie walked up to me and pulling my shirt closed at the front, said, "You okay there, Cos?"

"Fine as frog's hair. It's all that running that about killed me," I said and coughed a few times for good measure.

"That was that A-hole, Chuck," Steve said, sharing the obvious.

"Did you catch all that blood on Weasels face? What the hell happened, Cos? You give him what-for?" Brian asked.

"Ah no, he fell down. Smacked his nose on the pavement, he did. I don't think he's going to forget about that or… the big dent I put in the hood of his precious car."

They all laughed. I felt a weird sense of accomplishment. It was like I had actually done something worthwhile. But those things weren't going to help. It wasn't over. Those guys would want revenge. So, it was only a matter of time.

"You young fellows better go on home now before the marshal shows up," Arnie said as he stepped inside, letting the door shut behind him.

When he was out of earshot, Harry growled, "Fuck that, I ain't going home."

I watched him move across the street as lightning flashed above the trees up on Snob Hill, to the west. Harry sat down on the corner and lit up a smoke. We followed and sat with him, everybody pulling out cigarettes, but me. When my breathing got back to normal, Harry offered me a Kool, but I turned it down. He made a face, and I thought he was going to give me crap about it. But all he said was, "So what was that all about, Cos? Where'd you run into them, at?"

"I was walking down the street up by the library and…"

"What were you doing up there? The library's closed," Steve said.

"Shut the hell up, Steve, you moron. He wasn't at the library," Brian answered for me, giving Steve a shove.

"I was out riding around with Mike T. He didn't want to bring me back downtown because it was dark, and his headlights didn't work, so…"

"You mean that A-hole couldn't bring you back?" Steve added, now getting mad at Mike T.

"Steve! Dammit! Let him talk!" Harry shouted, throwing him the evil eye. Steve just looked away and took another drag off his cigarette.

"Yeah… so… those guys were doing a football practice, and we drove by up there. I think they must have seen me in the front seat of Mike's car. You know that Chuck and I haven't been getting along, not since he did that thing to Tammy."

"What thing to Tammy?"

"STEVE! Shut your big mouth!" Harry shouted, nearly deafening my left ear.

"Geez, Harry! No, it's okay. Steve, I'll tell you later. Why don't you guys calm down? Damn!"

Harry huffed and mumbled something to himself. His adrenaline was up now and he wanted to hurt someone. I saw him give Steve another dirty look. Steve kept his eyes down and after scuffing out his cigarette butt, he went to nudging a bottle cap around with the toe of his cow crap covered ranch boot.

Brian leaned forward to look around Harry and asked me, "So, why does Chuck hate you so much? It's been months since the Tammy thing. You'd think he'd gotten over you pushing him around that one day?"

"Well, he started the whole 'freak' thing tonight. That got the others going. Before I knew it, they were ready to kick my arse. So… I don't know.

"Well, next time he calls you a freak… you ought to call him a redneck and see how he likes that," Brian blurted out. He went to nodding his head and looking around at us, like he thought we'd all agree.

"Yeah, great, Brian. Start some shit like that and the whole town will be fighting because practically everybody here is a redneck," Harry said, adding, "Hell, Steve's a redneck."

"I ain't no redneck! I may be a farmer, but…"

"Steve, you're a redneck. They are the same thing, idiot! That's what I'm saying, we don't want to start that crap."

I watched Steve's face and I could see he was trying to sort it out. So, I said, "Don't worry about it, I'm not going to do that. That will only make it worse. Maybe Chuck's had enough and we can call it even."

"Cos, I think you're dreaming," Harry said, slapping my knee and grinning.

"I saw Chuck and his brother up at the Coogan auction and…"

"Steve, why don't you shut the fuck up?" Brian said, flicking Steve's ear lobe through his bushy hair.

"Yeah, shut the…" Harry started to say before I interrupted with, "No! Let him talk."

"No… the hell with this," Harry said, and standing up, he flicked his cigarette butt at Steve and without even a, "See you, later," he walked away down the street toward his house.

"Where you going?" I asked.

"Home, I've had enough of that moron."

"Ah come on, Harry, give him a break."

"Nope, I am going home now. I've had enough of Goofy's shit for one day. See you, Cos."

"What about me? I'm sitting here too!"

"Oh, yeah… sorry Brian… kiss my ass! How's that? Feel better now?"

Harry turned around and started walking backwards, making a weird face at Brian.

"What the hell did I do?" Steve whispered.

"Don't worry about it, he's uptight right now. He'll get over it." I said, as I watched Harry spin back around and walk the two blocks to his place.

"I don't know about that," Brian said.

When he was sure Harry wasn't looking, he raised his middle finger in that direction before dropping it quickly. Leaning toward me, he said in a low voice, "Well… to be honest, Steve is kind of an annoying doofus."

"I heard that! Why don't you eat shit! You trying to yank my chain, too?"

"Steve! Just ignore him.' I said, "What about the auction?"

"I was just gonna say that I was at the Coogan auction with my dad, and I saw Chuck there with his older brother, Micky. They were hanging out at the cattle barn with old man Kelly, and guess who else?"

"Ummm… Captain Kangaroo?" Brian said and laughed.

"No! Shut up! I'm talking to Cos! So… guess, Cos."

"Nope, not going to guess. Just tell me or I'm going to go all Harry Fulton on you."

"Okay, damn! You don't need to get crazy! It was Seymour Henton."

"So what? Who the hell are they, and why does that matter? I mean…"

"No, wait, Brian, it does. Steve are you sure it was ol' man Henton?"

"Yeah, I'm sure! I know that guy. He buys more cows than all my relatives put together."

"So… why does that matter?" Brian asked, sounding annoyed.

"Because… that's Kathy's da, ummm… father."

"Oh! I get it," Brian said, looking disappointed now that Steve was making sense.

"Yeah! I was trying to tell you…"

"Ah shut up, you're still a ditz," Brian said, and picking up the bottle cap, he bounced it off Steve's forehead.

"Hey!" Steve said, and they started tussling.

I got to thinking real hard about what Steve had said. It left me wondering if there was some kind of connection between the Griffins and the Henton family. It could have easily been a bunch of farmers just shooting-the-shit, as they say. But even when I tried to convince myself it was okay, it didn't make me feel any better. I didn't want Chuck in my business. So, I figured I'd simply ask Kathy the next time she came down.

I also wanted to ask Steve, why, if he was familiar with ol' man Henton, how come he didn't he say so sooner. But I figured he either hadn't known Kathy's last name, or maybe he wasn't smart enough to sort it out and make the connection. If I said anything, he'd just feel bad. He was getting enough crap from Harry and Brian as it was. Steve didn't need it from me, too. I figured I'd wait until there was a day when we were alone together, then we could talk.

We were on the corner up until about curfew, with Steve and Brian still going at it. The lightning was close enough that we could hear the thunder. Every time it flashed; we could see the huge clouds boiling above our heads.

Marshal Tylor soon rolled through the square, giving us a wave. That was our cue. Looking over at the clock on the Standard station sign, it said we had about two minutes left. The thunder cracked, and it was so loud, it gave me goose bumps. I got up to go home and the others got up too. Brian and I started walking together toward our apartment building with Steve saying, "See yah!" as he started running the other direction.

He had the farthest to go because his farm was out on the edge of town. We knew he'd use the backyards and alleyways to keep from being seen by Marshal Tylor. He had done it enough times in the past that we didn't have to worry about Steve getting home. Except, tonight, he was probably going to get that much needed shower.

"Hey, Brian, we need to talk," I said, stopping at the stoop in front of my place.

He kept walking but turned and waited at the corner of the building where there was a set of old, wooden steps that ran down to his. I figured he would come back over to where I was standing, but he just stayed there in the creepy shadow of this old apple tree. It overhung the steps and in the late summer you had to try to not trip over the apples that fell there.

"What do you mean?" Brian asked.

"The tavern, remember? You were pretty pissed off."

"Not going to talk about that, right now."

"But I thought…"

"Nah, got to go. See you… someday."

Then he disappeared down the steps, leaving me alone on the street. He didn't seem to care about the situation as much as I did. Now, I had no choice but to wait until I could corner him again.

Going inside my place, I went to my room and got undressed. Trying hard not to worry about Brian only brought me back to Chuck. That guy wasn't going to quit until he had me bloody. There needed to be a plan to deal with him, but I was too tired to come up with one. Laying on my bed in the dark, I listened to Brian arguing with his mother, downstairs. There was a loud, "I don't want to go." A door slammed and then it got real quiet.

It was the time of night that I missed my sisters the most. Fiana would let me sneak into her room when I was younger, and we'd listen to her records. The last time, was just before she left with our da. She had bought the *Hair* album for that really popular rock opera, and we learned every song by heart. *'Aquarius'* was her favorite because that was her astrology sign. Mine was the main song, *'Hair'* and I don't think I need to explain why. Shauna was too young for that kind of thing to be fun for her. She'd always get cranky because we didn't want to play house or tea party.

I started humming that song, but it made me sad. I needed real music. So, reaching over, I turned on my radio. I wanted to focus on something new, not the past. Music could help me do that. Sometimes I'd forget to turn off the old Philips portable and it would play for days at a time. I kept it low and tuned to KAAY 1090 AM, Beaker Street. Good ol' Clyde Clifford was going on about the band '*It's A Beautiful Day*'. Then playing the next song on his list, I fell asleep to '*Girl With No Eyes*' wondering what Brian meant by, 'Someday'

Chapter 7

<u>Without You</u>

I remember waking up to the rain beating against the big windows. The wind was whistling around, causing the screen door to bang. A hook and eye kept it from blowing open, making me glad I'd set the thing after coming in. There was a couple of minutes when I hoped there wouldn't be a tornado. But deciding I was too tired to care, I fell asleep.

It wasn't until much later that I almost fell out of my bed because of a nightmare. Kathy had come to pick me up on the corner, and when she took off her sunglasses, I saw she had no eyes. Instead, they looked like Little Orphan Annie's in the comic pages. She had been staring straight at me and when I got close, I saw myself reflected in them. There was something different about me though, almost like, it was me looking—but not exactly me, looking back. Like a more grown-up version of me in those reflections.

I tried to focus my eyes so I could read my brass alarm clock. The glow-in-the-dark hands told me it was 4:30 in the morning. Raindrops were still beating against the glass. I wished I could switch off the annoying streetlamps to make the room darker. Cursing the windows for being too tall and the curtains, for being too short, I rolled over to face the wall and dozed off again.

When Kathy actually did show up at the corner later that day, there were no sunglasses. Her green eyes twinkled, and I felt relieved. For the first time since we had met, she parked her car in a proper spot and came over to sit with me on the curb. Chatting about how our nights went, we got around to the nightmare. She teased me afterwards by sticking a quarter on each eye, and shouting something about lizards jumping (or maybe it was leaping). Then after calling by the names of every character from the orphan Annie comic page, I made her stop.

Getting bored with the corner, we got in the Pinto and drove around. We finally ended up at the county park. She wanted to go up to the top floor of this huge rocket-like piece of playground equipment. Three levels of steel bars, red paint, and a slide that came out one side. It seemed kind of silly to be in children's playground equipment at our age, but we were the only ones around and it was a good place to make out.

The storm had passed out of the area about sunrise. With the sky clear, the day heated up fast, drying everything out. I decided not to tell her about Chuck and his mates chasing me, figuring I could bring it up later. She didn't need to know right then. Besides, it might sound like I was feeling sorry for myself and trying to get her pity.

So, we sat cross legged on the floor and I asked if she knew the Griffins, not mentioning anything about Chuck hating me—or about Tammy. She told me they sometimes did business with her da. But she didn't know them personally. She had never met Chuck, but she remembered someone that looked like the guy I described. Whenever they stopped by her place, they stayed out in her father's office in the barn. She had seen him hanging around out there, just staring at her when she was doing chores.

She just ignored him and always made sure her shirttail was hanging out so he couldn't see her backside. Sometimes she'd catch him peeking around a corner at her, giving off a creepy vibe. After a while, she didn't want to talk about that anymore. Changing the subject, she asked me, "What's different about you?"

"What do you mean?"

"Hmmm… is it your clothes? Did you get new clothes?"

"I did. So? Just a couple of jumpers and some bellbottoms."

She was asking about the clothes that were given to me by the community center. The local dentist's wife was the person who ran it. Ol' Wilhelmina Theobald figured she knew what a kid, my age, might like. I couldn't argue because she was right most of the time. So, Wilhelmina had stopped by to check on my ma and dropped off a good pair of Levi's and two black, turtle necked jumpers. They were pretty nice, so I wore them to impress Kathy. It didn't go as planned.

"Jumpers?" she shouted, laughing. "Jumpers are for girls, silly. They are like dresses with straps." Reaching out, she ran her fingertips over the material of the jumper.

"That's just a… really thin sweater, or… something."

"This is a jumper. It's for men. That's what we called them in Ireland."

"Oh! I see, okay, so… we are not in freaking Ireland! Okay? So… so maybe we can just call them turtlenecks. And isn't it a little warm for one of those? I mean, it's July already."

"It's okay. If we hadn't come up inside this contraption, it wouldn't be so toasty right now."

It was not a good time for a bad mood, but it was coming. I was still practicing trying to be a nice guy, but I was failing. My goal had been to impress her, but she had made fun of me. I'd usually go off on somebody for that, sometimes even getting up and walking away without a word. But I didn't. It was like my patient side always came out when I was around her and I vowed I wasn't going to push her. So, I didn't lose my temper. What you have to understand is, there weren't too many people I could say that about at the moment.

Kathy noticed my mood had changed. Laughing softly, she said, "Ahhh, you're such a sweet boy." Sliding over, she put her arm around my waist. Planting her chin on my shoulder, she stared at the side of my face, crossing, and uncrossing her eyes.

She was trying to cheer me up, so I suspect she felt guilty about poking at me about my clothes. I was trying to pull myself out of my funk, and then it came to me that I didn't always have to be on top of the world when we were together. I was sure it was okay with her if I were blue sometimes—just not mean.

"Cos?"

"Himself," I whispered without looking at her.

"What was it like to live in Ireland?"

"Before I answer that, let's get the fek out of this hotbox. We can go sit under the trees. I'm roasting up here."

"Okay, let's get the fek out of this feking oven, but first… let me put my feking sandals on my feking feet, before we go, okay?"

She grinned, raising her eyebrows at me, her face saying, 'Well? What are you going to do about it, huh?' Not knowing what to do, I stuck my tongue out at her. She returned her version of a raspberry, making a weird face. Slipping on her Birkenstocks, she gave me a light punch on the shoulder before scooting her backside across the floor to the exit. She tried to get down the ladder before I came for my revenge, but I wasn't trying too.

I followed her over to the hatch, and we squeezed our way down through all three floors of the USS Galaxy before dropping out at the bottom. Walking down to a long row of huge trees on the river bank, we sat down in the grass with our backs against one of the trunks. Because she was taller than me, Kathy had to push her backside out a ways from the tree to put her head on my shoulder. Wrapping my arm in hers, she sighed and closed her eyes.

It always made me feel good when she did that. It was like I was the most important person in her life. What she didn't know—because I never said—was how important she had become in mine. I was getting used to her rough, sometimes crazy, ways and at that moment, nothing could hold a candle to her. I was willing to fight anyone who'd try to keep me from her. Thinking about that, brought me out of my funk.

"So, tell me about Ireland? You're not getting off the hook this time. Sure, you don't like talking about it, but… you have too, now."

"Okay, fine. There isn't that much to tell. It was all very green and very different from America. But… Iowa, in some ways, is a lot like Ireland. Except… you-all, talk funny."

"Oh, you idiot! We don't talk like that!"

She laughed and grabbing my arm, gave me a little shake She then made up for it by giving me a quick smooch on my cheek.

"What do you mean, 'idiot'? Don't you mean, 'eejit'? That's how we say it… eejit. Kind of like: Kathy Henton, yer such an eejit!"

"Ohhh! Youuu!" she said, pinching the end of my nose. Then she stuck hers in my hair and sniffed.

"Mmm… baby shampoo. Your hair smells like baby shampoo. Oh man! That's so sexy! So, tell me Cos, do you remember any of your friends from back in Ireland?"

"Well, I came here when I was all of eleven years old. It's only been about five years since… so… yeah… I do remember a few. Especially, Orlin. She was my best friend. Her hair was almost pure white hair and cut like a pixie's. She had these pinkish-red eyes and fangs. Like… ummm… what do they call them? Ummm…

"Canines?"

"That's it! She had extra-long canine teeth kind of like a vampire. She always wore this short yellow dress and went barefoot just about everywhere she went. I remember she always had dirty feet."

"So… she was an albino? You had an albino girlfriend once? Man! That must have been weird."

"Well… but I liked her. She was tough. If kids made fun of her, she'd kick their arse and I'd help. I guess people were so used to her being around that they stopped caring about what she looked like. Her skin wasn't that much lighter than yours, though. It was mostly her hair and eyes that were different."

"Yeah, I get you. So… you had lots of sex with your pink eyed pixie vampire? Did she try to bite your neck?"

"Well, we did. Ummm… just one time."

"What! You were having sex when you were only eleven?"

"Ten actually—and it was Orlin's idea. I honestly didn't know what was happening. Even at that age, she knew how to do it. Her ma was the village tail… uhhh… prostitute? That's how she paid her bills. There were always fishermen and sailors hanging about her place. Her ma didn't hide it from Orlin, either. I don't hold it against her, though, times were hard."

"So, Cos, tell me all about it. I mean… you and Orlin. If I remember correctly, you said you had never been naked in front of anyone, before?"

"Oh, I meant I was never completely without a stitch of clothes. Unless you think having your trousers down around your knees is naked. Okay, so one day we were out playing in the bog. Orlin snuck up behind me and whipped my trousers down around my ankles. At first, I thought it was a joke. But she pushed me down on the grass and when I rolled over, she pulled up her dress and jumped on me. The rest is all a blur. It was all very strange. She told me it was how her ma did it. I'm not even sure you can call it sex."

"Is that all true?"

"Cross my heart."

"Well, I have a confession. Ummm… I had sex for the first time when I was fourteen."

She got quiet after that. Her face told me she was afraid I'd get mad about what she had to tell me. Her eyes got real big and I think she may have thought it was a mistake to say anything. Staring down at the ground, she started pulling out blades of grass and tossing them into the breeze. She seemed ashamed.

"My first time wasn't so great, either. But—it was actually sex. No doubt about it."

"So, are you going to tell me more or… is that all?"

"Oh, I'm going to tell you. It's just… hard to find the words."

"It's okay, I won't make fun of you. Was it bad?"

"Well, because I didn't want to, and because it was with an older boy who really didn't care about me... yeah, I suppose."

She was quiet for another moment, like she had to sort it. Finally, the words came, and she said, "It happened in the hayloft of my dad's barn. My relatives were over for Thanksgiving dinner. They had an older, adopted boy who came along. He and I were up in the haymow, goofing off, talking, and swinging on a tire swing. I fell off into the hay, and was laughing so hard, I hardly noticed that he had come over and was sitting next to me. Then he pinned me down and started kissing me real hard. I tried to make him stop, but he was too strong. He sat on top of my legs, covering my mouth with one hand while he pulled up my dress with the other. The next thing I knew, his pants were down and so was my underwear. Oh man! Did that hurt! I'll never forget that."

"So… he raped you? The maggot, raped you."

"I suppose you can call it that."

"No! There's no supposing. That's what it was, plain and simple. My sister Fiana would've ripped his bollocks off. Or… at least, that's what she told me she'd do."

"Well, I didn't. So, I believe he still has his—whatever those are. I remember I had trouble walking straight for a couple days. I had to tell my mom that I'd pulled a muscle in gym class. If I said anything about what he had done, I'd be the one to get in trouble. So, I kept my mouth shut, well… until now. I mean, I feel like I can tell you anything and you won't judge me. You make me feel safe. I trust you."

Her voice sounded like it was coming out of an empty closet; kind of hollow and far away. I looked at her, not knowing what to say. I imagined her being held down with a hand over mouth so she couldn't scream. It gave me one of those bad chills.

My ire was coming up. At first, I didn't understand why she didn't go berserk on that guy. Memories of my da holding me down while he slapped and punched me, came rolling through my head. I realized that I did understand. It was all very clear. After he got done with me—I didn't want to go berserk—I wanted to go hide. Sitting underneath that tree by the river, I realized for the first that something had been taken from me. I just wasn't sure what. But I figured if I worked on it long enough, I'd sort it. So, the same for Kathy. Something had been stolen from her and she was never going to get it back. Sure, I did know what it was like to be forced, but I believe for Kathy—it was twice as bad.

I was looking at her, but it was like I wasn't seeing her. When she finally came back into focus, I saw a single tear rolling down her cheek. She wiped it away quickly and with her voice sounding like it was cracking, she said, "Damn… here I go again."

Turning her face to stare down the river, she got real quiet. I sat there, not knowing what to say or do. Because I felt so helpless to do anything about it, I started to get madder. Not wanting to feel that way, I finally pulled my arm from hers and put it over her shoulders. I needed to do something, anything, to let her know that I cared.

She turned back to me and pushed her left arm between the tree trunk and my back. Laying her other arm over my belly, she scooted her backside down even farther. Snuggling her face into my chest, she hid her eyes. We stayed that way for a long time, with me stroking her hair and her weeping.

After she calmed down, she sat back up and wiped her eyes. Bringing her knees up to her chest, she wrapped her arms around them and rested her chin on top.

"I don't understand why that still bothers me. It's been four years, but I still cry when I think about it. That's why I am so happy with you, Cos. I never met anyone like you before. You make me feel like there are still some nice people in the world. I really don't understand why my parents don't like you."

"What? Your parents know about me?"

She made an 'oops!' face, saying, "Well… there is something else I need to tell you. You're probably not going to like it. They asked if it was true that there was a boy. I suspect Averell opened her big mouth."

"Or maybe… Chuck Griffin! I'd think Chuck before Averell."

"Well, there's a good chance you're right. But anyway, we might have to start being more careful. My dad doesn't want me to get mixed up with any local boys. But honestly, I'm sure he believes that there isn't anyone good enough for me. So… the hell with him! Because… well, I know he's wrong about that. He hasn't ever met you, so… he doesn't know that you're a nice guy. You should also be aware that I don't care about anybody else's opinions. But, if you think it's too dangerous, or you're afraid… you can get up right now and walk away. I'll understand."

It was I who didn't understand. I was not so sure she did, either.

If I got up and left her, she'd probably freak out. It also seemed like she was trying to break things off with me. That hurt more than anything her da might do. Right now, I wasn't in the mood for it. My ire was already up about the rape thing, and I was trying not to lose my cool. Kathy was looking right into my eyes and her pupils were huge. Her bottom lip was quivering a wee bit, which told me she was about ready to start crying again. I still wanted to test her, though. So, as mean as it was—I stood up like I was going to be off.

She tipped her head back, watching me with a surprised look on her face. But I quickly reached down, took her hand and pulled her to her feet. She just stood there, looking down at me, hugging herself. I quickly put my arms around her waist and pulled her to me. Pressing the side of my face against her chest, I squeezed. She wrapped her arms around me and sighed.

"Oh my! I was so afraid you were actually going to leave."

Laying her cheek on the top of my head, she trembled. I felt bad for testing her, but it needed to be done. We stood there until the sun was gone. She seemed to be all cried out and for about five minutes, there was only the noise of the river along with cars whooshing by on the highway's trestle bridge a short distance downstream.

"We should go, I mean… I don't want to, but I have a dinner tonight. Or I should say, my family does. There's this stupid Cattlemen's Supper up in Delaware County and my dad's supposed to get an award of some kind."

"Shouldn't keep em waiting, I guess."

I needed to be alone, anyway. So, I figured it was a good time for her to go. She stepped back and cupped my cheek, looking sweetly into my face. The watch she normally kept hanging on her rearview mirror, was now on her wrist. I watched her eyes move to it and she said, "Oh crap, I'm going to be late! Crap! Cos, can we go? Please?"

"Of course."

"Race me?"

She took off across the grass without another word. I held back a second but closed the gap in no time. Even though her legs were longer, I was still faster. Passing her up, I got to the back of the car first. Bending forward with my hands on my knees, I waited, trying to catch my breath. She was there two seconds later. Laying back against the rear window of the car, she stared up into the sky, panting.

"Cos! Kiss me. Kiss me now while I'm out of breath."

I didn't know what to say because that was so daft. We had been in such a hurry to go and now she wanted to make out. The look on her face said, 'Just do it!'

I had to crawl up on her to get to her lips. All the time I was there, I was afraid that we were going to crash through the glass of the hatchback. I found myself hoping that Ford had taken that into consideration when they designed the car.

We kissed for a moment, then sliding back down, I grew dizzy with little white dots swimming around in front of my eyes. It was a strangely, good kind of feeling. So, I could see why she liked doing it.

Straightening her clothes, she said, "Let's go!" But I was already on my way.

We both jumped into the Pinto and starting it up, she raced backwards all the way across the parking lot. Spinning around out onto the main road of the park, she shifted into a forward gear and we zoomed away.

Nilsson was on the radio singing '*Without You*' and there couldn't have been a worse song for the moment. It brought me back to when she said I could just walk away if I needed too. I told myself, no. Not going to happen. I was going to hang on for dear life and she'd have to peel me off like a tight-fitting tee shirt.

I sat looking at her face as she drove. When she finally looked my way, I saw the sadness in her eyes. It left me wondering if the song was having the same effect on her. Music had always been important in my life. If anything were going to stir me up, it would be music. The song in the background made things seem weird. My nose was starting to numb up and that was a bad sign. She had softened me up, and now, Nilsson was going to finish the job. I was going to cry. I tried forcing myself to get mad, because if I did, the tears might not come. The problem was—she noticed.

"What's wrong?" she said. "I can see something in your eyes. Something kind of..."

"It's nothing."

"Okay, fine, but Cos... I need to tell you something."

"Well?" I said, trying to not to let her see my face.

"I'm not totally sure, because I've never felt this before, but... I... uh... I am pretty sure I'm in love with you. No... no doubt about it, I love you."

Now, I heard her words but, it was like my brain had melted. It seemed my skull was a hive full of bees, buzzing away. That wasn't something new though. It had always been like that. The buzzing meant that I was going to freak out, but not always in a bad way. It depended on the situation. I had a choice of either, getting really mad, or really goofy. Leaning my head back, I looked out my window. The tears were forcing their way out. Then I had to go and sniffle. That's when she put her hand on my arm. Now, there would be no hiding it.

There is something you need to understand, no one in my family had ever told me that they loved me—period. I was pretty sure, if they had, I'd be a whole different person. It was so strange that I could be happy, but still be crying. I remember my aunt talking my ma, saying, '*Oh, Mae, I just cried tears of joy.*' This must be what she meant. I wasn't going to cut loose and start blubbering or anything like that. It was simply my nose numbed up and the tears just started leaking out. I was trying to pull myself together as we came up on Highway 13. That's when Kathy slammed on the brakes and pulled over onto the shoulder, just short of the stop sign. The red paint reflected the sun, and the glow lit up the inside of the car with a weird, orange light.

"Are you crying?"

"No," I said, still looking out my window.

"You're crying, I can tell."

"No, I'm not crying! What gives you that idea?" I lied.

"I see the tears through your hair. You're trying to hide them. You're not fooling me, Cos McDhai!"

"Forget about it," I said, still not looking her way as I wiped at my eyes.

"Forget about what?"

"Ohhh, nothing. I mean, it's… well… no one has ever said that they loved me before. My brain is kind of freaking out right now."

"Well, is that a bad thing that I am in love with you?"

"NO!" I snapped and quickly wiped at my cheeks like I didn't think she would notice.

Something else had taken a hold on me, it was the goofiness. She had caught me and here I was trying to fool her. Now I had to wait and see what she was going to do about it.

"It's okay, Cos. It's just me here. Why can't you let go? You are always trying to be so strong, even when you don't want to be."

I finally turned my face to her. The hand that had been on my arm, moved up to push the hair out of my face. Then it went to my cheek. She struggled to get up on her seat, and sitting on her knees, she leaned over to hug me. I didn't say anything, and I didn't hug her back. I went limp in her arms. It was like the times when I was a little kid after my da had beat the crap out of me. My ma would take me aside and start talking real sweet to me. She was trying to make me feel better. But all she had to say was, *'Ya just gotta stay out of yer da's way, lad.'* It didn't help.

I wanted to jump out of the Pinto right then. I needed to go somewhere to be alone, but I wasn't sure where. I could easily take off across the open field, but if I walked too far, I'd still have to walk back. I decided my bedroom might be the best place, least no one could bug me there.

"Oh, this sucks so bad that I have to be somewhere else right now. I should stay with you. The thought of having to go hang out with a bunch of stinking cattle men and their wives really bums me out."

With a heavy sigh, she fell back into her seat. She started to say something but stopped when I swung my door open. She froze, her jaw hanging down like she couldn't believe what I was doing.

"I can walk from here. You need to get going. So, don't worry about anything. We can talk later."

I gave her my best smile and shut the door. Stepping back, I leaned down, looking in through the open window. There was this moment of awkward silence. A thought came into my head that made me feel like a total arse. Leaving me to wonder why I couldn't have said it earlier. It was so simple. What she had said about me not letting go, started to make sense. It was like I wanted to be the boss all the time. I was always trying to make everything go perfectly.

The first time Orlin's ma ever met me, she said, '*Oh! Look at dis one! He's de serious one, he is! Look at dat face!*' I remember grinning, trying to show her that I wasn't. Also, to be polite to the woman who my da always called, '*...dat whoor!*' Orlin was my friend. I owed it to her to be nice to her ma. She had never done a mean thing to me. I had no reason to treat her poorly. Besides, I've always believed in that thing about, 'Do unto others...'

I needed to calm down, but I didn't know how. There was a voice inside my head that sounded a lot like Fiana, saying, "*Just tell her, you eejit!*" So, sticking my head part way in the window, I ended up squeaking out, "Just so you know... I think... ummm... uhhh... I'm in love with you, too."

Stepping back, I waited for her reaction, my hands now stuck in my pockets. I watched her mouth go from hanging open, to showing that wonderful smile. She just said, "Oh, Man!"

Spinning around to face forward in her seat, she excitedly slammed the stick shift into gear. Then popping the clutch, the car squealed away as she let out a long whoop. Turning left on the highway, she headed north.

Shoving her fist up toward the sky through the open window, she whooped again. Then she honked her horn a couple times before going behind a long row of pine trees. When she came back into sight, crossing the trestle bridge, she laid on the horn, waving. I raised my hand, hoping she could see it.

After she was gone, I walked to the highway. I had to wait for cars and that gave me time to think and then realize, I should have been happier about the situation. But I just felt kind of worn out, like I wanted to go and sleep for a really long time. Growing up was something that just happened, and you never seemed to notice until way after it did. Maturing was what, Mr. Ward, my guidance counselor at school, called it. Something that was supposed to be a good thing. I remember as wee lad waking up in the night because my legs hurt so bad. My ma would come in and rub them, saying, *"Oh, it's just dem growing pains. Yer bones are stretching and so are yer muscles. Ya will be just fine in de morning."*

Now, I felt like I was having growing pains of a different kind. Take my word, it wasn't such a great feeling.

From where I stood, the Dairy Dreem was catty-corner to my right on the other side of the highway. It was a couple hundred yards away, but I could still see Shelagh standing in the open door with her broom. She was waving me over, but I couldn't handle her at the moment. So, heading down the hill, I ignored her, hoping I wouldn't run into anyone else before I got home.

Chapter 8

<u>Showdown</u>

Kathy and I had now been going together for well over a month. At this point, I felt things were going pretty well and that there was hope for us as a couple. I supposed this was what people called, '*Getting serious*' I had come to a place where I wanted to hear her say, "I love you" all of the time. A certain look would come into in her eyes when she said it, and it was right then I figured I knew exactly how a car battery felt after being recharged. I was sure it was the same for her. She'd start acting silly afterwards like she was a kid again.

This was my dream come true, and I couldn't get enough. I wanted to see her even more often, and I told her so. So, she started using the Sunrise Girls as an excuse to come to Clarksburg on Tuesday and Thursday nights. She had always avoided lodge as much as possible in the past. We were hoping her folks wouldn't get suspicious. She simply told them that since she was to be off in August, she would be willing to help out a little more at Sunrise Girls, mostly for Averell's sake.

The problem with that was, it also put her da close by. Something that we hadn't thought much about. Well, least until after the first night. Kathy convinced me it would be okay. She was always telling me that we shouldn't let being afraid get in our way. We agreed that it would be best if we weren't seen in the same place, at the same time, though. Our goal was to keep them guessing.

So, there was a part in the middle of the program where Kathy had to sit in the back and watch. She said it was an unbearable two hours. It made her want to go jump out a window. So, she'd tell them she was going off to the toilet, which was in another part of the building, and then she'd sneak out.

I always waited on the corner. When she showed up at the bottom of the stairs, I'd follow her down to what she called, 'The Kiddie Park' It was located on this end of the river bridge, just across the street from the path that led down to my fishing place. You had to go down a grassy embankment and the park ran along the water's edge for half a block or so. There was a playground at the far side with a wading pool in the middle. Everything was surrounded by little trees and among them, were places to sit. We always hung out on a wooden bench by the pool, talking and kissing.

There were was no light except for the streetlamps up on the bridge. So, we could get pretty cozy down there in the dark. This made our rendezvous, as she put it, magical. Kathy would always be wearing some kind of big, fancy gown, like the kind that girls wear to prom. She always made sure I understood why a dress like that was so important, if you wanted to be in SG. I finally had to ask her to stop talking about that. I was never going to be an SG girl. So, I didn't care.

It was also the only time she ever sported a serious hairdo. It was all very strange to me. Too much like a Cinderella cartoon. I felt she was actually embarrassed about it, but I never said anything. I tried to ignore all that stuff, waiting for the moment when I would see her as just normal Kathy.

Sometimes we'd wade around in the pool, talking nonsense and telling jokes. She had to avoid getting too playful because it would be bad news for us if she fell down. There was no way she'd be able explain how she got so wet from being in the toilet. I figured, though, if someone were to make that stupid comment, "What took so long? Did you fall in?" she could freak them out by saying, "Yeah!" and she'd have the wet dress to prove it. The other problem was, the bottom dragged on the ground. It was always getting dirty from the grass or the pool. Her da probably wouldn't notice that kind of thing—but her ma sure would. So, everything was going super for us—until the night Averell showed up.

We were on our favorite bench with Kathy dressed in her big, red gown. She was lying with her head in my lap and we were trying to name the star constellations. Suddenly, somebody was standing at the top of the embankment looking down at us. That was when we heard, "Kathy? Cos? Are you down there?"

Kathy panicked. Jumping up, she yelled, "Averell! You stupid ass, you can't be here! You've got to go back. You'll miss your part!" She then rolled off me and ran up the embankment toward her sister.

"Up yours, skin and bones!" Averell said, kind of dancing around, trying to stay out of reach.

"Averell, please. If you don't go back, mom and dad are going to know, and there's going to be trouble. Do you understand? You have to go."

"I want to come down there."

"No, I want to be with Cos alone and you're ruining it for me. Maybe we can go for some ice cream sometime soon, just the three of us? What do you say? Okay?"

"Really? No… you're lying. You're just saying that so I won't tell."

"No, Averell, really, I promise. Maybe we can bring one of Cos's friends and you guys can sit in the backseat together? What do you say?"

I could tell Kathy was desperate now. She had to be careful not to treat Averell too badly. Otherwise, she was going to spill the beans.

"No, I don't want that. I want to be with Cos, too."

"Averell! You can't, no way! Cos is my boyfriend."

"Fine, then!"

Averell suddenly pulled up her big dress, and plopped down hard, on the ground. It was a good thing that it was dark. The way she was sitting with her knees up, she wasn't hiding anything.

"Averell! Put your knees down, Cos can see everything you got under there, and get up off the grass, you're going to mess up your dress!"

"Well, you know… it's not much different from what you've got under yours! And… besides, I'm sure Cos has seen it all. So… hey, can you Cos? Can you see everything?"

Her face was in shadow, but I could see her teeth shining in the dark. She was smiling about it, which told me she liked the idea. I knew she was doing it to piss off Kathy.

"I can't Averell, it's too dark!"

I realized too late that what I said, might also make Kathy mad. That was when she ran back down and leaning over, she whispered in my face, "Tell her you can. She's wearing her new, polka dotted underwear tonight. So… tell her you can see every single dot."

"But that would be a lie."

"Oh, it's okay. You can do it. Let's make her embarrassed so she'll leave."

"No… I'm not doing that."

"Oh crap! Dammit! Okay, fine… don't then."

I was in a bad spot. No matter what I did, Kathy was going to get mad. I thought of what ol' Ernie B was always saying about, '*Hell if you do, and hell if you don't*' Then memories of the day at the pond came roaring back and I prepared for the worst. I watched her stomp back up the grassy hill. She stopped in front of her sister and putting her hands on her hips, they talked real low at first so I wouldn't hear.

"If you hit me, I'm gonna tell mom," Averell whined, putting her hands up to block her face.

"I'm not going to hit you. Well… not in front of Cos, anyway."

Kathy crouched down and I could have sworn she reached in under her sister's dress and pinched her on the bottom. Averell yelped, and started scooting up the hill backwards and that's when I knew it wasn't my imagination.

"Averell! Stop! You're going to get grass stains all over your gown!"

Standing up, Kathy reached down and gave Averell her hand. Her sister took it, and Kathy pulled her to her feet. They were having some kind of heart to heart, now.

They soon walked away, with Kathy nodding her head as if she agreed with stuff Averell was saying. They walked with their arms around each other's waist. When they stopped, Averell suddenly took off running up the street toward the lodge, trying to brush off the back of her dress while she did.

Kathy came back to me with her arms and head hanging down, pretending to be exhausted. She got back into her spot and without thinking, I bent down and gave her a kiss. When I finished, she said, "That a boy! That's what I want. Just keep them coming."

"So, how'd you get rid of her?"

Giggling, she winked, but said nothing.

"Come on, Kathy, tell me."

She giggled again, and reaching up, she pinched my nose.

"I told her I'd let her kiss you—someday."

"You did? Bollocks! You didn't?"

"Bullocks, I did too, and… what is bullocks, anyway? Isn't that like a big cow or something?"

"It's bollocks, and no, it's not a big cow. It's like, balls. You know? Nuts? Like big, hairy bull nuts. I know, you know what those are. It's used kind of like, '*Bullshit*' and I know for sure, you know what that is."

"Oh, okay."

She hollered out, "Bollocks!" at the sky, keeping it up until I put my hand over her mouth. She started licking my palm, so I pulled it away.

"Yum, salty."

"Oh shite, girl. You're gross sometimes."

She laughed, kissing at me.

"So, you're not going to make me kiss her, are you?"

"Ah, no, but she thinks I am. Wouldn't you want too, though? I mean Averell's cute, right? Just because you think her butt sticks out. I mean, don't you think her butt makes her sexier?"

"I'm not going to answer that," I said, knowing it was a trap.

I knew if I said yes, then it would only get me into trouble. It's not that I'd mind kissing Averell, it was more that I wouldn't want the trouble that comes with having two girlfriends. Worse yet—girlfriends from the same family.

"Good! Now… kiss me, instead."

Latching onto my hair, where it lay against my shirt, she pulled my face to hers.

The full moon had come up over the trees and its reflection was now on the surface of the wading pool. We could see just about every star in the sky. It was like being in a fairytale. Kathy said it was enchanting. Not something you can experience riding around in a car. I changed my mind about the Cinderella thing, deciding that it wasn't so bad, after all.

We stayed in the park until about ten o'clock. I didn't want to go home, but Kathy had to get back to the lodge. So, she put on her shoes and we walked back up the street toward the square. We said our goodbyes just down the block with a long kiss right out in public. Then grabbing up the bottom of her dress, she skipped away up the street, the massive red gown swishing like crazy.

Walking to the corner, I sat down to wait and watch, all the while, wondering if it was such a good idea. It might have been safer if I went into the Blue Front. But I was curious and wanted to get a look at her da. I figured I was far enough away from the lodge that I could be there without anyone making a connection. I was simply just some kid, sitting on a corner, not bothering anybody.

When the big clock at the Standard gas station read, ten thirty, a mob of girls suddenly came piling down the stairs. All sorts of girls, in different colored prom dresses, went in all directions. Some were running down the street, going into houses that I walked by every day. Others were getting into cars that showed up all of a sudden and left just as quickly. A few I recognized from school. Some of those were brave enough to smile and wave. They even called out my name, almost like we were friends.

They were girls who normally wouldn't give me the time of day. I figured they must have felt some excitement in yelling out to the local hippie on the dangerous streets of Clarksburg. All because it was against the rules. Then there was Poppy Johnson. She was one of those girls who was nice to me all the time and I didn't know why. I sorted that she just didn't see any sense in being mean to people. She went about her way, minding her own business, smiling, and saying hallo and goodbye to everyone. Her twin brother, Aspen, was the same.

Aspen showed up in his Ford Torino to give her a ride and saw me sitting there. He waved like he was truly happy to see me. It took a few seconds for Poppy to get over to the car, which gave me a chance to listen to '*Showdown*' by ELO which was pouring out of the car's windows. Aspen liked his music loud.

Poppy saw me, smiled really big and waved before she got in that green Ford. Then they drove away with the chorus of that song kind of drifting back saying something about it raining all over the world and tonight being the longest night. It was a good song and I played it sometimes on the jukebox at the Blue Front. But tonight, for some reason, the thought of it raining all over the world left me feeling sad. It wasn't the first time I'd felt that way since I started seeing Kathy. In fact, I have to admit, it was happening a lot more than it used too. Kind of like that vibe I got the first day. I suddenly felt sick for all of about ten seconds and I wondered if maybe there was something else going on that I wasn't seeing. Like, because I wanted things to be a certain way, I wasn't seeing them for what they really were.

The girls stopped pouring out of that stairwell for about a minute or two and then came the old men and their wives. Getting into big Buicks, Lincolns, and Chryslers, they drove away, leaving the Henton's huge, burgundy Cadillac behind. Kathy's folks had to clean up, turn off all the lights, and lock the door. So, they stuck around longer.

The street was empty when they came down. Kathy was busy getting an earful. Mrs. Henton looked like your typical ma, but still dressed like it was the '50s. Her reddish-blonde hair was made up just like Kathy's, and even at this distance, I could see she was wearing horn-rimmed glasses. She was carrying a large white purse and wore a flowered dress with a pink sweater draped over her shoulders.

Kathy stood with her back to me and lowering her hand down behind her bottom, she gave me a little wave. Averell saw her do it and laughing loud enough for the whole town to hear, she did it too. That's when I noticed the big wet spot on the back of Averell's yellow dress. My first instinct was to get the hell out of there, but like the fool that I was, I didn't.

Mrs. Henton stopped talking all of a sudden. Then they all turned to look at me. Kathy and Averell were grinning, but their ma looked like she might be getting mad. That's when the ol' man showed up.

He was a big, John Wayne type, and I decided that must be why Kathy was so tall. He looked my way over the top of the car when he was reaching for the Cadillac's door handle. I smiled and nodded at him like I'd do with everybody. He looked down at his feet for a few seconds and shook his head like he couldn't believe what he saw. The girls climbed into the car along with their ma, but Mr. Henton did something I didn't expect—he walked over to me. I thought about what Kathy had said about running, but I wasn't afraid. I truly thought I'd be able to just say hello. I was wrong.

His fancy cowboy boots sounded loud on the street. The closer he got, the taller he seemed. I stayed sitting when he stopped in front of me. His big hands were on his hips and he smelled like Brut aftershave. His blue suit looked expensive and his tie was red with little cartoon cows all over it. It looked like something a kid might get their da for Father's Day.

"Hallo," I said, smiling.

"Why… you aren't nothing but a little hippy boy. Well, little hippy boy, you had better just stay away from my girls or there is going to be trouble."

So, it was true. Either Chuck had described me, or Mr. Henton simply decided I was the one, and that, was that. I mean, I was the only kid in Clarksburg with hair this long. So, it was a dead giveaway. Also, what I thought or said, didn't matter to him. Just like with my da.

I didn't know what to say. He sounded pretty serious. Normally, that wouldn't stop me from saying something that would get me in trouble. But I decided to play dumb.

"Who are you, and what in the hell are you talking about?"

He pointed his finger at me, taking a step closer. Even in the light of the streetlamps, I could see his face was turning red. His finger started to shake as a car door creaked open, followed by Mrs. Henton saying, "Kathy! Get back in this car."

"Dad… Daaad! Don't you hurt him, dad!"

"Get back in that car, Kathy, I'll handle this!"

Looking back at me, he said, "You heard me mister. I mean what I say. If you want trouble, you just keep sniffing around and I'll give you trouble. I know people who can have your greasy little butt in the hoosegow before you can blink."

He backed up a couple steps, still looking at me like he was waiting for me to jump up and take a poke at him.

"I'm not trying to cause any trouble. Besides, you don't even know me."

"Oh, I know your kind, and that's enough. You're just another welfare kid, sucking off the government teat. I can just bet on it."

"Well, uhhh… I've got a job and…"

"Oh, I don't care! Just stay away from my girls!"

He scuffed his boot in my direction, spraying me with sand from the road. He startled me by spitting on the ground, and turning around, he clonked back to the car, saying, "Scumbag."

Kathy was still standing next to the Cadillac, and when he got there, he grabbed her arm and tried to force her back inside. She jerked away, yelling, "Don't!" and started to walk toward me, but stopped when her ma said, "Kathy Lillian Henton, you listen to your father. Get back in this car."

She did as her ma told her, with Mr. Henton slamming the door behind her. He then got into the driver's seat and started the engine. The transmission clicked into gear and the big car backed my way, stopping just a few feet short. I jumped up onto the sidewalk to get out of the way just in case he really wanted to nail me.

"Seymour!" Kathy's ma yelled as she looked back to make sure he hadn't run me over. Putting it into drive, he floored it. The tires squealed, covering me with grit, and filling the air around me with smoke. As the car roared away, I could see Kathy and Averell's faces staring at me through the rear window. Their eyes were big and afraid.

"Asshole!" I hollered.

Sitting back down, I realized that I was shaking. Looking over at the Blue Front, I saw Arnie standing in the open door with his baseball bat. When he saw me looking, he nodded, shut the door and went back behind the bar. He had been watching out for me.

I stayed where I was and lit up my last cigarette, trying to calm myself. Greasy butt? Where did that come from? I started wondering why people always had to be so damn mean. Kathy's da was judging me before he even knew me. That didn't make any sense. It didn't seem fair, but I knew he didn't care about that. It was like there was a bunch of different kinds of 'fair' and his was more important than mine.

I thought of my da, figuring there must be a lot of fathers that were like that. Then I started to worry about what he might do to Kathy after they got home. If he were anything like my da, he'd smack her around a bit, kick her a couple times, and then lock her in a closet. If he did that and I found out—I might have to do something about it.

Something that would surely get me tossed into that hoosegow he was talking about.

Chapter 9

<u>I Heard It Through the Grapevine</u>

I didn't see Kathy at all the next day. The waiting about drove me crazy. I don't think I'd ever wanted to see someone as bad as I did her. So, the day just dragged. The night was worse. I spent most of it sitting at the little desk in my bedroom, worrying, my imagination running wild. I wished I could hear Brian and his ma going at it downstairs. At least that would be something. But it was as quiet as a tomb with only ma's snores coming through the curtain that hung in my doorway.

I tried to write Kathy that poem, but it kept coming out all wrong. Then I got a crazy idea about calling her. But I couldn't get up the nerve until about two in the morning. Realizing a minute later, that if I called, it might make things worse for her. I decided it was a stupid idea. So, I just stayed in my chair and stared at the few words I had written. I gave up worrying around four in the morning and fell asleep with my face in my notebook.

I woke up with my poem stuck to my face. Peeling it off, I saw I had slobbered away much of what I had written; ruining it. Crumpling it up, I tossed it in the wastepaper bin and went to shower. Not sure why I did that, though. I had no plans other than to go fishing. Neither the fish nor the fishermen would care what I smelled like. I guess I wanted to be prepared in the case Kathy showed up, since that could be just about anywhere. My ma was still snoring away. Seconal will do that to you. Grabbing my pole and tackle box, I headed down to the river.

Walking over to the roller dam, I said hello to the regulars I fished next to; the ones I had mentioned earlier. They were these two old guys who spent their whole day sitting in lawn chairs, casting their hooks into the boils the rushing water made, coming over the dam. They were out to catch carp, and believe me when I say they were good at it. Over the past few years, they had showed me some of their best tricks for catching those huge bottom feeders. The cost of that education came in the form of patience, they constantly poked at me.

The thing you have to understand is, for every one fish I pulled in, the old geezers would give me a quarter for it. I always sat along the short end-wall of the dam. It sloped up to a narrow road at the top and then down the other side. It put me high enough to see all the good holes and to avoid tangling lines with the old guys.

After about three hours and six fish later, I had enough of that kind of thing. Gathering up my stuff, I headed down to sell my fish. I had been coming here a long time, but I still didn't know the names of those old guys, and I don't think they knew mine.

"So, what are you going to do with all those fish?" I asked the one fellow with the red face who must have been about a hundred years old.

He laughed, and looking over at the huge, red cooler overflowing with gasping suckers, he said, "Well, boy, we are going to take em home… and smoke em!"

He laughed again and winking at me he nudged the old, fat man sitting next to him. That guy looked up at me with a trickle of tobacco juice running out of the corner of his mouth and said, "Probably not what you're are used to smoking, huh boy?" He cackled like an ol' hen and winked at the first guy.

I supposed, since I had long hair, they thought I smoked marijuana. I feared they were going to start in on me about that. So, I got ready to defend myself, but all the old guy said was, "Say… aren't you that young feller that works for Ernie B, down there, fixing lawnmowers and such?"

I didn't answer and just looked at the ground, kicking at a stick caught between two rocks. Going fishing might have been a mistake. I just wanted to leave. They were both staring at me and things got a little awkward. I decided I'd better say something or get the hell out of there. The problem was, as soon as I opened my mouth to talk, the first guy took it as his cue to jump in.

"You are… aren't you?"

I looked up, and they were both grinning at me. I felt my ire coming up because I was ready to answer the question, but he kept interrupting. Then the old guy let me know he could tell I was getting upset.

"Calm down, sonny. Don't take yourself so serious, huh?"

Reaching into the chest pocket of his bib overalls, he pulled out a couple of dollar bills and shoved them at me.

"Here, take these, you deserve 'em. You did a good job catching all them fish."

He nodded toward the stringer of carp that was swinging from my hand and then looked back to my face. It dawned on me that he was trying to tell me to leave the fish so we could close the deal.

"Oops! Sorry!" I said and taking the money, I stuck it in my pocket with my quarters. I thanked him in a whisper and walked over to their cooler. Pulling the fish off the stringer, I let them fall in with the rest of the carp. That's when the fat guy said, "You know… you all talk funny. Where you from there, little feller?"

There it was.

I flashed back to the fifth grade and the first recess period with my new classmates. I remember the boys standing around me in a circle, making fun of my accent. When I got fed up with that, I punched the biggest one, Brett Hader, right in the nose. Of course, I spent a wee bit of time in the principal's office after that. But it only lasted until I had worked my way through the entire lot. It took about a month.

What you have to understand is, I couldn't do that with these ol 'geezers. In fact, I couldn't even imagine punching some ol' guy in the nose. It seemed, well… just wrong. I looked over at the fat one and wondered when the last time was he had changed his filthy white tee-shirt. He was what my ma would call a slob. I figured if she were going to get upset about me leaving my shirts untucked—she'd have a field day with this guy.

"You one of them there, Brits? One of them there, Beatles?" he said and cackled some more.

"Ah geez, Stu! Leave the young feller alone, he ain't no Beatle. He's just a lawnmower fixing man down at Ernie B's place."

"Now, John… don't you be telling me, what's, what!"

They started in arguing about who should be telling who what, and being able to tell a Beatle from a lawnmower fixing man, a farmer, or an auto mechanic. I turned and hopped away from them across the tops of the big rocks that covered the shore. Problem solved, and I had also learned their names without having to ask. I don't think they even noticed I'd taken off.

Stashing my gear out of sight underneath the bridge, I headed up to the Dairy Dreem. I decided to splurge on a banana split since I wasn't sure when I'd get another chance. I lived mostly on PB&J and Kool-Aide. That's all my ma ever had in the house. I was in charge of delivering the grocery list to the Royal Blue, but I never looked at it. I'd simply drop it off, and they'd deliver everything to our front door. More often than not, they'd leave the bags in the entryway for me to stumble over when I came home in the dark.

So, I had this big ache to try something different. Something to help me take my mind off Kathy. I was worrying twice as much now, wondering if maybe something bad had happened to her. Something terrible like a farm accident, a cattle stampede, or that she had gotten thrown from a horse. My imagination was running wild. I pictured her da locking her up in the basement to keep her from coming to Clarksburg. When she showed up, there would be rope burns on her wrists where he had tied her to a steam pipe. She'd have to wear long sleeves or a bunch of bracelets to hide the marks. But I'd see them, sooner or later. Then of course, I'd have to plot my revenge.

It was one long block uphill to the Dairy Dreem. The sun was beating down and my face was getting all sweaty. I could feel the wetness on my back, so I undid a few more buttons, wishing all the while there was no such thing as humidity. When I finally got there, I opened the door and saw Shelagh Bennett behind the counter.

What Mike T had said about her during our historic car ride, ran through my head. I almost turned to leave. The air conditioning felt good, though, and I wanted that banana split. Buttoning up my shirt so as not to tempt her, I strolled in like I hadn't a care in the world.

Now to be totally honest, Shelagh wasn't so bad. It wasn't like she would jump on me or force me out on a date at the point of the knife she used for splitting bananas. She was always nice to me, but being around her was kind of nerve racking. The other kids said she was, '*Really sexual!*' and take my word for it, they weren't kidding.

Shelagh had this pretty, triangular shaped face with really, really, bright blue eyes. Not the pale kind, like Averell's. She had light brown hair just down past her shoulders and she parted it in the middle. Sometimes she wore these little flower barrettes, to keep it out of her face. She was curvy, not like Kathy. But girls came in all kinds of shapes and sizes. To be completely honest, I liked them all.

Some of my friends called Shelagh, '*Bubble Butt*'. It kind of pissed me off because, well, she was nowhere near that. They were only exaggerating to piss her off. Probably because they tried to put the make on her and she turned them down. I couldn't see how Shelagh's body could ever hurt anyone except for Shelagh. So, it was no one's business but hers.

"Hi Cos! What happening!"

"Hallo Shelagh," I said, trying to sound like it was no big deal we were in the Dairy Dreem alone. I tried not to look in those beautiful eyes, so, I looked everywhere else.

Talking to a rack of potato chips, I said, "Could I get a banana split, please?"

"You know… you are kind of nice for a long-haired boy. Most long-haired boys are pricks."

"What? Oh! Ummm… okay. Thanks?" I said, continuing to avoid her eyes. I went to playing with a toothpick dispenser, wishing she'd get to work and quit looking at me like I was one of those treats listed on the wall behind her.

"English Leather, right? Hmmm… I love it!" she said, commenting about my cologne. Throwing her head back, she closed her eyes and took a long whiff.

I got the urge to tease her, so I said, "Uh, no… Irish Leather. The English ran out of leather, and the Irish weren't sharing so, they had to switch to English Vinyl."

I could see by the look on her face she was believing my blarney. So, I took it a step further.

"Next time you go down to Nordon's, you can look for it by the shaving stuff."

"Really?"

"No—not really. I'm just giving you a hard time."

"Oh… I'll let you do that… but… only you! So, anytime you want to give me something hard…"

There it was, she was starting.

I could expect that for the rest of the time I was in there. She giggled, moving away toward the prep counter. When she finally got there, she stopped but didn't turn around.

"You want to know something?" she said, now talking to the ice cream machine.

"Ummm… sure, fine. What?"

She looked at me out of the corner of her eye and reaching out, she put her hands on the counter like she needed to brace herself for what she was going to say.

"It was my birthday last week, and ummm… my dad said I could start dating, now that I'm sixteen. I was kind of wondering if maybe we could go out?"

She didn't wait for me to answer, but nervously picked an extra-long banana from the bunch and held it up in front of her eyes. Running them up and down the piece of fruit, she slowly turned her face to me and grinned, raising her eyebrows a bunch of times.

I pretended like I didn't notice and getting tired of waiting for me to laugh, she went to peeling that banana, splitting it, and putting it in the tray. The little white portable radio on a back shelf was blasting away with the Doobie Brothers singing about a long train running.

I was so caught up in what Shelagh was doing, I forgot to answer her question. Just as she was getting ready to pump on the ice cream, she stopped. Looking back over her shoulder, she gave me the, 'I'm kind of waiting!' look.

"Oh, uuuh… sorry. Ummm… I have a girlfriend. I mean, you're nice and all, and you're real pretty, but I have somebody."

A big smile came across her face at the pretty remark. She flipped her hair, but it got caught on some spatulas hanging on a rack above her head. She jerked her hair loose and some of the spatulas fell onto the metal counter making a hell of a racket. She gave me the 'Oops!' face and setting down my banana split, she picked them up and hung them back on the rack. Blushing, she went back to work on my order.

After putting on the nuts, sauces, and pineapple, she brought it over. Setting it down in front of me, she picked up the whipped crème can and put one huge mound, right in the center. After that, she leaned over and putting her face in mine, said, "Isn't she that really tall one? That rich girl from up in Coogan? The one with no boobs?"

"What? Oh… Kathy has boobs… it's just that when they were handing them out, I think you butted in line, and took part of her share."

Shelagh looked down at her chest and then back at me. "Yeah, they are kind of big, aren't they? But I like em. I mean… I think a girl should like herself, and that should be everything, including her boobs, right?"

Now she was asking me something I knew nothing about. I hadn't any idea what it felt like to be a girl. So, I said, "I suppose. I mean, I don't know what it's like to have em, so I can't really say. But… yours are real nice and all…" When I realized what had come out of my mouth, I shut up.

Her goal was to bring my attention to her boobs, but it was almost like we were talking about a new pair of shoes, or something. I thought it was kind of weird we went from joking, to talking serious. She stopped staring at me with that hungry look for a minute and reaching over, she opened the lid to a clear plastic box, pulling out a cherry by its stem.

"Here's my… ummm… here's a cherry, if you want it… uhhh… want one… I mean."

Giggling, she plopped it into the whipped cream, and then adjusting it so the stem stuck straight up, she talked to it, saying in a sexy whisper, "Ooo! Such a big boy!"

All the time she was doing this, she was looking at me out of the tops of her eyes. I was well into the nervous zone by this point. I needed to come up with something to say. Anything that would change where I suspected this conversation was going.

"Did you just want me eat it with my hands, or… could I have a spoon, please?"

She threw her hand over her mouth and said, "Oops! Sorry! Sorry!" She went to snorting, but I think that was how she laughed. Pulling a long, red plastic spoon from a jar that sat beside my banana split, she bumped my arm with her hand. She grabbed me in apology, saying, "Sorry!"

"It's okay… just stop saying you're sorry."

She didn't let go right away, and stood there, looking at my face. It was when she started rubbing it that I pulled it away. I smiled to be nice, but I wanted to go. I saw her face go red again as she finally got around to sticking the spoon into the whipped cream.

"Two bucks, right?" I asked, pulling the money from my pocket.

"Uh, no… only one dollar for you. We get a discount for working here, so I'm giving you mine, okay?"

"Are you sure?"

"Yeah, I'm sure—it's okay. I'd do that for you."

"Uhhh… well… thanks!" I said and turned to leave.

"Cos? Can I tell you something?"

Her voice was real serious now and it made me turn back. I almost lied and told her I had to be someplace, but she didn't give me a chance to say one word.

"You know, Cos… I heard that your girlfriend, uhhh… Kathy? Has other boyfriends up in Coogan."

That froze me right on the spot. I grew as cold as the little plastic tray in my hand and goose bumps started popping up all over my arms.

"Who told you that? I don't believe it."

"Well, I shouldn't say, but… Peggy Bowman."

"Peggy Bowman! She hates my guts and I feel the same about hers. I think that girl may be rotten inside."

"Well, I'm just saying what she told me one day in Home Ec. We were talking about dating, and boyfriends, and I mentioned how I was thinking about asking you out. Then she did the gag-me thing. You know? Where you stick your finger in your mouth and make puking sounds?

"Yeah, I know it. So?"

"Well, anyway, she started going on about how she was up in Coogan for a hair appointment at Ruthie's and she saw Kathy. She was sitting on a bench out front of the Creamy Cone. You know, the other place that Mr. Goldsberry owns? You know, my boss? Well, anyway, Kathy was sharing ice cream with some guy and they were sitting pretty close together… some big guy in a Coogan football jersey. I mean… for just being friends, don't you think that's kind of strange?"

I did think it was strange. Right then that Marvin Gaye song came on the radio where he was singing about a grapevine and how his girl wasn't going to be his for much longer. I needed to say something to drown him out, so I said in a loud way, "Bowman's probably making that crap up so everybody will think Kathy's some kind of a slut. She did that to Tammy, remember? You know, Shelagh, I wouldn't believe anything that Peggy Bowman says, or try to be friends with her."

"Oh, I wasn't trying. She just came over to me. I mean… she might be popular and all, but she's not my friend. I think she was telling the truth because she knew so much about Kathy, and Coogan. So, I thought since Kathy was with some other guy and that maybe you two had broken up. Which, ummm… is why I asked if we could go out sometime."

"You know, Peggy is pure evil. So evil, in fact, that I'm surprised she can even come outside in the sunlight."

That was all I had to say about that. I figured Bowman was just trying to get at me and was using Shelagh to do it. She had talked about Shelagh in a bad way before, and I figured Shelagh wasn't lying when she said they weren't friends. I also didn't think Shelagh would make up some crap about Kathy. Not if she wanted to stay friends with me. But what bothered me the most was that Bowman was familiar with Kathy. I mean, how would she even know what Kathy looked like? Now those bees were back in my head, filling my head like a hive, and they were buzzing big time. They must have been the killer kind because they were extra loud.

"I'm sorry, Cos. I guess I shouldn't have said anything. Peggy Bowman truly is a really bad person, but I can usually tell when she's making crap up and when she's not."

I barely heard Shelagh's words. Reaching out, she patted my hand like she wanted to get my attention. She talked some more, but I'd fallen off the face of the planet. She didn't seem to notice and just yakked on. I felt like I was floating away. I could still see her face with her mouth moving, but all I could hear was that buzzing. She patted me on the back of my hand again and flipped her hair. Then cocking her head, she looked at me in a worried way.

One of the outside doors suddenly flew open and I snapped out of it. Looking that way, I saw a noisy bunch of guys in Clarksburg football jerseys come tumbling in. Some cheerleaders were following them, laughing at something that one of them said that was probably stupid, but they thought was funny. I checked for Chuck or Weasel, but didn't see either. Looking back at Shelagh, she rolled her eyes.

Those kids were a little too rowdy for me. So, I laid the dollar on the counter and Shelagh took it, whispering, "If you ever breakup with that girl, or just change your mind, let me know, huh?"

Showing me her perfect teeth in a big smile, she turned sideways and stuck out her chest like that's how she wanted me to remember her. Grabbing the banana split, plus a handful of napkins, I headed for the opposite door.

"Bye Cos, see you around," she said in a dreamy kind of voice.

"See yah, Shelagh."

When I looked back, I caught her leaning forward over the counter, watching me. Suddenly my Levi's felt a wee bit too tight across my backside, and I got a little tingle up my spine. So, I walked faster.

"See yah, Shelagh," one of the jocks said, mocking me. Then all of cheerleaders laughed on cue.

I pretended like I didn't hear anything and hurried through the door before some crap got started. It wasn't that I was afraid of them, it was just, I didn't want to make a bad day worse by getting into a fray. Also, I didn't think Shelagh would be too impressed with us tearing up the place.

My mouth was watering for my banana split, but so many things were keeping me from it. I stopped outside the door, just so I could take a bite. Then I stood there for a minute just taking in all the flavors.

Revenge soon snuck into my mind and taking a second bite, I promptly spit it onto the rear window of one of the football player's cars as I made my way out toward the highway. It looked just a seagull had flown over and had mistaken the car for a privy. They probably wouldn't notice for a long time. I imagined the look on their faces when they found it. Laughing to myself, I sat down in the grass out in the corner of the lot by the highway.

The bees in my head had calmed down a bit, but what Shelagh had said was really bothering me. I needed to talk to Kathy so badly, I could barely sit still. If there were other boyfriends, I needed to know. I figured she wouldn't do that, though. It was supposed to be against the rules. I was her boyfriend and that was that. She even got upset whenever I mentioned Averell. But we had never really talked about it. I was trusting her to do the right thing. Kind of, the unwritten rules of going steady.

The cars whizzed by as I worked on my banana split. Deciding I didn't like being that close to things going that fast, I got up to move over to the closest table. Doing that, gave me a clear shot down to the trestle bridge and a familiar green car speeding my way.

Chapter 10

Dazed & Confused

The Pinto zoomed into the parking area, its wheels locking up as it slid sideways across the blacktop. It screeched to a stop, almost dead center in the lot. I could see Kathy inside taking off a dirty baseball cap and tossing it into the back seat. Then she undid her ponytail and shook out her hair. Without turning off the car, I heard her pull the emergency brake as she gave me the 'I'm fed up!' look. After throwing her sunglasses on the dashboard, she got out, not bothering to close the door.

Walking real fast around the car, she came toward me, her work boots loud on the asphalt. Her brown, sleeveless shirt was soaked with sweat, her face red and puffy like she had been crying.

"Kathy! What's…?"

Without a word, she snatched the banana split out of my hand and flung it on the ground. Then standing me up, she threw her arms around me and kissed my lips really hard. I didn't like the rough treatment, but I went along with it. I think mostly because I was grateful that she was finally here. When we finished, she stood there hugging me as I rubbed my hands up and down her sweaty back. It didn't gross me out like you might think it would, because, well… it was Kathy's sweat, not just some random stranger.

I caught Shelagh out of the corner of my eye, standing at the window. She looked kind of disappointed. I felt bad for her, but I figured she'd find a boyfriend soon enough. I had my own problems to deal with.

Kathy finally let go and stepping back, took me by the hand and led me to the car. She opened the passenger door for me and waited while I got in before closing it. When she got herself in the driver's seat, she let off the brake, and surprised me by not flooring the gas pedal or racing backwards out of the lot at high speed. Instead, she turned it around real slow and eased the Pinto up to the highway. We sat there for the longest time like she was trying to decide where to go.

In the side mirror I saw Shelagh come out one door as the jocks left by the other. She walked over and picked up what was left of the banana split and took it to the red garbage bin. Holding the remains over the open top, she stood for the longest time before dropping them in. It was like she wasn't sure if she wanted to let go of it. I wondered if maybe it was because she had made it especially for me, and now, Kathy had turned it into garbage.

Kathy soon pulled out, heading north toward Coogan. She still hadn't said one single word. I could smell her even more now and there was just a hint of cow crap along with sweat and patchouli. A filthy pair of leather work gloves lay on my side of the floor next to a weird looking set of pliers with a hook on one side. There was also a hammer, along with a box of big metal staples.

I wanted to ask what she had been doing, but she suddenly whipped the little Ford left into a country cemetery. Pulling into the grass, she shut it off before climbing out, leaving me behind, a wee bit unsure what to do. Without looking back, she walked to a gravesite with a big, black, shiny headstone. Plopping down beside it, she looked toward the car and said, "Cos, would you come here?"

I'd been sitting there in kind of a daze, watching her through the windshield. But when she called, I came. She pointed to a spot on the other side of the grave, saying, "Sit there." I didn't like that she was being so pushy about everything, but whatever was going on with her, must have been serious. I figured it would be best just to keep my pie hole shut. She was looking down and picking at little purple flowers that were growing in the grass. She had something to tell me— probably about last Tuesday night.

I checked out the tombstone while I waited. It was big and square. On the front it said, 'Averell Lillian Harrison, 1900-1970' There were a couple angels hovering above a little lamb, bordered by ribbons. Next to that was, 'Charles Dewitt Harrison, 1893-1969'. For him there was a cowboy hat, a coiled rope, and some cowboy boots. I began to suspect that they were somehow related to Kathy and then she whispered, "My grandma and grandpa… my mom's folks."

When I looked at her, she didn't look back. Tears were now dripping off her chin, making me wish she would tell me why. This was the third time the dam had broken when we were together. But for some reason, I didn't feel the same way about it as I did a month ago. I mean, I'd always get embarrassed whenever someone would start bawling. But now, I could deal with it. The first step is to throw an arm around anybody who broke down in front of you, or, at least, say something that tells them you're sad too about whatever the problem is; even if you aren't. That was the right thing to do. But… this wasn't the right moment. I needed to wait for a clue that she was ready.

After a few minutes, Kathy said, "She was my favorite grandma. We spent a lot of time together. When she died, almost three years ago, I was a total wreck. It took a while to get over it. When I get really sad or upset, I just want to be with her. So, sometimes I come here to sit."

"I'm sorry about that. I mean—that she had to die. I hardly knew my granny. We never heard from her after we left Ireland. She was a wee bit upset about us coming to America. So… what's wrong?"

"Oh… it's my father. The other night when he was being so mean to you. Well, it was terrible after we got home. There was a lot of yelling and he threatened to have you beaten up or something. I have never heard him talk like that before. My mom tried to calm him down, but he was so mad at you, it took a while. I think it was because he was trying to scare you and it didn't work. He kept saying that he didn't raise two girls so they could run off with a nobody like you. Also, how you were such an irritating, little bas… ummm… bastard. I tried to tell him that I wasn't running off, and besides that, you weren't a nobody or… a bastard, for that matter. I was telling him how much I cared about you, but he wouldn't listen. It's just… my folks are finally realizing I'm leaving the nest. They're afraid. They kind of acted this way when my brother was going off to college except, they didn't threaten to have his girlfriend beaten up. I guess… I don't think it's fair."

"It's not! So, what's he going to do? Get me arrested? Shoot me down like a dog on the highway?"

"It's not funny, Cos."

"Sorry. That's from a poem I read once. But… it's just… I'm the one who's going to get hurt. Physically, I mean. I am not sure I can do anything about it. Well, other than joke."

"Oh, he's not really going to hurt you."

"Well, we don't know that."

"What? Hey, my dad's not a bad guy!"

She kind of glared at me. It had been a good while since I saw that meanness in her eyes, but there it was. It was almost the same look that I saw in her da's eyes that night on the corner and hers at the pond. I started to worry a little. But I told myself that she was just protecting her da, and maybe she was watching out for me at the same time.

Also, I suspected this moment was coming. It only made sense that we'd eventually have a fight. What I was a little confused about was—if she suspected that her da was going to throw a fit—why was she so upset about it? She was acting like she was innocent, or should I say, 'we'. It's not like we didn't help it along. Harry was always saying, *'If you mess with the bull, you get the horn!'* and that's just what we were doing. I wanted to say something that might help, but all that came out was, "My da used to kick the shite out of me all the time. So, I'm a little shy about getting it from somebody else's da, too."

"I guess we never talked about that, huh? I wonder why?"

"Maybe… because you never asked?"

"I did ask. You said you didn't want to talk about it."

"That was about Ireland."

"No… that was me trying to get you to talk about you. Your life. Your family. Whatever. I tried to get you to open up to me, but I always got the impression you didn't want to. So, I needed to respect that. I even tried a second time at the park that one day, remember?"

"Why couldn't you just come out and ask?"

"Cos… I know you're poor. I know that your dad ran off and abandon you. I asked around. It's not like you're totally unknown. I even know you have two sisters, Fiana and Shauna. I found a yearbook for your school, and I looked you up. There are not too many people around here named McDhai. I just didn't have any idea how your parents may have treated you."

She was right. I couldn't argue with any of that. It was all true.

"So, you checked me out? What else do you know?"

"Where you live, and that you might be too ashamed to show me. Afraid that it would matter. It doesn't, though. Other people live in that same building besides you. I don't hang around with you because of your status, or your popularity. I get enough of that crap up in Coogan."

There it was again. That word—status. Something the popular kids at my school seemed to want so badly that they'd make trouble for the rest of us just to get it. I don't remember it ever being a problem before high school. But now, it was all about how popular you were, and spending a whole lot of time trying to make sure you stayed that way.

"Cos?"

"Huh? Oh, sorry, was just thinking about something."

"I was just saying how I was really attracted to you that day on the corner, and that first kiss—oh man! When I got to know the real Cos, you were nice, smart, and funny. I was hooked. But you knew we were just making the best of the summer, right? I made it clear that I'd have to go off to school in August. I haven't hidden anything from you. So, other than how my dad has been acting… well, everything's been great."

"So, it wouldn't make any difference to you, if you knew my ma had been in a mental institution? Or that my da knocked me around when he was drunk? Which was… all the time. He used to make me get these stupid butch haircuts every other week. I had to wear second hand clothes just so he could spend all his money on shots and pints. It was more important for him to buy his friends a round at the pub than get us things that we needed."

"Yes, I saw your picture in the yearbook from back when you first came to Iowa. I thought you were cute. I'm sorry you were forced do something that you didn't want to do. But it doesn't change how I feel about you. Besides, that's all in the past. I want to live for now, Cos."

"Well, I think it's going to take me a lot longer to get over it. So, it's not quite in the past for me."

"I just want you to be aware that I can live with it. We have less than two weeks left and…"

"And… I stop existing?"

She sobbed then. It kind of broke out of her lips and she caught herself, putting her hand over her mouth. Closing her eyes, she squeezed out more tears. Opening them after a minute or so, she sat looking at me like she was waiting for me to say something. I suddenly felt bad because of what I said. It sounded selfish. I could see that it hurt her. I felt like a fool because, well, that sob was for me. Simply because she had to leave me.

Her face looked like she was in a lot of pain. She finally pulled herself together enough to say, "No! Cos! Please, I'm not going to stop loving you! But I won't be around here as much. The summer will be over and even though I am only going to school in Des Moines, I can't drive back every weekend."

"So, what if I came to you? What if I came to Des Moines? Would that be okay?"

The pain suddenly left her face. I could see she was sorting it. Trying to decide if it would work or not. Then she said, "I suppose that would be okay. I mean, every once in a while. But you have to understand, I will be having classes. I will be busy. The first year is always the toughest, and if I want to pass, I'll have to work really hard. My parents are forking over a ton of money. I can't let my family down. There… there may not be time for a boyfriend. You'll get tired of waiting. Nothing will be the same."

The pain of it all, hit me like a kick in the chest. Kathy suddenly clapped a hand over her mouth as another sob tried to escape. After a minute or so, she kind of squeaked out, "I thought about it a lot yesterday and… I think it might be better for the both of us, uhhh… if maybe you… found someone else. Someone who could be here for you."

There it was. The thing I was afraid of most.

"What? Someone else? There's no one else. I… love you. I want to be with you."

"Well, of course you do. You won't stop loving me, sure, but… you might want to move on. You will get tired of waiting. People get tired of waiting."

"Kathy… I don't want anyone else."

"I'm not sure there is any other way to say it… to make you understand."

"What's there to understand?"

"Cos, we have less than two weeks, then I'm gone. I was hoping we could just move on. I mean, I figured it would hurt, but… that's the way life is. Life is not going to end because the summer does. Neither is my love for you. But now, our lives are splitting into two different directions. It all seems so simple to me. It all makes sense. There's also something else that might help… ummm…"

She stopped then and took a deep breath. Letting it out, she said, "There's always Averell. She'll still be here. You both are the same age. So, you two could hang out together. She really likes you. The two of you could be together for a couple of years before anything changes. I mean… college or… whatever. You could get to know her and… maybe you will fall in love with her?"

"You make it sound like it's completely over for us."

"Well, it kind of is, isn't it? Things are going to change again for us like they did at the beginning. I mean, we knew this time would come, right? Cos… it's just… it's time for me to go."

I didn't say anything. My nose was starting to numb up and I couldn't look at her. She was right, but I didn't care, or, I simply didn't want to agree. That would be too much like making it final. That would be like—quitting.

The bees poured in, filling my head, making me feel a little crazy. It was like I was looking at her through a telescope from the big end. Everything around the picture was fuzzy, and I was getting a headache. I didn't want to bash the Averell idea, but I didn't feel so great about it, either.

"I like Averell, she's a great girl, but… I remember you saying I was your boyfriend and… Ahhh! It just won't be the same not seeing you around Clarksburg."

My voice sounded weird. Almost like it belonged to someone else.

"Can't we still just make the best of it, like we planned?" she begged, "I've got a lot of loose ends to tie up before I leave. So, let's just go with the flow. Let's see how things work out. What do you say?"

I had run out of words. The tears were coming, and I was too busy fighting them. I didn't want to look like a whiney little kid who couldn't have his way. The fact is, my nose had numbed up more times this summer, than in the all the years before. I tried to look away from her, but it was like a magnet kept pulling my eyes back. If I stared too long—I was going to break. One long look at that sad, sweet face and I was going to fall apart. I played with a dandelion in the grass, trying to think of good things.

I needed to change the subject. What Shelagh had told me, came to mind. I stopped messing with the dandelion and slapping my hands on my thighs, I rubbed them up and down real fast. Focusing on her peace sign belt buckle, I said, "I have something to ask you, but I don't want you to get mad. I need to know… are there any other guys besides me?"

I brought my eyes slowly up to her face and saw she looked kind of stunned. Turning away from me, she started pulling out tuffs of grass and tossing them into the breeze. I could have sworn I heard a clock ticketing as I waited. Why was it taking so long to answer?

After a minute or so, she said, "Sure, I have guy friends. But they are those boys… those people that my folks think I ought to be hanging around with. So… it's all for show. None of those guys mean anything to me."

"So, there are others?"

"Yeah, but there's no hugging or kissing or… anything like that. Just old fashioned hanging out. I always have to make sure that everyone sees us together, just for the sake of my parents. It's all a trick… you know what I mean? All for show. All for a stupid show."

"That's all? So, there's no one else like me? No old boyfriends from school, or…"

"Of course, there are old friends. I mean… you have old friends, right? Girls that came before me?"

"Well, no… not really."

"Oh, come on? You're not serious, are you?"

"Yeah, well, maybe like back in elementary, or jr. high."

"See, so there! That's what I mean."

"So, can you promise me that you won't see anybody else besides me?"

I realized what I had asked, and then wished I hadn't. I was trying to get her to promise herself to me. That may have been asking too much. I got a bad feeling, and I expected a big fat, no.

"Cos! I have friends, and… I'm leaving soon. It's going to be hard enough to leave you and… it's like I already told you, I think you'd be happier finding somebody else. Summer is over."

"I… I don't want no one else, Kathy."

"Oh Cos…" she said and whimpered a little before throwing her arms open for me.

I hesitated a second before I crawled across the grave to her. It was kind of weird for me because there were dead people beneath that grass. I slid in between her legs, hugging her tightly, trying not to think about anything. The buzzing in my head grew less and finally went away completely, the bee's taking off for places unknown.

After a while, she let go of me and I moved around beside her. We sat with our legs stretched out, leaning back on our arms. She soon kicked off her work boots and pulled off her socks. Laying down, she crossed her arms behind her head and stared up at the sky. After a while, she closed her eyes, leaving me to watch and wonder.

It was a shady spot, so we didn't have to worry about getting cooked by the sun. The light flickered through the leaves and danced around on our skin. I had a thousand things I wanted to ask her, but I was afraid it would start the crap all over again. So, I thought about stuff that we might be able to deal with at the moment. Hoping she hadn't fallen asleep, I asked, "So, what are we going to do about your da? I mean… for the next couple of weeks?"

She opened her eyes, sighing. Looking at me, she said, "Nothing. We don't need to do anything. I think I need to let him cool off. He'll get tired of fighting me, just like he always has. Then he'll let it go. He truly wants me to be happy. The only way he can be happy is… if I am. So, we'll just wait."

"Nothing changes? I don't have to worry about being killed or crippled or anything like that?"

"Of course not, his bark is worse than his bite. He'd never do anything against the law. He wants to put on a big show. You know that macho man thing? That, macho… DAD thing!"

I knew what she was talking about. Guys were always trying to outdo each other. Most of the time, it came down to how long the thing was between our legs—like that would really matter. Girls were the same though, they just went about it differently. Like the boob talk with Shelagh. I figured she brought it up to try to make Kathy less than human for not having big ones. Like she'd be less of a woman, and because with some guys that would matter.

I started to wonder what she meant by tying up loose ends. I was going to ask, when she said, "I think we are through the worst of it. He's punished me by making me do the hard jobs around our place. He knows how much I hate that. I finally just had to throw down my hammer and say, enough is enough. When I came in to grab the car keys off the rack, he didn't say a word. Besides, in less than two weeks, I'll be gone. Then I will be completely in control of my own life. No more mending fences or… CLEANING UP COW SHIT!"

My arms started to hurt from leaning on them, so I lay down. We laid there for a while with our feet out toward her grandma's grave. I could see she was thinking real hard. She had on the kind of a face that people have when they are making plans. I was thinking about taking a nap, but she reached over and pulling my face to hers, she kissed me lightly on my forehead.

Something started bugging me and I said, "Don't you think it's kind of weird, lying here together, next to your granny's grave in a cemetery?"

"Oh, no. It's okay. She wouldn't mind. It's too bad my dad wasn't more like her. But my mom is. Sadly, most of the time, mom only does what dad wants."

"What about your grandda? He's lying here too."

"Would you just shut up and kiss me?"

Rolling on to her side, she pulled me to her, and we kissed for a moment. Then laying back down, she stared into the sky. I gave her the once-over, thinking how lovely she looked, her hair spread out around her head, her skin almost like milk against the green grass. She licked her pink lips and looked at me out of the corner of her eye before closing them completely.

I told myself I needed to hang on to that memory. But I was feeling sad that there wasn't going to be too many more. There was something about the way she looked at that moment that made me get kind of solid between my legs. It got me to thinking about sex, and I wondered if that might happen before she was off for Des Moines.

We never talked about it. But like I said, I think she had planned it for that skinny dipping day. Stupidly, I had messed that up. I wanted to kick myself for being so dumb and why I was always doing stuff like that. Back when my ma was a normal person, she'd always say crap like, '*Oh, don't trouble yerself about it, laddy. Ya,ll grow out of it*' I was wishing I had learned how to do that before I met Kathy.

Her eyes popped open, and she saw me looking at her. She grinned and said, "Cos… the Harvest Fair is coming to Coogan this weekend. I want you to come up and be with me."

"What? Come to Coogan? What about your da?"

"Oh, he won't be around. He's going off to an auction over in Illinois. He won't be back until the next morning."

"Can you come pick me up?"

"That's the bad part, I can't. I have to work a booth for the lodge and before that, I have to help set up. Can you get someone else to give you a ride?"

"I suppose I can, or… maybe I can hitchhike?"

"Good. My booth is going to be right in front of the Hitchin' Post. It's that tavern on the main street. Don't come until after seven, though. Averell will be there at that time, and if I'm not, you can always sit and talk to her until I come back. She'd really like to talk to you, anyway. You two would make a good… ummm… I mean… you'll get along fine. Just talking and all. I don't give two shits anymore if anyone from there see's you around. Soon, I will be free. They won't be able to do anything about anything."

There was that Averell thing, again. I was hoping that wouldn't come up anymore. It was like she was trying to send me a message that I didn't want to accept. So, I ignored that part, asking, "What kind of booth is it? I mean… what's it for?"

"Oh, it's an SG thing. I'm supposed to recruit and get moms and dads to join the lodge. I'm doing a favor for my father, or more like, a promise, since he can't be there. Cos... he might be mean to me sometimes, but he's still my dad. I still love him."

"You mean... more than me?"

"Oh, I don't know about that," she said and reaching over, she messed up my hair. "But I do love you, and... you know that, right?"

"I do. I don't think you'd be throwing hammers around or running off to come find me, if you didn't."

"So... you'll come, right? Maybe we can go out and goof off afterwards? I only need to be there til eight. Averell will take over until nine when the fireworks start. There's a cool place up on the hill behind the old high school. We can go up there to watch them and be alone."

She grew quiet for a few seconds and then added, "A good place to get cozy, if you know what I mean?" She grinned real big and raised her eyebrows a bunch of times as if to hint at something.

"Sounds brilliant."

The eyebrow thing started me to wondering. Was the invitation to come to Coogan, part of the '*tying up loose ends*' thing? A chance to make up for that day at the pond.

"Oooh! It's you that sounds brilliant!" she said, teasingly.

Giggling, she tickled my ribs, then kissing at me, she slipped on her socks and boots. I stood up and after adjusting my Levi's, I helped her to her feet, and we walked back to the car.

She took me down to the Clarksburg square and dropped me at the corner. Before I closed the door, she told me that there would be no SG that night. So, I wouldn't see her again until the Harvest Fair. Blowing me a kiss, she raced away.

"Love you!" she hollered out the window, the sound of the engine nearly drowning out her words.

She was gone before I could yell it back. I watched her disappear down toward the river bridge, feeling a little cheated. Sitting down on the corner, I was still thinking about all she had said earlier. Along with that 'cheated feeling' there was something else. Almost like when the sun is slowly going behind a cloud and its shadow comes creeping up on you. I couldn't sort it out. Something was wrong. The 'three things rule' suddenly popped into my head.

"Not again…" I whispered to myself

I should have asked more questions. I was trying to sort it, but it was more like beating my head against a wall. Even though the bees were gone, I still had that headache. I needed food. I didn't get to finish my banana split, but Shelagh's discount had left me with a dollar fifty in my pocket. I'd still be able to afford Arnie's 'Toasted Cheese Special'. It came with a glass of beer, or root beer if you were a kid. There were chips, too. I didn't want to go home because that meant PB&J, and who knows what else might happen there. I really wanted to wait until I was sure my ma had gone to bed.

As I sat there, trying to push the worry out of my head, a junker of an Oldsmobile came up from the river bridge. It stopped for the intersection and the old hippy driving it, gave me a wave. "Hey, brother!" he called out. Then bringing his free hand into view, he showed me what I knew wasn't a normal cigarette. It was like he was saluting me with it, and then taking a big toke, he grinned at me, as the smoke rolled out of his teeth.

Moving on, he headed toward the east end. Half way down the next block, Led Zeppelin's *Dazed and Confused* suddenly poured out of the car's windows. The whining notes of an electric guitar moved slowly down the scale, bouncing off the buildings and rolling down the street as the Oldsmobile, like it's driver, smoked away.

Dazed and confused was right. Ever since Tuesday night and meeting Kathy's da, my world seemed to be falling apart. I needed to get my head on straight. I figured supper would be the best place to start. I was hungry. Once I had food in my belly, I'd be able to sort it better.

Walking over to the Blue Front, I saw Steve looking at me through the 'O', waving his hand. Crap! Oh well. I could put up with him for a little while, but eventually, I'd have to make some excuse to get away. Eating with somebody to talk to, was better than not, even if it was Steve. Sitting there alone, while the old farmers talked, belched, and farted at the bar, wasn't my idea of a lovely supper time. Maybe Harry would show up, or even Brian, who had mysteriously dropped out of sight.

Chapter 11

As I figured, there was only a couple of old farmers, and Steve, inside the Blue Front. Arnie was washing out glasses as usual, his eyes on the TV. Steve was playing himself a game of pool and grinned like he was really glad to see me.

"Man! Am I glad to see you. This place is so boring!"

"You could always get your silly ass out of here? Don't you have homework to do, or… some hubcaps to steal?" Arnie said. Letting his eyeglasses drop to the end of his nose, his eyes bulged as he stared at Steve, his short, gray flattop looking even grayer. "Maybe you can spend some money and help me forget you're even in here?"

The two old farmers laughed, grinning back over their shoulders at us. That pushed me into the trouble making zone. So, walking over, I jumped up on the rail between them, and looking back and forth, I gave them a sneer. Slapping my dollar-fifty on the counter, I blurted out, "Here's some money for you, Arnie. How about that grilled cheese special with a root beer?"

Arnie walked over, looked at the money, and rolled his eyes. The farmers laughed again. Then one of them had the nerve to pat me on the back.

"A few more years and you can take the root right off that beer, hey, young feller?"

"Looking forward to it, hey, old feller?"

He stopped grinning, and taking his hand off of me, he went back to watching the TV, mumbling something about smart-ass longhairs. I looked left at the other guy who was staring into his beer mug, looking like he was sad because he had run out of beer.

"Five minutes, then you can come back up for that sandwich," Arnie said as he set the can of root beer down in front of me.

I knew if a deputy sheriff wandered in while I was up there, Arnie could get into trouble. I didn't want that. When I was in there alone, he treated me differently than when the guys were in there with me. I figured it might have something to do with him being a McKay and me being a McDhai. My da used to come in there a lot and the bartender was the only one he ever got along with. Arnie knew my story. I think he felt sorry for me and my ma.

I took my root beer over to sit down in our favorite booth by the door. Steve threw his cue on the table and came over. We both sat down just as the bell rang on the toaster oven. I climbed out to head back up to the bar. Steve got this look of confusion on his face, saying, "What the fuck? You don't want to sit with me?"

"I have to go get my sandwich, dimwit. There's no feking waitress, you know!"

He had to think about it. His mouth was hanging open, *'Doing the codfish'* as Fiana used to say, his eyes glazing over. Turning around to go back to the bar, I saw the two farmers were leaning toward each other, talking low. Since Arnie had set my paper plate on the counter between them, I pushed my way through, to pick it up. They looked a little shocked at my bad manners. Tilting away from me, they stared like I was the worst kid in the world. That's exactly what I wanted. They stank of moldy corn and diesel fuel. It kind of gagged me, reminding me of how Steve smelled sometimes.

The farmer on the right said, "That sandwich looks kind of good there, little fella, mind if I have a bite?"

He reached out a hand, but I jerked the plate away, saying, "That hand looks kind of tasty there, big fella. Mind if I take a bite?"

I chomped my teeth a couple times at him, and licked my lips, looking straight into his watery, gray eyes. He was shocked, so I grinned. Looking back at the other one, expecting him to say something, all he did was look at the bar top and shake his head.

Arnie leaned toward me, and said in a gruff voice, "You got your sandwich, now git!" Motioning with his head for me to get back to my booth, I walked away without arguing.

The farmers must have thought it was hilarious because they both burst out laughing. I stopped and shot them my best Clint Eastwood squint. But the one on the left raised his beer mug, saying, "Here's to you, kid. Don't take no shit from nobody!"

That didn't make any sense. Here I was trying to make trouble, but they didn't seem all that bothered by it. Looking at Arnie, I saw the old guy nod at me, a big grin on his face. Pushing it out of my head, I went back to my seat.

"What the hell are they laughing at?"

"Well, Steve, I have no idea. Just something I said, I guess. You know… I am kind of a funny guy."

"Funny looking, maybe."

"Ahhh, what do you know? You're dumber than a box of rocks anyway, Steve Clark. So, shut your pie hole."

"I'm not dumb! Hell of a lot smarter than you are, anyway," he said and mumbled, "Geez—pie hole?"

I said nothing and took a bite out of my sandwich. If I let him have the last word, he'd shut up. It seemed so strange that he was related to the people who had settled this town. His family had been here for over a hundred years. I started to wonder if he had a part missing and that made me think about my ma.

Brian was always teasing how Steve was two bricks shy of a load. I looked hard at him as I chewed away. He had dumped out the salt shaker and was now making pictures in it with his fingertip. I decided I would be nice to him. It wasn't going to be easy. There was no doubt he was going to say and do some of the dumbest stuff imaginable.

Arnie surprised me by bringing over my chips. "Forgot these," he said.

Dropping the little bag on the table, he stopped to stare down at Steve and his art work of salt. Steve got nervous, giving him the 'What?' look. Arnie just walked away, shaking his head and chuckling.

"Can you believe that guy? Man… sometimes he gives me the creeps."

Ignoring his remark, I opened the bag of chips and offered him some.

He made a face like I was handing him gold. I dumped a bunch into his cupped hands, and he said, "Thanks Cos, you're alright." He pulled them out of his hands with his teeth, one at a time. Then he chewed each one as loud as possible, throwing me a grin between each one until they were gone.

I took another bite of my sandwich, waiting for him to finish. I thought he'd ask for more, but instead, he made a terrible face. One, I had hoped to never see again after the first time. I quickly swallowed and blurted out, "Don't you dare!"

But it was too late. He let go with a fart he had probably been holding for hours. It was loud and long, vibrating the wooden booth. All heads turned. I pointed a finger at him, but he just pointed back. It was a rotten eggs and beer fart. It made me feel like puking. I wasn't sure I could finish the rest of my sandwich or my chips.

"You skunk! Thanks a bunch for ruining my supper."

He just grinned, doing his 'he-ha' laugh. I stood up, and grabbing my food, I moved two booths away.

"Hey, young fella, you keep that up and you're going to have to come up here with us," the farmer on the right, said.

"You keep that up, and I'm going to drag your silly ass out into the street, and you won't be coming back in here. Hear me?" Arnie said, his eyes bulging. It made me wonder if he had serious eye pain at the end of a day after dealing with us.

"Ummm... sure enough there... Arnie," Steve grumbled. Afterwards, he did that thing where he curls up, sideways in the seat, hiding his face behind his knees.

Changing booths didn't help much. That smell wasn't leaving anytime soon. It was when it rolled up to the bar that everybody began to look uncomfortable. Arnie reached up and turned on the exhaust fan above the oven. Taking off his glasses to rub at his eyes, he left me to think there was no escape for any of us.

"What is wrong with you? You rotten inside, or something?" I whispered across the backs of the booths.

"No. We had pickled eggs and beer last night at home. Oh man, was that good!"

"How many did you eat?"

"About a dozen or so… and drank three beers with my uncles and my dad. We had a real good time playing cards til midnight. You should've been there, Cos, you would've had fun, I'm sure of it."

"Uhhh… yeah sure. You know what a dozen pickled eggs will do to you?"

"I do now! Make you break wind like a twister."

He laughed, squeaking out another. Arnie looked our way, shaking his head. I ate faster, trying to get it all down before Steve let loose with another. Then he got up and I frowned at him, thinking he was going to move over into my booth and bring his stink with him. But instead, he walked past me to the old jukebox sitting by the back door. Soon, 'With A Little Help From My Friends' came blasting out of the speakers. It was a Beatle song, but it was Joe Cocker doing the singing on this version. It was a good tune, but it was loud and overpowered the television. I don't think Arnie, or the farmers, liked it as much as me and Steve. Walking back to his booth, he left me alone so I could eat. I looked at Arnie and the farmers. They were all giving Steve their version of a Clint Eastwood squint, because the music was interfering with the weather forecast. Arnie finally slammed his dishrag down on the top of the bar and stomping over to the cash register, he stopped and looked back over his shoulder at Steve. The old guy grinned in a wicked way and looked like he was making sure he had Steve's attention. Steve was watching him, his eyes wide, his mouth hanging open. I figured he was probably thinking, "Don't you dare!"

Then Arnie's hand moved slowly toward a little silver toggle switch on the back wall beside the register. It hesitated there for a couple seconds just short of the switch and then shot out and flipped. All the pretty lights on the jukebox went out and the music stopped.

It grew quiet in the tavern with only the sound of a big, white floor freezer raising a wee bit of a ruckus in the back room along with the weatherman.

"Hey!" Steve shouted. "That's my quarter, you know?"

The farmers laughed. Arnie grinned, shrugged, and turned up the tv.

"Dammit," Steve said and curled up in his booth, picking at a string hanging from a rip on his jeans.

I wanted to say something to make him feel better, but sometimes I think he just asked for it. That was his curse—we all had one. I sat there watching him, wondering at what point in his life things had all gone to crap. Then it dawned on me. My da used to always say, '*Make yourself useful*' and then he would give me something to do like, mow the grass or paint the shed. As much as I didn't like the work, it made me feel good about my life. Kind of like going to work for Ernie B. I thought it was weird that work could make you feel a lot less worthless.

So, anyway, I was aching to do something that would make Steve feel important so he would stop the pouting. I still had a problem of how I was going to get to the Harvest Fair—Steve was going to solve that problem for me. I wouldn't even have to ask; I knew he could sort it.

"Say Steve, you know anything about the Harvest Fair up in Coogan?"

"Uhhh… yeah, sure. My whole family goes up there every year. My dad's going to sell some horses and goats, and my mom's got a bunch of chickens she wants to get rid of. I always go up later with a second cattle truck just in case they overdo it at the auction."

That's when I realized he was gritting his teeth and the veins were popping out on his forehead. Steve looked like someone sitting on the toilet trying push one out, except for him, it was the opposite. He was trying to hold it in, letting it build. Steve was going for revenge.

Before I could gather up my food and move out of the range of the explosion that I knew was coming, he let go with one I swear would've registered on that earthquake measuring thing. Looking back at Arnie, he grinned and shrugged just like the bartender had after shutting of the jukebox. The old guy's face went from surprise to pure anger and slapping his flyswatter down, he started around the bar. Steve ran for the door and leaving it wide open, he jumped down the steps and stumbled out onto the sidewalk.

Arnie ran over to the opening, moving faster than I thought an old guy like him could. He didn't go out, though, instead he just stood there shouting, "Your done in here for the night. You got me? I don't want to see your face around here until tomorrow. Are you hearing me, Clark?"

"Loud and clear!" Steve hollered.

I watched through the doorway as he backed out into the street. Arnie propped the door, and walking back to his favorite spot, he fanned the air with his bar rag. Steve was real good at getting back at people, but you had to push him pretty far, before he'd react. Maybe that was his curse—he was too nice.

I couldn't let him get away before he solved my problem, though. So, I got up and dumping my paper plate in the trash bin by the door, I took my root beer outside. The farmer on the right, hollered out, "Getting too close in for you, sonny?" Then they all laughed, sounding like a bunch of old crows.

"Hey Steve," I said, walking out to the curb.

"Don't get too close, Cos, I'm liable to get some on you," he said, and went to doing a little jig.

"Hey! Pay attention! I got a problem and need I need your help. I need a ride."

He stopped everything and stood staring like he couldn't believe what I had said.

"Oh! You're going to the Harvest Fair, I'll bet? You're going up to see your girl!"

"If you must know…"

"Sure! I can give you a ride—no biggy. Hey, we can grab some beers and head up around seven thirty. I have to meet my uncle at eight, but that will give us some time to hang out. Maybe toss back a few cold ones."

There, problem solved, and Steve could tell everybody it was his idea. Also, I wouldn't have to be the one to come up with an excuse to get away from him. He had to be somewhere else afterwards. I sure didn't want to drag him along when I met Kathy. That would turn my night into a disaster. It started me wondering why I couldn't put up with him. He wasn't that much different from a lot of other kids, and I truly didn't want to be cruel and chase him away. That would go against what I was trying to do tonight; trying to be a nice guy. I knew all about being a hypocrite and I didn't want that reputation. But Steve sure didn't make it easy.

"Well, I'm going home," he said. "Saturday, seven thirty, on the corner, got it?"

"Okay, seven thirty."

"Oh! Can you bring the smokes? Even some of those Pall Malls? My dad only smokes a pipe. So, I can't get any."

"Sure, yeah, I can grab a few. Can't get too many, though. We're kind of on a budget. So, you bring the beer—I'll bring the smokes."

He didn't say anything else and walked away like he was in a hurry. I figured if he had to go number two, he wasn't going to make it. When he got up to the drugstore, I heard, "Ah, damn!" He stopped all of a sudden, and changing directions, he ran across 4th Street and jumped into the horseweeds next to Slade's. He was going back into our hiding spot. I cringed at the thought of what he might be doing back there. Moving over to the corner, I sat down, thinking how he had worked so hard to gas out the Blue Front, and now, he was paying the price.

Fishing a crumpled cigarette out of my shirt pocket, I realized I didn't have any matches. Putting it back, I just sat watching the moon rise. It was coming up in the opening between the trees where the wee railroad bridge crossed over the street. I could hear the sound of the TV coming through the open tavern door, and for some reason, I kind of loved it all.

It was one of those perfect moments. You know what I mean? Like when I got up early to go fishing at the Pits and the sun is just coming up, shining through the trees and the mist is laying in the fields. A ton of birds would be singing, along with some cow mooing because it wanted to be milked before it exploded. You could even hear the clanking of the metal lids on the pig feeders as they ate their breakfast at some of the farms that sat close to Clarksburg.

There was this one time I camped out at Eddie Beltzer's. We were sitting together in his backyard, watching a thunderstorm way off in the distance. It was right about the time when the sun was going down. The lightning flashed crazily among the big clouds as they rose up to hit, what I think is called, the stratosphere? Turning into greenish-yellow anvils, they let the rain go, and it came down in weird, gray beards, moving across the sky.

Now, here I was sitting on a deserted street, watching the moon rising up, and wishing I could share the moment with Kathy. Sadly,

Arnie had to ruin it by coming to shut the door. He had it half way closed before he saw me sitting out there by myself.

"Where'd your pal go?" he yelled across the street.

"Home, I think. Probably to change his trousers."

I heard him chuckle and say, "You want to come in here with us? Got some old cokes in the fridge that have to go. I'll give you one, on the house?"

"Uhhh… no, thanks," I said, and showed him my can of root beer. "Still have some left, besides, I think I'm going home."

"Alright than, you behave yourself, huh?"

He let door shut and the loneliness came rushing in. That terrible feeling that fills you from your feet to your head. Something that never seemed to bother me before I turned sixteen. Now, it felt like a disease. I realized at that moment why I hung out with guys like Mike T, or a moron that reeked and told stupid jokes. Poor company was better than no company. I was missing my family. Thinking I should go check on my ma, I got up and went home.

Chapter 12

<u>Roadrunner</u>

The next morning, I walked down to Ernie B's to see if he had any work for me. It had been a while since I'd checked in, but there were no regular work hours. It all started one day just after my da had run off. I was hanging out down there in the big open door, watching him do his thing. So, he put me to work. There was too much for him to do, anyway. I got the feeling he was glad I was there.

"Where you been? I could've used you a couple days ago. Got two lawnmowers and a snow blower need prepped. Ol' lady Edgerly needs a new mower, so she's taking one. The dentist needs the other. He's already paid for his and gave that old piece of crap in trade," he said, pointing toward the crappiest push mower I had ever seen sitting just outside the open door. "So, you'll have to run the new one up to his office."

"No trouble, a-tall, Ernie. I'll get on it."

"The mower for Doc Theobald is late. I promised it early yesterday. So… do it first. Boy! I wished you'd come down before now."

"Sorry, I'll check in more often."

I would have told him to come and find me if he wanted me so bad. But what you have to understand, Ernie was what everybody around there called a gimp. It was a war wound, they said. He got a foot run over by an M4 tank in Germany, way back in World War II. He had to slide around on one of those mechanic's creepers all day long. It had these little metal wheels that scraped over the rough concrete of the floor, and it used to drive me nuts. It made me wish I could get him something that was quieter. He was pretty fast though, but he had a lot of practice. Ernie was one brilliant mechanic and I'd heard stories how he fixed stuff that no one else could.

"That snow blower needs to go up to Ralph Steward's TV shop. But you can walk it up when you go home since he's right up there next to your place. I don't think it's going to start snowing anytime soon, so… we're safe for a while."

I said nothing. He sat there staring at me from under his greasy, green army cap. He looked as old as the standing stones, as my ma would say. But I knew he didn't miss a trick.

"Well? Did you get all that?"

"I did! Lawn mower to ol' Doc Theobald's, snow blower to Ralph at the TV shop and… what about the other one for that old crone?"

"Don't worry about that one, just get it ready to go. She said she'd send her own boy down, didn't want you coming up there. Was saying something about how you and some girl ran down her mailbox in a little green car last month. I told her, bullshit, you don't know anybody who owns a green car, let alone, a girl. She said she recognized you by your long hair. I didn't believe her, though. She don't see worth a hoot, anyway."

Ernie winked at me, clicking his tongue. He had been sticking up for me and I got to thinking I was spot on about me being like a son to him. He went back to working on a boat motor that he had laid out on the floor. So, I went to work. Then he had to go and say it, "Speaking of long hair… you might want to tie that back while you're running those engines. You get that caught in a flywheel and… well…"

"It'll rip it right off my head! Yeah, I know! Heard you the first hundred times."

"Well, you know… I seen it happen once to an indian friend of mine up in South Dakota."

"Ah, bollocks, Ernie… you don't have any friends."

He cackled like crazy at that. But now, I had a picture in my mind of that poor indian with his hair ripped off. It was pretty bloody. Then another picture came of me meeting Kathy on Saturday with only half my hair. I wasn't sure how I'd explain that. So, I made a ponytail and tucked it under my shirt collar, like before.

We worked for about an hour, with Ernie mumbling, "Bollocks..." every once in a while, and then cackling about it. The radio was on, but he never listened to music, unless it was the old-fashioned kind. So, there was the news, and people talking about Vietnam, along with how President Nixon didn't want to give up some stupid tapes he had. They were going to impeach him for it; whatever that means. The same, old, boring crap, over and over. It got better when the music came on, but it still made me antsy. I wanted some Creedence Clearwater, or even better, some Van Morrison. So, I secretly changed the channel.

I was standing next to the radio, waiting for Frank Sinatra to end. Ernie B had his back to me, and I pretended to be sorting through the general hardware drawer. When '*My Way*' faded out, I quickly turned the dial to 106.5 and found Bo Didley singing, '*Roadrunner*' Ernie either hadn't noticed that I changed it, or just didn't care. Then he went to bouncing his head to the beat, and I quit worrying about it.

I kept on digging through the nuts and bolts, just listening to the words. It was a hopping tune and there was nothing bad about it, but after about a minute, it brought a dark cloud to hang over my head like that Charlie Brown character in the funnies. It felt like doom. I couldn't sort it, though. It was like that vibe, it left me feeling like something was going to happen. I kept hoping it would go away and leave me alone.

I went back to work on Doc's lawnmower so I could get the hell out of there for a wee bit. The second I thought I was free, and started to push the lawnmower outside to the street, Eddy Beltzer came putt-putting up to the back overhead door. He was riding his Cushman scooter. It was this big, blue, clunky thing with a huge lawnmower engine on it. It was fun to ride, though. Eddy's da was the official motorcycle mechanic of Clarksburg. I figured if Eddy was down to Ernie B's, he was getting spark plugs and stuff for his da.

Ernie didn't do motorcycles. That way he wouldn't interfere with Eddy's da, and vice versa. They traded stuff, though. Because the Cushman had a lawnmower engine, they let Ernie work on it once in a while when it had a problem. But that was only when Eddy couldn't sort it out. If it came to a 'throwing up your hands moment' they turned it over to Ernie. Eddy wanted to be a mechanic, too. He didn't like anyone else working on his ride.

"Eddy! What's happening!

"Hey, Cos! Had to come down for spark plugs and stuff."

"Yeah, figured as much. When are you going to get a real motorcycle and quit messing around with this kiddie bike?"

"Hey! Don't knock it! It's a great scooter. Hell! Someday when I'm older, I might have it bronzed. Then I'll stick it in the corner of my living room so my kids can see what a great bike I had."

"Well, you have to get a girlfriend before you can get married and have kids. Honestly, Eddy… I don't see that ever happening."

He sat there grinning at me with his big buckteeth. I could tell he was trying to decide if he should punch me, or just laugh it off. The sun was almost blinding me as it shined on his red hair. He always greased it back like a, *'true biker'* as he put it. He had really white skin like Kathy's. The freckles on his face were so thick that sometimes when he was far away, it looked like he had a tan. He was a tough kid, though. So, I was glad we were friends, otherwise he would have nailed me. Sometimes he'd come to school in the dead of winter without a coat on. I figured he thought the cold air might help toughen him up. Other people said Eddy was just stupid.

"You going to get that mower up to Doc sometime today?" Ernie asked.

"I am, just give me a minute… busy talking with my friend."

"Busy talking with my friend," he mocked. That was followed by an almost perfect imitation of me, "Oh Cos, we know better… you don't have any friends." We all laughed, but when Ernie turned away, Eddy made a face and flipped him off.

"Saw that, punk," Ernie said without even turning around.

Eddy made his 'Oops!' face and because he was still sitting on the scooter, he rolled it forward a wee bit, in order to put me between him and Ernie.

"So, Cos… working today, huh?"

"Yeah, right, hah! Working…" Ernie said aloud to himself.

"I am, got two lawnmowers and a snow blower to prep."

"Well, you ought to come up some time, so we can go riding. Now that you mention it, that real motorcycle you're so worried about, well… just got here from Germany. A Sachs! Dad's working on it right now. Soon as it's done, I'm heading for the Pits. You can ride the Cushman if you want?"

"Sure, yeah. Ummm… maybe next week? Going to the Coogan Harvest Fair tomorrow. So, maybe on Monday?"

"Oh… that's right! You got that girlfriend, now. That rich one from up there in Coogan? I saw her picking you up at school. Man! That girl's a looker. Wish I had a girl like that. I think I may have seen her in town this morning. She was riding around in a big red Plymouth Roadrunner. One of them big, motorhead cars. I was thinking maybe she finally got rid of that piece of shit Ford."

"A red car?"

"Yeah, a loud sucker, all jacked up and everything. If Mike T saw that car… he'd jizz in his pants."

"A Roadrunner?"

"Yeah—how many times do I have to say it?"

"You going to get that mower up to Doc, soon, or am I going to have to do it myself?"

"I'm going! Later, Eddy, got to get back to… WORK!" I said, throwing Ernie a look.

"Alright, Monday! Meet me at my house about ten in the morning, huh?"

"No problem, a-tall," I said, but my mind was somewhere else.

I didn't know a single person with a big, souped-up Roadrunner. What if Kathy had gotten another car? I didn't think that would happen, though. That made me worry even more. Maybe she was out with a girlfriend, who had a boyfriend, who had a muscle car.

"I'm off, Ernie, heading up to Docs."

"About time, what the hell am I paying you for, anyway?"

I didn't make any jokes or argue. I needed that money for tomorrow night, and he always paid me cash. He'd slip me a greasy twenty and a five, before I left for the day. That was a lot more than he was supposed to pay me. More than we agreed, anyway. He knew me and my ma had only a wee bit of money coming in. So, I always gave her the twenty, keeping the five for myself. She didn't have a clue how much I made. I suspect she thought the twenty-dollar bill that I left behind on the dining table had come from the money faerie.

Saying see-ya to Eddy, I pushed the lawnmower out through the front door. Crossing the street, I headed up the hill toward the dentist's office. It was right across from my place, so I could see my ma washing the big windows on the inside, a cigarette hanging out of her mouth. Her grayish-black hair had gone wild, as usual, and her glasses were hanging crooked on her nose. I waved, but she just kept on wiping, throwing her head back to signal she noticed me.

I pushed the mower around back of the tiny office building and came to peek through the window in the side door. That was Doc's private entrance. He didn't like coming in the front. I could just make him out through the open curtain that separated his little office from the teeth pulling room. He was sitting in his dentist chair, drinking from a little silver flask as he swiveled slowly, back, and forth. Opening the door a crack, I yelled, "Got the new lawnmower out back by the cellar door, Doc."

Dropping his flask out of sight between his legs, he hollered, "Okay Cos, I'll get to it."

I watched him stand up and slip the flask into the pocket of his long white, dentist's coat. He pushed his glasses up, and rubbing the top of his bald head, he started my way. He staggered a bit, and I grew afraid he might try to talk me into letting him pull some teeth. So, I didn't stick around.

There is only one thing worse than a drunk barber, and that's a drunk doctor. I quickly closed the door, but instead of going back to the shop, I ran across the lawn toward the alley behind the office. Turning left, I went up toward the main drag. The alley came to a T behind the hardware store, so I squeezed between it and Davis's Café. Popping out onto the sidewalk, I stood there, watching the street, listening for that Roadrunner. After a few minutes of hearing nothing, I walked to corner just outside the Blue Front's door.

Now, what you have to understand about Eddy Beltzer is—he's a liar. And a good one at that. He was also a good storyteller and was as full of blarney as anyone I'd ever met. He's what they call here in Iowa, *'a real bullshitter'* There was a good chance he had made that whole thing up about the car. He'd do that, just to mess with me. I don't think he had any idea he was hurting people when he did that.

He was a funny guy, though. I liked him a lot, but he couldn't be trusted.

It was right then I heard the roar of a souped-up engine. A red Roadrunner flew out of a side street, five blocks up and zoomed up toward the high school. The driver floored it and the huge rear tires smoked. The four-barrel carburetor opened up, making that strange moaning noise like they always do. I watched the Plymouth come out of the cloud of smoke, the driver running it through the gears. I could see the car swaying on its springs as it picked up speed. Then came the 'down shift' at the school as it squealed around the corner. Once it was out of sight, my ears picked up the sound of it going back into fourth gear. I imagined it speeding out toward the highway and wondered if they would leave town or come back around for another go.

So, Eddy hadn't been lying about the car. The thing is, unless it came back, I'd never know if Kathy was in there or not. It certainly wasn't a Clarksburg car. Nobody in this town drove anything like that. But I was sure there were guys in this town who would give their left kidney to get their hands on it.

I headed back down toward the garage. Ernie would be missing me, and I still had work to do. The bee's swarmed inside my head, the buzzing growing louder. I wondered if I'd be able to finish my work without going crazy with worry.

Even though I didn't see who was inside the Roadrunner, if Eddy was telling the truth about the car, maybe he was also telling the truth about seeing Kathy. I felt my ire coming up, but I wasn't surprised because that usually came right after the bees. I tried to calm myself down, thinking about what Kathy told me at the cemetery about hanging out with guys just for show, to make her parents happy.

But maybe it wasn't Kathy that he saw, just some girl who looked like her. It could even have been Averell in that car. She looked a lot like a small version of Kathy. Someone who didn't know those two, could easily mistake one for the other. Especially, if they only saw them through a car window. I wasn't going to find out today, though. I'd have to wait until tomorrow night.

When I got back to the shop, Ernie yelled out, "Took you long enough! What did you do? Sit down and have a drink with Doc?"

"I did, we finished off half a bottle! But I left when he opened the second. Why?"

Ernie laughed so hard, it kind of scared me. I'd never heard him laugh like that before and I was afraid he might break something. Then he got the hiccups. The whole situation became hilarious, and I laughed too. It actually helped me feel better, making it easier to get back to work. But when I tried to push that red car out of my mind, it kept rolling back in, smoke and all, leaving me to curse Eddy for having brought it.

Chapter 13

When I got home, ma was asleep on the couch as usual. The afternoon soap operas were blasting away from the little orange Motorola on the sideboard. With all the noise, I didn't have to tip-toe around just because she was snoozing. Putting the twenty-dollar bill on the table, I went into the long, narrow room that was part kitchen and part bathroom.

I spent close to half an hour trying to get my hands clean. I wondered about Ernie and how his hands probably never got clean. It was a good thing he had a wife. He'd never get a date with those filthy paws. This made me happy with my decision to become a writer. Ernie, Eddy and all those others could have this mechanic stuff, ink was whole lot easier to wash off.

Showering up and putting on clean clothes, I made sure there was enough food in the fridge for ma to eat. I hadn't eaten since breakfast, but if I ate something, there wouldn't be much left for her. Slipping out the rear door and down the rickety stairs, I came around to the back of Brian's apartment. The shades were all pulled and there wasn't any noise coming from inside. I worried that something bad had happened, or worse, that they had moved away without telling me. I figured it might be best if I asked around to see if anyone knew where they were off too. Snagging an apple off our tree, I headed down to the river bridge.

It was about five o'clock and that's when the square was the busiest with all the farmers coming to town to buy their groceries and stuff. I didn't want to be sitting up on the corner right in the middle of all that. Especially by myself with no one to talk to.

The bridge had a thick metal railing that hooked onto a short concrete wall at both ends. It was a good place to rest and watch the world go by. I sat down on the end by the kiddie park where Kathy and I had hung out in the dark. The apple was good, and I wished I had snagged a second.

I was there for about an hour without seeing anyone go by that I knew. All I got out of it was a bunch of crap from people shouting things like, "Get a job!" or "Get a haircut!" About the time I decided I'd had enough; I saw Mike Ts' red Chevy roll slowly up to the square. The fenders where on now and I got the feeling he had finished the hardest part of his project. All he had to do now was go out and get himself killed in it.

The red car suddenly whipped right and came tearing down the block toward the bridge. It screeched to halt right in front of me. Mike was all sweaty and still wearing his football jersey. His eyes were wild, like he was afraid, or something.

"Meet me over at the substation!" he yelled, and not waiting for an answer, he floored it and squealed away.

I watched him turn right and go down a maintenance road at the end of the bridge where he disappeared behind a row of old cedar trees. The substation was a place owned by the electric company. It was where they put all of their huge, green transformers and then built a tall chain link fence on three sides with a short wall concrete wall at the front. We used to go there and sit on that wall and goof off. One day this worker with a hardhat showed up and told us he would have us thrown in jail if we didn't leave. So, we moved down the river to hangout out at the old, rusty railroad bridge. But then some guy in a pickup truck that drove on the rails, showed up, telling us the same thing. That was when the corner became our new place. It was the best of all the places, and no one tried to make us go away.

I thought it was weird that Mike T wanted to meet me over at the substation since we didn't go there anymore. Jumping down off the bridge railing, I walked over. I could see the two old fishermen sitting in their usual place. I had learned by accident that they were called John and Stu, but I still didn't know which was which. I didn't bother to wave since I was sure they couldn't tell who was doing the waving, anyway.

Mike had pulled in behind the cedar trees, and was outside the car, leaning against the fender. He was hugging himself and wouldn't look at me when I walked up. "What's happening, Mike? Oh… and you couldn't just give me a ride over to tell me this big, important thing?"

"No… listen… this is serious. I don't want them to know I told you. If we ride around, they'll see us together, and if anyone ever asks, please don't tell them it was me, okay, Cos? OKAY? PLEASE?"

"OKAY! Stop freaking out and tell me what's going on?"

"Chucks coming after you."

"So… what else is new?"

"No, listen to me! I heard him tell Weasel to get as many guys as he can because he wanted to come downtown and beat your ass. He asked me if I'd come along, but… I told him I had an Eagle Scout campout this weekend. Which is true… so… I have to get going, but I just wanted you to know."

He kind of rubbed at his face for a few seconds like it hurt. Then he said, "I know Weasel got his nose bashed the other night and that he blames you for it. So, he and Chuck are teaming up to bring you a world of pain. That's what they said, anyway. They are going to try to get you alone. And Cos… there's something else. He and his brother were with old man Henton at the Coogan auction house. That's Kathy's dad, right? Well, I guess he was complaining to everyone about some kid that Kathy was seeing in Clarksburg. Chuck told them he had seen you riding around with Kathy in her car. Chuck was bragging how he could make it so you'd never want to see Kathy again. And well… I think old man Henton took him up on it. There were a bunch of Coogan kids hanging around the football practice today. I have no idea why. I wasn't going to talk to them, though. I mean… hell, Cos, they're our rival team!"

"What? What the hell are you saying? I mean… about Kathy's da?"

"I'm sorry, Cos, I'm really sorry."

He wouldn't look at me all the time he was talking. When he finished, he started to get back in the car. I grabbed his arm, but he jerked it away and climbed into his front seat, shutting the door. Looking straight at me through the window, I watched tears roll out of his eyes. Starting up the Chevy, he floored it and zoomed backwards all the way to the street, spraying gravel as he went.

I was having a tough time sorting this out. He wanted to warn me, but he also wanted to keep them from knowing he had. He always wanted to be my friend, but he wanted to be theirs too. I wasn't sure what he was up to. One thing I finally sorted out was that he was putting himself in a bad spot just for me. If he was going to start bawling about it, I knew it was serious. I started to feel different about him, like maybe he was a better friend than I thought. He seemed pretty mixed up, though.

Another thing that bothered me was—it all seemed so unfair. This whole thing got started because Chuck believed it was okay to treat Tammy in a bad way. Now, there were bad feelings all around, with people acting crazy. Honestly, I just wanted to get along with everybody. But I guess not everybody wants that. It seems some people aren't happy unless they're causing trouble.

I waited a few minutes, then walked back up to the bridge. There was a weird feeling in my gut and my ire was coming up. I really wanted to hit somebody and figured it might as well be Chuck. So, I'd let him find me, then we could have it out. I knew he and his mates wouldn't hurt me too much. Not if they wanted to keep their normal life. I figured it might be best if I stayed out in the open, though. Least that way, I'd have witnesses. I figured I'd better tell Harry and Steve about what was supposed to happen. So, I headed up to the Blue Front.

When I crossed the bridge going back up to the square, I saw Mike T's Chevy parked at our corner. It looked like he was talking to Harry. So, maybe I didn't have to broadcast it because Mike was doing it for me. He then jumped back in his car and raced away. Harry ran across the street to the Blue Front and went inside. I walked faster, but he was back out the door in seconds and was now running toward his house. When I was about a block from the corner, I heard a car coming up behind me real slow and loud. It was the orange Duster, the big dent in the hood, a reminder that it wasn't only Chuck who had a bone to pick with me.

Passing me, I saw Weasel at the wheel. Chuck stared real mean like from the front seat, and of course, Kevin and Bobby were in the back. Following the Duster was a green, two door, '64 GTO decked out as a Muscle Car. I didn't recognize it.

Inside, there were five guys and a girl with bright red hair, in pigtails. They were all looking at me, grinning. The kid in the front seat on my side of the car, said, "Hey little girl." They all laughed as the driver gunned the engine several times. Rolling up to the square, they stopped and someone in the back seat stuck their hand out a window and flipped me off. My ire hit the top about then, but happily for me, the bees never made an appearance.

Driving on through the square, they went for three or four blocks before making a U turn. I thought about going to the tavern or even home, but none of those ideas would help stop this. Besides, that was too much like running away. I mean, I couldn't tell if I was excited, afraid, or maybe both. It didn't matter, though, I was now spoiling for a fight and I figured it might be in my favor that they knew that I was getting excited about fighting. That would make me seem a little crazy. So… more dangerous. Maybe they'd back off because it wasn't worth getting their faces smashed in.

Back in Ireland, I'd have stood my ground. Besides, running always made you tired which made it harder to fight. Better to be fresh and ready to go when trouble showed up. I turned around and headed back the way I'd come.

There was this huge, sloping lawn that ran up to the back door of the Dairy Dreem. It was covered in old, oak trees and there was a big, open pavilion right in the middle of it. I heard it was the Clarksburg's picnic place, but you had to pay to be in there. The town always locked away the picnic benches, so the kids wouldn't carve stuff into them. If you got caught hanging out in there without a permit and the town maintenance guy drove by, he would make you leave. He told us one time we needed to have a reservation, and if we didn't get one, (of course) he'd have us thrown in jail.

The pavilion sat on this huge concrete slab that was about two feet high off the ground on the river road side. If we hung out there, it was usually at night. We'd sit along the high side so we could see if anybody was coming, then we'd run away to hide in the backyards up on Snob Hill.

I sat down on the edge of the slab with my legs hanging off. The orange Plymouth rolled onto the bridge and headed my way. The sun was out of sight behind the Dairy Dreem, and creepy shadows were everywhere. The street lights started popping on and along with them, the single light bulb on the pavilion's ceiling. It gave me a start because it lit me up like a billboard, saying, 'Here I am, come and kill me!' It made me realize that I might be hiding after all.

Weasel wheeled the Duster around the corner and then slammed on his brakes like they had seen me. It was too late to escape without looking like a chicken. He gunned the engine and whipped the orange car over to the curb. The GTO finally showed up and pulled in behind him. I sat watching them, trying to figure out what I was going to do next. I was sweating and my whole body seemed to be vibrating.

They were revving up their engines, yelling, and laughing, trying to scare me, and of course—it was working. I reminded myself about my plan to go where there'd be witnesses, not alone in a dark place where no one would find my body unless they were looking real hard.

The cars emptied out and everybody just stood next to them, talking, and pointing. I didn't know the kids from the GTO, but a couple of them had on Coogan football jerseys. That made sense. I wondered if the big guy had been the one sitting outside the Creamy Cone with Kathy. The very kid that Seymour believed was good enough for his daughter.

There was a bit of an argument between Clarksburg gang and the Coogan kids. It looked like Chuck was trying to convince the big guy to come up the hill and kick my arse. Then the Clarksburg quarterback, threw up his hands, turned, and stomped toward me with Weasel close behind. All my wondering went on hold as I prepared to defend myself.

The other kids stayed put, just leaning against the cars, and watching. Chuck turned around and seeing they hadn't moved, yelled out, "Aren't you coming?"

The big Coogan kid shouted, "We can see the show from here. You just holler if you need us. I don't think you're going too, though. I mean… it's just one short kid, right? How dangerous can that be?"

Kevin and Bobby had gotten out and leaned with their backs against the Duster. They stood with their arms crossed, looking back and forth between the Coogan kids and Chuck. Those two guys didn't seem to want to get serious about anything. It was like they only wanted to keep doing kid stuff. Maybe—being mean and fighting—wasn't their thing. But Chuck was their quarterback and they didn't want to piss him off. I figured they hoped just hanging around would be good enough. All they really had to do, was show up.

Chuck kept coming. I could see Weasel was holding back a little. It was almost like he didn't want to get too close to the action. Probably thinking now that the big dent in his hood wasn't worth it, after all. The look on his face told me he was afraid.

Jumping off the slab, I whipped my hair back out of my face. Chuck stopped when he was just out of reach and taking off his glasses, he put them in his shirt pocket. He stood staring at me, gritting his teeth, and clenching his fists. I figured I'd do, what I'd seen Harry do. One quick punch to the nose, then one to the stomach and then maybe kick him in the bollocks for good measure.

"Freaking weirdo," he whispered.

"Come on, boyo, let's get this over with."

"You got this coming for all the shit you've been pulling."

"What shit are you talking about? You mean, Tammy? I think you're the one whose got it coming."

I got ready to punch him in the snot locker, but the problem was, his fist was already on its way to mine. It seemed to be coming at me in slow motion. So, I tilted my head to the right just in time and it bounced off my ear. That still hurt like you wouldn't believe.

"Yeah! Chuck! Give him what-for!" I heard Weasel say.

Chuck laughed and got into a boxer stance. The guys at the curb started in whooping and I wondered for a second if that was just a Coogan thing. Chuck started to bob and weave like he had boxing experience. I threw a punch at his nose, but I only caught him lightly on the cheek as he bobbed back. He laughed, saying, "Ah shit, you hit like a girl."

"Well, I know some girls who could knock you on your arse."

"Yeah, right… freak. Come on, let's get serious."

I started to feel like maybe I was going to get the worst of this. All his farming and football practice had toughened him up. On top of that, I could tell he liked to hurt people. Watching him dancing around like he was Muhammad Ali, left me wondering if all bets were off for the Harvest Fair.

I wasn't going to back down though, even if the feeling I had was telling me I wasn't going to win this. That was about the time a rattle trap of a pickup truck came clattering and smoking across the bridge. The back was full of people and one of them was standing up, facing forward over the cab's roof. Blonde hair waved and flashed as the truck passed under streetlights. It was Harry.

I knew that truck, too, it was Harry's cousin, Vaughn. He was this guy who worked summers roofing houses and went to university for the rest of the year. He was a weight lifter. A muscle-bound monster of a man, who always walked around without a shirt on. Along with his dark tan, he had this wild, brown hair and a crazy, Fu-Manchu mustache. Harry told me once that Vaughn was an activist and was always starting protests about the Vietnam War. He really liked to stir shit up. We all thought he was a little nuts. The kind of guy that you wanted to stay on the right side of.

The truck squealed around the corner and slowed down. Elton John's new song '*Saturday Night's Alright For Fighting*' was blaring out of the windows and even though it wasn't Saturday, one day's difference wasn't going to hold them back. I am sure Vaughn would have been happy to fight on any night of the week.

I expected him to slam on the brakes and stop right there in the street—but he didn't. The old truck slowed to a crawl and rolled right into the back of the GTO. The Coogan kids jumped away and started yelling at Vaughn. The truck backed up, the engine died, and the music went away. Vaughn climbed out of the driver's door and everybody else hopped out of the back.

There was some tough-looking older woman, two old guys that I didn't know who had tire irons, and then there was Harry and his da, Richard. They stood in a group looking over at the Coogan kids who were still hollering at Vaughn and pointing toward the back of their car. Vaughn reached inside his truck and pulled out what looked like a large roofing hammer.

He had everyone's attention now. When Chuck looked their way, I thought about sucker punching him. That was when I heard Vaughn yell, "You get your asses back in that car and get the hell out of my town, or you're going to regret it. Got it, twerps? I don't ever want to see another Coogan jersey in this town again, unless it's at a football game, or being burned in the street after we win. Got it, dipshits?" The big kid started to argue. Vaughn raised that hammer above his head and said, "Go!"

I figured that kid wasn't smart enough to sort it out. He started stuttering something, and that's when the hammer came down on the trunk lid of that GTO. Those guys didn't know Vaughn, but I knew they weren't ever going to forget him.

The girl screamed and jumped back inside the car. The others followed. The driver started it up, but accidentally hit the Duster as it tried to turn out. I heard Weasel make a weird little squeak, along with, "What the…"

He started back to the car, leaving Chuck alone with me. Vaughn started toward Kevin and Bobby who jumped inside the Duster and went to rolling up the windows and locking the doors.

"Where you going, Weasel?" Chuck hollered. His friend didn't answer.

Chuck turned back and looked at me. That's when I realized I was grinning like a madman. There wasn't much light, but I could still see Chucks eyes. They went from being tough guy, to being afraid, and I mean the, 'Oh shit, I think I picked on the wrong hippie' kind of afraid.

Looking past him, I watched Weasel running down the hill. Harry and the others were now coming up and Vaughn jumped at Weasel, pretending like he was going to smack him with that hammer. Weasel sat down real hard in the grass, and covering his head, he started crying, "No! No! Not me! Not me!"

They kept coming, with Harry right behind his cousin as they ran. Chuck turned to face them, backing up as he did. I pushed him hard from behind, and he nearly ran into Vaughn.

The big roofer stopped and looked down at him. It reminded me of a picture out of a little kid's book that I saw at the library. Something about Jack and the Giant. I figured it was about then that Chuck wished his name were Jack, because Vaughn asked in his deep, scary voice, "You Chuck?"

"Uh… yeah," he answered, backing up now and forcing me to step aside.

"You're the one that raped that little girl?"

Vaughn then looked over at Harry, who was grinning the evilest of grins and nodding away.

"What was her name? Tammy?"

"Yep, that's the one," Harry said in a voice I hardly recognized. His eyes were glittering. But Vaughn's were crazier, making me real glad that I wasn't Chuck.

"Rape? No… wait…" Chuck stuttered out, looking around for help.

"And now you're going around calling people freak and threatening to beat them up?"

"Well… I… you know… ummm… Hey! They've got it coming."

"Yeah, well… you know what, you little prick, you got this coming." He hit Chuck right on the top of his head with that hammer.

Now, it wasn't that hard, just kind of a tap. Like all those years of roofing had given Vaughn the ability to decide just how hard to hit someone to make them drop like a rock—but not die. Chuck fell straight down. I couldn't tell if he was hurt or just so scared that he had passed out. Then, almost like Vaughn hadn't noticed that he'd just hammered a guy, he looked over at me and said, "You okay, kiddo?"

"Uh… yeah, I'm… uhhh… fine! Got a sore ear, is all."

He roughly grabbed my chin and turned the side of my face toward the light.

"Ahhh… you'll be okay."

Turning away, he yelled at Weasel in his booming voice, "Get your ass up here Fiesel and get your pal before I hit him again… and bring those other two with you."

Walking over to me, Harry threw his arm over my shoulders and said, "Come on, Cos, let's get the hell out of here before the cops come."

Weasel got to his feet and started yelling at the Schupp boys to come help. Kevin and Bobby got out of the car, but had their eyes on us, not Weasel. The looks on their faces said they wanted to come along, and maybe, become friends.

Harry's da and the other three had followed us and climbed back into the truck to wait for Vaughn to finish his business. They never said a single word during the whole thing. But they sure laughed like crazy when Vaughn dropped Chuck.

I could hear Vaughn harassing Chuck and the others as Harry and I started across the bridge. Looking back, I saw them help Chuck to his feet and walk him to the car. I actually felt relieved that Vaughn hadn't killed him.

"Man! Harry… that Vaughn wasn't messing around. He's one crazy guy."

"Yeah, he's kind of my secret weapon," he said, and taking his arm off my shoulders, he laughed and slapped me on the back.

We headed up toward the tavern and just before the houses blocked my view, I looked back to see the Duster roll slowly down the river road toward the Pits. This left me to wonder what kind of story Chuck was going to make up about this whole thing. He was always going to have to worry about Crazy Vaughn, now. But that seemed to balance things out. I mean, if you're going to go around making people's lives miserable, I guess, well… like Ernie B was always saying, "*What goes around, comes around.*"

Chapter 14

<u>Look What They've Done To My Song, Ma</u>

I ended up over at Harry's place. It was a really small house, with only a living room, a kitchen, and a bathroom on the first floor. There were two of the smallest bedrooms in the world, upstairs, and Harry's ma must have been a wee bit too busy for housework. Vaughn, those two old guys I didn't know, and that tough-looking woman, were all there with Harry's ma and pa. They gathered around the kitchen table, talking, and drinking beer inside a cloud of cigarette smoke. They were all relatives, or as Harry put it, '*Kinfolk*'

In Concert was on the TV and Melanie was singing, '*Look What They've Done To My Song, Ma*' It was about how other people were screwing up her life. I felt like I was right there with her. She was cute, and I wondered if she would talk to me if I ever met her at a concert. When the tough looking woman and Harry's ma started singing along, I left the room. I didn't want to hear them try to do the French part. It was a little embarrassing. They might have done a better job if they weren't so drunk. But I wasn't going to count on it.

Every time I came through the kitchen for a soda or some chips, they'd all carry on like I was some kind of hero. But I figured they were trying to make me feel better because I'd come close to getting my arse kicked. Vaughn got really drunk and kept throwing his arm around my waist, saying things like, "Don't worry, little buddy, those jerks aren't going to bother you no more!" Then he'd go back to drinking and forget all about me. At least, until the next time.

When Harry's da passed out on the couch, everybody left for the Blue Front. His ma didn't go with them and got busy with her hair, putting in curlers and waving around a blow dryer while she was yakking. She was trying to do her make-up, smoke a cigarette, and talk to us, all at the same time. She wanted us to go with her over to the dance hall in Prairieville. They were doing a fund raiser and the Wally Waltzers were the band for the evening. I tried to convince Harry that it might be fun. But he made big eyes and shook his head no, saying under his breath, "Oh no, not a chance," trying real hard to make sure his ma didn't see or hear him. Grabbing me by the front of my shirt, he pulled me up the stairs to his bedroom.

After his ma took off, we snuck a couple of beers up to do our own bit of drinking, chatting, and smoking. Our talk was about girls, with Harry doing most of the talking. He wanted to know about Averell, or anybody else I might be familiar with that was boyfriend-free. But I changed the subject because I wanted to talk about Chuck. I was worried what might happen now, and what we should say if the cops took us in for questioning.

He changed it right back to girls, and how he had trouble talking with them. It seemed every time he tried; he'd get nervous. I think he thought I knew something he didn't.

"You know, Cos, I can't figure out why I can't talk to girls. I mean… some girl looks at me and I am like, 'Hey, I might have chance with this one.' Then, I open my big mouth and—pow! So, I either scare them off or they end up laughing at me and walking away."

"So… you think I do any better?"

"Well… yeah! I mean, look, you have Kathy. You almost had Tammy, but she left. Now, I hear Shelagh Bennet's hot for your bod. I'll bet if it weren't for Kathy, it would be her, or… Averell. Wouldn't it be great if we could go out together, then you could talk for me, at least in the beginning, anyway? You know what I mean? So… introduce me, will you?"

"Yeah, I know what you mean, but do you think that's a good idea? I'm not so sure... You blew your chance tonight, though. There might have been someone over at the dance hall. Hell, a lot of girls go over there."

"Yeah, well… just not there. I've had bad experiences over at Prairieville, besides, it's the Wally Waltzers, for fuck's sake!"

"So, what kind of bad experiences?"

"Rather not say, just… anywhere, but there."

"So, how about the dance coming up at the County Fair? There's always a room full of girls out there and mostly our age, too."

"Yeah, maybe there…"

"Okay, so I'm thinking… Keli Hale, or Saleena Birdsong? You've seen them, right? They're in my grade at school?"

"Yeah… I think so. But if I remember correctly that Hale girl has a smart mouth. But… Saleena is okay, even though she might be part indian, or something. Somebody told me once she moved here from a reservation up in South Dakota. She hangs out with Willowbough Boyd that other indian girl."

"Don't tell me that's going to matter? I mean you want a girlfriend, right? Quit being so picky!"

"Hey! I'm not."

I looked over at him, noticing he was having trouble keeping his eyes open.

"So, how about when Kathy comes home on a break, from college… we can double date? If you invite Saleena, I mean."

"I don't know, Cos… and now that I'm thinking about it, the county fair? A lot of farmer kids go to that."

"Listen, Harry, how difficult are you going to make this? Who are you thinking? Raquel Welch or… ummm… Farrah Fawcett? Come on!"

"Oh… alright. So, do you think Saleena will like me?"

"What am I, a mind reader? We are simply going to have to try, okay? I think your chances are pretty good with one of those two. I mean, you have a smart mouth, too, right? So, you and Keli might go good together. That is, if Saleena doesn't work out."

"Okay, boss. Whatever you say."

Harry's eyelids drooped and popped back open a bunch of times. He was lying on his bed, with his boots off. I was sitting on the floor across the room so I could see the TV. He started to snore.

"Harry!"

He snorted and sitting up, looked around like he was expecting to see Chucks gang busting through the door.

"What the hell!"

"A quick question before you pass out, again. Ummm… what happened to Brian? Haven't seen him in like… forever."

"You! What the hell! Cos, you scared the crap out of me."

"Yeah, well… do you have any idea?"

"Uhhh… yeah, he told me at the Blue Front, that night you were out with Mike T, that his ma was going to send him over to Paris. Something about spending the summer with his relatives or something."

"Paris?"

"Yeah! Now, quit bothering me."

I went back to watching the TV, thinking about what he said. I was a little confused. Brian had relatives in Paris? That kind of surprised me because he never said anything about it. That's when I heard the snoring again and saw Harry was dead to the world. I wanted to question him some more, but I was afraid he might punch me if I woke him up again.

I stayed long enough to watch some old horror movie called, '*Nosferatu*' Afterwards, I took off for home because I didn't want to sleep on the floor. I was hoping Marshal Tylor or the deputy weren't sitting up at the Standard gas station. I decided to sneak down the alley that ran behind the Clarksburg Bank, Whitcomb's, and Slade's Autobody. That way I could sneak into our hiding spot and take a look.

Pushing the weeds apart, I was able to make out the back of the deputy's car parked over in front of the gas pumps. I didn't want to wait for him to leave, but here was no way I could get to my place without crossing Main Street. He'd see me for sure, and then, maybe, come to my apartment and haul me out for curfew violation.

There was a chance I could cut through yards and work my way down to the river. I'd be able to sneak in the back, but that would take forever. I was too tired. I decided to cut back to the alley. Coming around to hide at the side of Doctor Brandhal's office at the west end of the Royal Blue, I made sure I stayed in the shadows.

Peaking around the corner of the office, I could see the side of the car. Marshal Tylor was sitting in the front passenger seat, talking with his hands, as usual. I was afraid they were looking for me because of the Chuck thing. On top of that, I'd been drinking. I didn't think they'd go easy on me if they caught me smelling like a brewery.

Main Street lay in front of me. I could race across, run down the alley behind my place and maybe hide in the garden shed. I kept telling myself over and over again that I could do this. Counting to three, I took off.

The alley on the other side of the street was offset to the right, just a wee bit. So, I had to run across a corner of the Sawyer's front lawn to get to it. Sadly, that was as far as I got.

Chapter 15

The red lights came on, along with a wee bit of siren. It scared me and I tripped, falling face first into the Sawyer's front lawn. Getting to my feet, I looked back to see if they were coming. But the lights were off, and I could hear them laughing.

"Go home, Cos," Marshal Tylor yelled out his window.

Brushing off my jeans, I waved like it was no big deal. Then walking away down the alley, I felt like the biggest fool in the world.

Was there something I wasn't getting? I was breaking the rules, and they thought it was funny. It seemed like I was always going around worrying about getting caught at something, and fretting about all the trouble I'd be in. Then I'd go and get caught, but they wouldn't do anything. I was worrying for nothing. Someday I was going to walk right up to Marshal Tylor and ask him what the deal was. I mean, who else could I ask? There was a chance he'd be nice enough to explain what I was missing.

Guys like Eddie, or Mike T, could just ask their folks. But that wouldn't work for me. My da would have slapped me for asking such a stupid question. My ma, well—she wouldn't get it. As always, she'd ignore the question and ask me if I wanted a cup of tea. Her solution to every one of life's problems.

I finally made it to the safety of my bedroom and got ready to go to bed. Sitting on the end of my bed in my underwear, a million thoughts filled my head. It had been a long day. A lot had happened and it had me wondering about tomorrow night. When my eyes got heavy, I lay back with my bare feet still on the cracked linoleum of the floor. Clyde had the Moody Blues on the radio, and I drifted off to '*Isn't Life Strange*', finding myself in total agreement with the singer.

I didn't sleep too well though. My ear was hurting, and there were a lot of bad dreams. The one I remembered most, was of me driving the red Roadrunner. I was speeding up toward the school when Chuck pulled up beside me on Eddy's Cushman. Kathy was on the back and I thought it was weird she was with him. But what was even weirder was that the scooter could out run that car. Kathy was wearing a tight, red tee shirt. On the back it said in large, white letters, 'Hi! I'm Chuck's slut, Kathy' Tammy had been written above her name, but it was crossed off with a long white slash.

I remember looking down at the speedometer and saw the needle sat right at a hundred miles an hour. When I looked up again, Chuck had turned into some kind of a freaky skeleton man, kind of like the Grim Reaper. Then Kathy went to whooping, like she does, with one fist raised to the sky. Her jeans had slid down and her backside was hanging out.

Gunning the engine, Chuck zoomed away from me. Kathy looked back and grinned at me with Nosferatu teeth, her eyes going from green to completely black. I floored the gas pedal and went after them, the engine roaring like crazy. I still couldn't catch up.

The scooter didn't turn at the T intersection. Instead, it zoomed straight up the walk toward a mountain of concrete steps at the front of the high school. A second before they crashed, I woke up yelling, "Stop!"

My legs were still hanging off the edge of the bed. I was sweating and breathing hard as I sat looking around the room. My legs below my knees were all pins and needles. Rubbing at them, I noticed the sun was now shining in through the curtain that blocked my bedroom door. That meant it was at the back of the apartment. It was already afternoon. Standing up, I wobbled a bit as the blood rushed into my legs.

Going into the kitchen, I found my ma with her head stuck in the refrigerator, and I felt grateful that it wasn't the gas stove. All the wire shelves were out of the fridge and were now stacked beside it on the floor. They were keeping company with about a dozen loaves of bread, a bottle of ketchup, a dried-up old apple and a couple of candy bars. The jars of peanut butter and jelly were out on the counter next to a box of powdered drink packages. Along with them, something that just about turned my stomach; PB&J mixed together in a single jar. Stripes of purple and brown spiraled down from the lid to the bottom. I didn't catch the brand, but I figured sooner or later somebody was going to invent that. It left me wishing for real food. I was missing my aunts home cooking back on the farm.

Ma was wiping away inside the fridge with her rag, talking to herself. As always, she was dressed in her faded, summer nightgown and fuzzy slippers. Doctor Brandhal still had her on Seconal and she was sleeping for most of the day. That is, when she wasn't watching soap operas or lying curled up in her bed, crying.

"Morning, ma."

"Morning, lad," she said from inside the fridge.

"Nice day out, huh?"

"Tis… nice and cool in here, too. I was sure we had some food, though."

"Is that it, over there on the floor?" I said, pointing to the bread.

Pulling her head out for second, she said, "Well, I'll be… tis!"

Because of my creepy dream, I was hoping for a normal day. She had to ruin it by saying, "Ya get Fiana and Shauna to help ya go borrow some pratties from the McGuire's. We've run out, ya know. Can't find a single one in this kitchen."

I walked out, not saying a word. Going back to my room, I got dressed in yesterday's clothes and went out front to sit on the stoop in my bare feet.

I was kind freaked out and not sure what to do. My sisters weren't here anymore. Pratties are potatoes, and we hadn't had one in this place for ages. As for the McGuire's, they were our neighbors back in Ireland.

My ma wasn't getting any better.

I wanted to be out of there. But I had no place to go except for my uncle's farm. Not that I minded it there, they were good to me. The problem was, when I was there, I had no one to hang out with except, Coop, their watchdog. Besides that, the farm was a couple miles from Clarksburg, so getting into town was a pain. I supposed I could run away or go live with Harry. But I couldn't find it in my heart to leave my ma.

The way I figured it, as long as I kept coming home and making sure things were kept straight and that our few bills got paid, we were fine. I also had to see that her monthly check got to the bank from the post office, and that some food got delivered from the Royal Blue. That way, she could go on cleaning, sleeping, and watching TV all day without starving or freezing to death.

She never left the place except to go get cigarettes and chocolate. She always ran like crazy over to the Royal Blue every time she needed those things. I'd be in the tavern and she'd dash by across the street with her big winter coat flapping and her fuzzy slippers slapping on the sidewalk. It didn't matter if it was summer or winter. Then, she'd come back twice as fast with a big, brown bag in her arms, never stopping to talk with anyone.

The first few times she did that, somebody would yell out from their bar stool, "Hey Cos! There goes your ma!" Everybody would gather at the windows, and me with my ire coming up because my ma was on parade. I was always ready to punch anyone that made fun of her. But that only happened once. Arnie saw to it that it didn't happen again.

After everyone got used to her doing her thing, then only Arnie would say something like, "Oh! There goes Mae." I figured he did that just so I'd know she was out of the apartment. I finally realized it only happened when she found that twenty-dollar bill I left for her. So, it was kind of my fault, but I didn't know how else to give her the money without her parading herself. It bugged me for a long time, but then I figured it bothered me more than anybody else. So, I quit worrying about it and soon felt a whole lot better.

When I felt less like screaming and more like eating, I got up and went back inside the apartment. That's when I saw the huge pile of candy bars and Pall Mall cartons sitting in a heap on the seat of our big, ratty armchair. Ma must have found the twenty.

Sneaking up to the kitchen door, I heard her singing an old Irish song. If she was singing—than she was happy. I didn't want to mess that up by bothering her. Besides, I really wanted to get out of there. I just couldn't go without saying goodbye.

"Ma, the McGuire's are out of pratties."

"Okay, darlin', ya can go play wid yer sisters now. Yer such a good lad for yer ma."

There was a pain in my chest like my heart was breaking. I thought back to when she was normal, and my nose grew numb. I fought the tears because there was no way I was going to let that happen, not right now. Grabbing up my shoes, I got the hell out of there.

Stopping long enough to slip on my sneakers, I headed for the corner. I needed to get my head on right and put on my happy face, otherwise, people were going to ask questions and I'm not very good at lying.

My stomach was now making noises loud enough for other people to hear. I had Ernie B's five dollars in my pocket, but the Blue Front wouldn't open for an hour or so. I didn't want to face Shelagh at the Dairy Dreem, and even though the Davis Café served breakfast all day, the food was too greasy for me. Besides that, the place was always full of farmers and their families. There'd be a lot of staring, with people asking each other, "Is that a boy or a girl." I went over to the store, instead. There were plenty of things I could eat right off the shelf or out of the coolers.

So, I came in fast. Grabbing up hotdogs, a pint of milk and a small wedge of cheese, I paid and left just as quickly. If I hung around too long, Phil and Grandma would start asking questions. Especially if it was on a day when my ma had just shown up in her nightgown. I wasn't sure why they needed to know anything at all. I figured it was for the gossip.

Juggling my food as I walked, it dawned on me that I only had a couple bucks left for the harvest Fair. Wanting to kick myself for buying too much, I'd have to come up with a plan to make more money. I'd either have to collect pop bottles, work more down at Ernie's, or go fishing and sell everything I caught to John and Stu. It had to be one of those three, and fishing seemed to be the best bet. Hunting pop bottles made for a lot of walking and lawnmowers meant grease and smelling like an exhaust pipe for the rest of the day.

Going up under the end of the bridge, I was surprised to find my pole and tackle box were still there. Tucking my shirt in at the front, I put the food inside. I had only a short distance to go, so I wouldn't have to worry about too many people noticing this weird shaped bulge at my belly.

Grabbing up my fishing stuff, I headed back across the bridge and down the path to the river. John and Stu were in their usual spot, with their lawn chairs and a case of PBR. I was trying to hide that weird bulge at my belly as I jumped from rock to rock. It changed shape every time I did and the cheese was trying to work its way around to my back.

"Hey there, little feller, how you?" John said.

"Just grand, big feller."

"You all here to fish with your best buddies?"

"Going up top to my favorite spot right this minute."

I noticed they had two, big red coolers this time. One was already full of fish, their mouths constantly opening and closing, their black eyes staring. Clear plastic baggies full of sweet corn were scattered around on the ground at the bottoms of those coolers it seemed like those carp, even though they were suffocating, were still trying to figure out a way to get to them. I was pretty sure if they had legs, they'd jump right out of that cooler and help themselves.

"What you got there at your tummy?" Stu asked.

"Lunch," I sang out and hurried away before they asked me anymore questions.

Finding my favorite rock, I sat down and drank the milk. After eating a couple of cold hotdogs, I took a big bite of cheese. I needed to get a line in the water and get to fishing or I would run out of time. My plastic baggy of sweet corn was still in my tackle box, but it was over half gone and had gone rotten. I figured the fish wouldn't mind though, since they'd eat anything; spoiled or not.

I caught about five Carp and two Redhorse before I ran out of bait. So, thinking I could trade cheese or hotdogs for corn, I hopped back down to Stu & John.

"Hey guys, I ran out of corn. Can I trade you some cheese or hotdogs?"

"What? Oh… yeah, sure! But you know… you can use cheese or hotdogs, too. You don't need just corn. Say… aren't you that, Cos? That kid that's all the gossip, right now? The one that Chuckie Griffin was going to beat up?"

"Huh? What gossip? Oh! Well… yeah… he tried, but…"

"Yeah, tried is right! But that stupid idiot went and got himself hit in the head with a hammer. You hear that, Stu? You hear how my stepson's kid went and got himself hit in the head with a hammer by Crazy Vaughn?"

"The hell you say? Boy, I wouldn't be messing with that crazy bastard. He's apt to take yer head off." Stu gave me a look like I was the one who had been doing the hammering.

"Yeah… my so-called, grandson, Chuck. You know, Chuck Griffin?"

"Yeah, I know! Get on with it before I croak off from old age," Stu said.

Here they were, yakking on, and I was trying to decide if I should be running away before it was too late. All this time I'd been fishing with Chuck's grandda. On top of that, I was now standing within grabbing distance.

"So, what happen?" Stu asked me and then spit tobacco juice in the river, leaving a shiny, brown trail down his rubber boot and trouser leg.

"Ah… well… ummm…" was all I got out because John interrupted with, "Oh! And that stupid little prick, he tried to beat up our little buddy, Cos. But that crazy Vaughn, he took a hammer to him. Didn't hurt him much, though… just a tap. Gave em a little goose egg, nothing more. My stepson, he never called the Marshal. He figured since it was ol' Chuckie that started all the shit. And then he couldn't finish it! Then there was some talk about ol' Chuckie raping a girl from the school. My stepson… well, you know… Leon? Well… he was telling me that Chuckie was going on about how some feller by the name of Henton, up Coogan way, had put him up to it. You know? Comin' after our little pal? Do you know that feller, Cos? That Henton feller, up Coogan way? Ol' Grandma Schneider, up at the Royal Blue, you know? She told me that he's a real A-hole."

I was now doing that codfish thing, my mouth hanging open and staring like those carp were, at that corn. But I wasn't seeing John and Stu no more. I was a million miles away thinking that what they were saying, fit right with what Steve had told me. I wondered if Kathy or

Averell might know something. But now, waiting to talk to her was going to seem like forever.

"Hey, Cos? Earth to Cos? What's up with you?" John asked.

"Oh… sorry, was thinking."

"Well… don't hurt yourself. So… any-who… since Chuckie didn't have to go to the hospital or nothing, they decided not to call the law and drag that Henton feller in to it. But you know what I think? I think it's because they're afraid that Crazy Vaughn's going to come after the whole lot of 'em, and you know… not even Marshal Tylor wants to tangle with that scary son of a bitch, and he's gotta a gun, no less!"

John looked up at me and winked as the bees made a grand entrance. They began buzzing pretty ferociously inside my noggin and it seemed I was looking at John and Stu through that backward telescope. My stomach went to hurting and I couldn't tell if it was the hotdogs, my nerves, or both.

"So, he didn't get you? Knock you around a bit? I mean… that Chuck feller?" Stu asked me, his face looking worried.

"Ah, hell no, Stu!" John bawled out, taking my turn. "Vaughn got em first! Besides, this little feller here… hell… he could probably take that lightweight—quarterback of the football team or not, it don't make no difference."

I wanted to tell them about the punch to the ear. But the thought that John and Chuck were kin, kept getting in the way. I couldn't figure out why he wasn't mad at me? Why wasn't he cussing me or Vaughn out for hurting his grandkid? I got to thinking it was some kind of trap. Maybe they were just being nice to me, so I'd get comfortable. Then, when I got closer, they'd grab me. I figured I'd better keep my distance, just in case.

Realizing I was still holding the cheese and hotdogs, I set them down on John's stack of newspapers. Then going back to my spot, I grabbed my stuff and the stringer of fish. When I came back down, they were just sitting there, looking confused.

I threw the fish by their cooler, along with the stringer and said, "You can have those, I'm going home. Got to go up to Coogan to the Harvest Fair tonight. So, got to get ready. You can have all the hotdogs and that cheese, too."

"Now, wait a minute there, sonny boy! I think I'm going to have to give you something for those fish and that food."

I was afraid what he was going to give me, might hurt. So, I said, "Naw, that's okay."

Stu picked up the hotdogs and stuffed a whole one in his mouth. Winking, he made a face like it was the best thing in the whole, wide world and said, "Love these wieners! They're Phil's, ain't they? That man makes the best!"

"Here, take this for em."

Looking back at John, I saw he was holding out a wrinkled five-dollar bill. Shoving it out toward me, he waved it around.

"What? No! That's a lot of money for just carp."

"Ah, naw, you can take it. You're gonna need it if you're going to the Harvest Fair."

It dawned on me that was the reason I was fishing today in the first place. I put my pole under one arm and walked over. Reaching out to take it from him, he gave me a start when he grabbed my hand with his rough, old mit. I tried to jump back, but he had me now and I stood there, kind of off balance, trying to pull away.

I thought I would piss my bell bottoms if he didn't let go. He gave me the, 'What's your problem?' look, and then turned my hand over and shoved the money inside. Then turning it back, he patted it with his other, saying, "You all be careful up Coogan way, Cos. That's Henton territory up there."

John winked at me and let go of my hand. I stood there, staring like I was stupid or something. He was grinning now, and Stu was trying to do the same, but his cheeks were so full of hot dogs and cheese, they were leaking out of his mouth. Even though he couldn't give me a proper smile, I could see it in his eyes.

I had been freaking-out for no reason. These old guys didn't have a mean bone in their bodies. 'You eejit!' popped into my head and my face got hot. I needed to say something, but that's when the little bell, clipped to John's rod tip, went to jingling. He spun around in his chair, and grabbing the pole out of the holder, he hollered, "Got one, Stu! Got one!"

He was acting like a little kid catching his first fish. Stu was sputtering, with food flying out of his mouth as he tried to help. John set the hook, saying, "Got you! You little booger! See that Cos? Got another!" He was grinning so big I thought his face would break. He went to fighting that fish as Stu got up to get the net, knocking over his lawn chair in the process.

It was time to go.

Turning around, I hopped back across the big rocks toward the bridge. Once I was back on the grass, I took off running until I got to the bottom of the path that led up the embankment to Main Street. Stopping there, I tried to catch my breath. I had so much to sort out. Even though ol' man Henton wanted me gone, and Chuck was the one supposed to get rid of me, I still wanted to take the risk of going up to Coogan.

On top of that, I'd been fishing with Chuck Griffins grandda for almost two years without knowing it. Then, I find out he likes me better than he does his own grandkid. I really wanted to stop thinking now. I wished I could find a way to shut off my brain. But since I couldn't do that, short of being dead, I knew I had to get on with it.

When I got home, ma was napping, a pile of chocolate bar wrappers on the floor, next to the couch. The TV was on as usual and there was a cigarette burning down in her fingers. Taking it from her, I put it out in the ashtray. Something made me stand there, just watching her sleep. Of course, the memories came, and I went into a kind of daydream.

After a minute or so, I heard, "Haven't you had enough?" and it startled me, like I had been caught doing something I wasn't supposed to be doing. I looked at the TV where a woman was holding up a large bottle with a bald man on the label. He was grinning at me, a bottle of the cleaner in his hands as well. "Well, try Mr. Clean for all those stubborn stains," she said and stepping over to a washing machine, she dumped some of it inside. Not caring, because I didn't have any stubborn stains at the moment, I went in to take my shower.

Even though I couldn't smell it, I figured I reeked of fish, and when did any girl, ever like that? If home plate was what Kathy was shooting for tonight, I didn't want to smell like I'd been on the river all day.

After I finished, I got into Fiana's old dresser and stole what she called her, 'Dashiki shirt' I think it was a boy's shirt, but being a feminist, she didn't care. It was my favorite of hers because it was tie-dyed and fit me perfectly. After putting on my best jeans with the biggest bells, I cleaned up my sandals with a wet rag. Then after slapping on a small puddle of English Leather, I brushed out my hair to make it fluffy. Taking one last whiff to be sure there wasn't any fish stink, I tiptoed back into the living room.

Ma was still asleep and now the news was on. They were talking about a huge rock festival that was coming up next weekend at some place called Watkins Glen. They said it was supposed to be as big as Woodstock and then showed footage of that concert from way back in 1969. I was wondering if maybe Kathy and I might go to Watkins Glen, together. I'd have to ask her when I saw her. Moving over to the TV, I rolled the volume down a bit. Then turning on a lamp, so my ma wouldn't have to wake up in the dark, I headed out the door, stealing my ma's open pack of Pall Malls and a book of matches on the way.

Chapter 16

<u>Bell Bottom Blues</u>

Sitting down on the corner, I put my back to the lamp pole and lit up my first cigarette of the day. It was becoming a habit, and I thought seriously about quitting, again. I knew the reason I smoked was because the guys did. It was the cool thing to do. If I quit, I would get a bunch of crap for it. I wondered if I had the guts to go through with it. It had been over a year since I started, and it was becoming a hassle.

Puffing away, I watched the street, listening to The Blue Front. It was going full blast with the music, the yelling, and all the laughing. As always, the rowdier farmers showed up on Friday and Saturday nights. I didn't go in there unless I had to. We could always count on at least one fight to break out. Eventually somebody was going to jail. Some townie from Slade's Auto Body, or Elsie's Construction Company would pick on a drunk farm boy, and that would start the fray.

Marshal Tylor was already on the prowl, driving around in his '64 Ford Galaxy. He was pretty proud of his ol' 390 Police Interceptor, as he put it, but I'd never seen it intercept anything. Waving as he drove by, I had to wonder why anyone would want to be a policeman.

More often than not, he'd stick to the backstreets on his evening patrols and walk the square area in the day. I figured it was easier for him to deal with kids out causing trouble than to have to put up with mean drunks. That would come later when the deputy sheriff showed up to help. He'd park his car up in front of the bank where it wouldn't get bashed by the rowdies and then he'd jump in with the deputy.

I watched his car come back into view, crossing 4th Street about three blocks up. As soon as he was out of sight, headlights come on in a side street up by the school. An old cattle truck with an open-topped box on the back, pulled out, and turning down toward the square, it picked up speed. When it pulled up alongside me, I saw it was Steve.

"Get in! The marshal's on the prowl. I think he's working his way up toward the school. So, let's go before he comes back."

I jumped inside without a word. He did a slow-roll away from the curb toward Ernie B's as I watched in the big side mirror, not real sure what Steve had to worry about. Turning right at the shop, he worked his way around to Main Street. After crossing the river bridge, he picked up his pace toward the highway.

Dressed in his best, I almost didn't recognize him. His hair seemed longer when it was combed out, and he had brushed his teeth. He wore new jeans with a black and blue, plaid shirt. He still had on those damn crap covered boots, though. I wondered if they were all he had. I could always suggest the wet rag technique, but I didn't think he would take the advice.

The truck wasn't too bad of a ride, but I figured it must have been built back in the early fifties. It was ancient, but the cab was pretty clean, well… except for a rusty old chain, some hand tools, and a roll of wire piled up on the floor underneath my feet.

"You're early. Why'd you have to come so early?"

"Does it matter?"

"Well, yeah! I mean… I'm not supposed be there til eight."

"Fine then!" he said, and whipping the truck left, he turned down a gravel road.

"Wait! You think this is a good idea? Now we will get all dusty."

"What the hell do you want? Damn, Cos…"

"Yeah, that's right… damn Cos."

"Ah jeez, I'm nice enough to give you a ride… what the hell? Do you think I run a limo service or something?"

"Could we at least roll up the windows and turn on the air? This thing has air, right?"

"Sure does," he said with pride, like he had been the one to invent air conditioning.

Rolling up the windows, he hit the button and the cool air flowed. I figured calling me a wuss would come next, and I was surprised when it didn't. There was now an awkward silence in the cab with only the engine noise and the fan on high. I turned on the radio and getting ready to switch from the country station to 106.5, then I changed my mind. Eric Clapton was on, singing *'Bell Bottom Blues'* and I really liked that song. Especially now, because I could relate. Eric was singing about how he didn't want to fade away, and that he wanted her, whoever she was, to give him just one more day.

I was getting into that song, when Steve ruined the moment by blurting out, "Going to get laid tonight, Cos. Going to find me a girl and… get it on!"

Annoyed, I said, "Oh, yeah, right! So, who's it going to be? Some lonely sheep named, Baaa-bara?"

"What? Naaaw! I wouldn't do that! In fact, my uncle Lew's going to bring his daughter, Lizzie. She's only fifteen, but she's good looking, and… she has some pretty nice boobs."

"Steve, ummm… didn't anyone ever tell you shouldn't have sex with your cousin? Great boobs, or not."

"No! Why not? A girl's, a girl."

"Yeah, but if you're of the same blood, there might be problems."

"Like what?"

"Like if she gets pregnant? There's a chance she could have a weird baby."

"Well… she's not! I got rubbers."

"I wouldn't tell anybody about this, if I were you. Some people will beat the crap out of you for having sex with your cousin. It's just, well… bad taste."

"I never said I had good taste, and… I'm not trying too, either. You know, Cos, Jerry Lee Lewis married his cousin, and they didn't have any weird babies."

"Wow! Steve, that's an interesting fact, but… you know… you're not Jerry Lee Lewis. I heard he even got in trouble for that, but… could we talk about something else, please?"

"Yeah! Let's talk about beer." Reaching down, he pulled a six pack of Olympia from under the seat.

"Filched this from my dad's supply. Pull a couple out, will you? I can't while I'm driving. Got to shift this pig at every frigging hill we come to. Push them back under the seat when you're done, huh? Don't want the deputy to see them if he stops us."

I pulled two cans out of the plastic rings and put the rest back under. Then popping the tops, I handed him one. We drove around the countryside for a while, just drinking. Even though I got lost after a few miles, Steve didn't, and he, somehow, found his way back to Highway13. I finished my can of beer by the time we got to Coogan. The trucks little dashboard clock said it was only 7:42, but I figured that was close enough.

Steve was still working on his beer when we pulled into the farmer's co-op. The lights were off inside, so I figured they hadn't even bothered to open for the day. Steve parked beside the other trucks that looked a lot like his and shut off the motor.

"If I park here, the cops won't notice a big truck out of place on the street. That way they won't get suspicious. Good idea, huh?"

"Brilliant," I said, shrugging and rolling my eyes.

He finished his first beer and chugged a second. Watching him do that, made me want to tease him. Thinking back on Thursday, I said, "You didn't have pickled eggs tonight, did you?"

Stopping mid swallow, he did his own version of my Clint Eastwood squint.

"No, we had my mom's homemade pizza, why?"

"Well, if you start in like you did the other night, you won't get laid, that's for sure."

"Don't worry about it! Not your problem. Maybe Lizzie will like my farts."

Giving him my, 'That's so disgusting' face, I watched as he tossed back the last of his beer. Climbing out, he took our cans and threw them into the box of somebody else's truck. I got out my door, and walking back to the tailgate, I stopped and tried to decide what direction to go in. Looking through the trees, I saw a small Ferris wheel come to a stop and a loud bell started ringing. There were the lights of all the different rides whirling around, and somewhere, a band was playing. Even though we were still two blocks away, I could hear someone calling a bingo game. There were a lot of people there for such a small town. It made me wonder why I had never come up here before.

Saying nothing, I headed toward the lights. Steve followed and when I looked back at him, he hollered out to the sky in a loud and obnoxious way, "Gonna get laid tonight!" Then he had to go and push me right to the edge of insanity by making up a song about it.

"Gonna get laid tonight! You knooow it feels so right! Oh, I hope she's kind of tight! Gonna be with-her til the morn-neeen light! Oh, gonna…"

I wanted to turn around to tell him to shut his pie hole. I was nervous enough without all his carrying-on. In my mind, I was begging for that beer to kick in because I needed to calm down. He kept his noise up for almost a block and I imagined myself turning around and strangling him right there on the street in front of some old lady's house. Instead, I slowed down and when he caught up, I asked, "Are you really going to have sex with your cousin, or was that just bullshit?"

He stopped singing and giving me a look like I was some kind of an idiot, he said, "Hey, Cos… pussy's pussy, right? It'll only be one time. So, it won't matter."

"You know something, Steve? You're screwed up."

"What? So! So, what? Just because I want to have sex with my foxy cousin?"

"No, not because you want too… because you are going to have sex with your cousin. Also… because you're an eejit."

"A what? Oh… its idiot, you idiot. Why can't you say it right? You're not in Ireland anymore, you know. So… say it right!"

Reaching into the pocket of his jeans, he pulled something out and slapped it in my hand.

"Take that. You might need it."

Looking at it in the light of the streetlamps, I read, 'Ecstasy-The Form Fitting Condom'

"What the…?"

"Don't ever say I never gave you anything."

He laughed and walked away down a side street. I stopped to watch him go, yelling, "You off to find your uncle, now?"

"Yeah, got to get down to where they park the horse trailers. See you… never!"

"Hey, Steve."

"Yeah?"

"Is this right? Is this how you flip someone off in America?" Holding out my left fist, the palm toward me, I pretended to crank with my right hand as I slowly raised my middle finger.

"Up yours, Cos!"

"Good luck with your cousin… EEJIT!"

He laughed and sticking his hands in his pockets, he hunched his shoulders and walked away into the dark.

Sticking the condom in my shirt pocket, I snuck back to the truck. I needed another beer to help me calm down. Chugging it as I walked toward the lights, I tossed the empty can into someone's garbage bin still sitting at the curb.

The Harvest Fair people had put up a snow fence along the main street. I supposed it was to keep cars out and the drunks in. Someone had smashed it down in one spot, though. So, I simply walked over it. Coming out onto the main drag, I stepped into a mob of people. It was kind of hard to stand in one place without getting run over. Looking left, I saw where the Midway stopped, and a line of white stalls with signs and banners, started. They lined both sides of the street, facing to the center, each one with a single lightbulb rigged to hang from the ceiling. Down at the far end, was another row of snow fence running across the street, blocking the way.

From where I stood, I saw people squeezing through a gap where it ended at the front of Ruthie's beauty salon. The street beyond that fence had become a parking lot. People had parked their cars every which way. I imagined it would turn into quite a mess if they all tried to leave at one time.

The first thing I wanted to do was walk the Midway, but there were too many people. I was afraid of getting knocked down. Being in a crowd when you're short was always dangerous. Especially, if you had a buzz starting.

There were carny's everywhere, and they were trying to outdo each other to attract the kids to their stalls. I didn't much like carnies. They were like tinkers, or travelers, as the Irish called them. You couldn't trust them not to steal from you. I figured what they were doing here at this fair, was a lot like that. It was a con game. But it was supposed to be for fun. So, I guess we were expected to go along with it, letting them take us for every, single, penny.

The buzz that had started, just kept going to become something worse. I regretted having downed that second beer. Things got a little strange. I didn't have much to eat before I came, so I suspected that's why I already felt drunk. Shaking my head to clear it, I took off to find Kathy.

I walked along the back of the stalls that started on my left and headed down toward the cars. I kept tripping over cables, people's lawn chairs, coolers, and crap like that. Most of the stalls were empty when I looked inside, and I had to duck back, when they weren't.

When I got down to the end, I peeked around the corner of the last one. That's when I saw the patrol car. It was just outside the fence, hidden in the shadow. Because my head was spinning a little, it took a while for me to see that it was empty. Which—wasn't so great. That meant the deputy was out on foot. It would be pretty damn easy to run into him just about anywhere.

He wasn't in sight at the moment and I really hoped he wasn't watching me from the shadows. So, I stepped over to the fence to peek inside the big, white Plymouth. It was all locked up, but I could still hear the police radio going at it. The deputy was talking to the dispatcher about how he would be escorting the bingo guy to the bank drop.

I didn't know where the bank was, but it sure wasn't at my end of the street. So, I figured I was safe for the moment. I scanned the inside of the car, but I didn't see anything of importance to me. But when my eyes came up and I looked through the opposite window, I got a surprise. Out there in the dark, parked in that mess of cars—was a big, red Roadrunner.

I slipped through the fence where I'd seen those other people squeezing by. Walking over to the red car to check it out, I noticed it had Oklahoma plates. All the windows were down, and it stank of beer with a hint of marijuana. The back seat was full of empty cans, along with a bunch of clothes. On the passenger side, in the front seat, was a stack of cardboard signs that read, '*Rheingold's Carnivals! Fun for kids of all ages!*'

I had my doubts about that last part, but they had to write something good about themselves. It's not like they could say, '*Rheingold's Carnivals! We suck!*' That just wouldn't sell. Now I knew why I'd never seen the car around before—it was a carny's car.

I scanned the rest of the inside like I did the patrol car and I saw a smaller box on the floor of the passenger side. My curiosity got the best of me. So, cracking the door, I hoped for a dome light to come on, and when it did—I regretted it.

One of the flaps on top of the box was open and I could see a double stack of pamphlets that read: '*The Trulla Lodge-Clarksburg, Iowa*' The bees, away on holiday, came back with a vengeance. Between their buzzing and the buzz that was already there, I felt myself getting a little crazy.

I kept telling myself that there was a good reason for all of this. If I could just find Kathy, she'd be able to explain. But no matter how many good reasons I came up with, my ire still kept rising. I realized that I was lying to myself. Something was rotten in Denmark, or should I say, Coogan. I kept trying to convince myself that it was still all sunshine and roses, and maybe, I was just being paranoid.

I slammed the door shut and stomped back toward the fence. Stopping halfway there, I threw my hands up in the air and hollered at the sky, "Damn it, all to hell!" Then stumbling forward, I bent the skinny metal fence post down in frustration as I went through.

"There! Better now!"

Moving in behind the stalls on this side of the street, I headed back the way I had come. I was so mad, I felt like puking. I knew now that Eddy hadn't been making stuff up. It was my worst nightmare, come true. I needed to sit down. If I kept carrying on this way, something terrible was going to happen, and it would be to be all my fault.

There was a concrete sidewalk on this side, but still, plenty of those electrical cables to trip over. After falling down a bunch of times, I actually started cussing out loud. There was a wooden bench out front of the Creamy Cone, so, I sat down.

Taking a few deep breaths, I closed my eyes and putting my face in my hands, I tried to will the bees to leave my head. This was just nuts. I kept thinking how much I wanted to go back to Clarksburg, or at least, somewhere quiet.

Sometimes when things got too crazy for me at home, I'd grab my sleeping bag after dark and go spend the night in some farmer's field on the edge of town. It had to be a clover field or a pasture, because corn and bean fields didn't make for a good night's sleep. I only did it on clear nights. I'd go to the very center and spread out my bed. Then I'd lay out under the stars, watching the sky until I fell asleep. More often than not, I'd wake up to a misty sunrise, always feeling a whole lot better. I wished I were there now. But you know what wishing gets you.

Suddenly there was a loud whooping, reminding me I was still in Coogan. I pulled my hands from my face and looking up the street, my eyes fell on the second stall from the far end. There was a big banner draped around it that read, 'TRULLA LODGE—JOIN US AND BE WITH GOOD PEOPLE!' I hadn't noticed it going the other way but, I had been busy tripping over stuff. Getting up, I walked over and looked inside.

There was a radio playing a song I didn't know, and an empty bar stool. Another box of those pamphlets was sitting on the front counter next to a clipboard and a small pile of ink pens. I figured it must have been only a little after eight. So, Averell hadn't come around yet, or Kathy had gone off to pee.

The whooping came again, making me want to go check that out. So, heading around to the back of the booth, I saw the place that Kathy had mentioned. It was a small, brown brick building with a sign on the wall no bigger than a loaf of bread. 'The Hitchin' Post' had been painted in small, goofy yellow letters, inside a border of gold rope on a black background. The front door had been propped open, so I stumbled over and peeked in.

There was some big guy sitting on a stool just inside the door, dressed in shorts and a shirt missing its sleeves. A straw cowboy hat was tilted back on his head and there was a mug of beer in his hand. He was sitting sideways to me and had his eye on the TV. Through the cloud of cigarette smoke, I could see there was a ball game on. The place was packed. Country music was pouring from the jukebox, mixing with the sounds of the baseball game. The cowboy turned his head to look out the door, so I ducked back out of sight. That's when I heard Kathy's giggle.

Stepping out past the edge of the door, I saw her with this tough looking, skinny guy. They were standing in front of the real estate office next door. He was as tall as she was. His long, blond hair was in a pony tail and tattoos covered his arms. They were facing each other, and she had a hold of his hands.

I was having trouble sorting if she was just holding them because she liked him or was trying to keep him from grabbing her. It sounded like they were arguing, or maybe, they were teasing each other in a mean way. Then he tried to put his hands on her hips, but she pushed him away.

When he tried to kiss her, it was all I could do to keep from exploding. I was going to holler at them, but the big cowboy stepped out, blocking my view.

"What's going on out here, Chas? You getting some?"

"None of your freaking business, fat ass! Get out of here and go get your own."

The cowboy muttered, "Asshole," and went back inside, leaving me in plain view. That's when they both looked straight at me. Kathy had a surprised look, almost like she hadn't been expecting me.

"Kathy! What the hell?" I hollered.

That's when the Chas guy said, "What the hell, is right! More like, what the fuck do you want, creep. Get out of here before I kick your scrawny, little ass."

This was the moment where I was going to write a check with my mouth, that my 'scrawny little arse' couldn't pay for. It was something, Harry told me to never do. But because of my ire, the beer, and all that buzzing going on in my head—I lost control.

The words, "Ahhh, up yours! I'm not talking to you… you tinker!" filled the air.

It took me a couple seconds to realize that they were mine. It took Chas about just as long to come after me.

I turned to run, but tripped over a big electrical cable and fell flat. Kathy screamed out, "Don't you hurt him, Chas!"

As I rolled onto my back, I saw the cowboy step out of the door again. He looked back at me lying there on the pavement and as Chas stomped by the door, with murder in his eyes, the big guy grabbed him.

"Ah jeez, leave him alone, Chas. He's just a kid."

"I don't give a shit. I'm going to mop up the street with his face."

"Uh, no—can't let you do that."

They big cowboy grabbed Chas and put him in a headlock. Kathy tried to squeeze by so she could come to me, but they were all over the place. Instead of waiting for her, I got up and took off, stumbling between the stalls and out into the street. I didn't want to talk to Kathy anymore. Plus, I was really afraid of that Chas guy. If he got away from that cowboy, I would be in for a world of hurt. There wouldn't be any Crazy Vaughn around to save me this time. I headed across to the other side to find a place to hide.

"Cos! What are you doing?"

Whipping around, I saw Averell was now sitting on the stool in the booth. Stopping, I stood and stared at her but didn't say anything. I wasn't sure if I wanted to talk to her, either. She was a friend, and I figured, maybe the only one I had there at the moment. But Kathy was getting close, but I knew if she caught me, I was sure to say something that would hurt her feelings. Besides that, if that Chas guy found me, I would not make it home. The voice in my head kept yelling, "Run! Just run!" The problem was, when I tried to do that, I'd trip over stuff.

I turned away and I tried to leave, but there was another big cable laying there, and for some reason, it seemed too high for my feet to get over. My knees hit the asphalt, hard, and it hurt like hell.

"Damn it! I hate this place!"

"Oh, crap! Are you okay, Cos? Where are you going? Come over here, I want to talk to you!"

"Well... I don't want to talk to you!"

Realizing that was not what I wanted to say, I felt I needed to go tell her I was sorry. But my thoughts were all twisted up now. There were so many bees in my head, I felt like a walking beehive.

Remembering why I should be running, I got up and staggered away between two empty stalls on the other side of the street. I started to feel like I might make it after all, then I had to go and crash face first into that snow fence. It gave way, and I actually somersaulted over it, through a hedge, and right into someone's backyard.

I lay on my back for a while, looking up through the leaves of a big tree. I could see the stars through the gaps along with a sliver of moon. Lying there in the cool grass, I thought about spending the night in that very spot.

I felt safe for the moment. Even though my nose was stinging, and I had a bit of a headache, I think hitting that fence had knocked the bee's right out of my noggin. I lay there in the dark, listening to Averell and Kathy having an argument, which I couldn't make any sense of. Then my ears picked up Averell raising her voice, saying, "Well? What did you expect? He's mad at you now. Isn't that what you wanted?"

"Yeah, well… not quite like that."

"So, your little plan backfired, huh, bean pole?"

"Listen… bubble-butt, it had to happen. It would be better if he were mad at me. Then we can go our separate ways. You know, Averell, it just wasn't going to work out. Remember what dad said about me making a big mistake? I suppose I can say it was simply a summer fling, nothing else. But that doesn't mean I don't still love him. I'm positive about that, but…"

"I think it was a mean thing to do, whether you love him or not. Now, you're just as bad as dad."

"Well, Cos and I talked about it, but he wouldn't listen to me. I didn't know what else to do. Besides, who are you? Little Miss Perfect? Oh, shit! Just tell me which way he went so I can go find him."

I didn't hear Averell's answer. The pain in my nose was getting worse. Now I had a sore nose along with an aching ear. My eyes were watering, leaving me to wonder if it was from the pain or if I was actually crying.

I had to get up and go before Kathy found me. Getting to my feet, I stumbled out of that backyard into the street. I figured Steve's truck might be a safe place to go. I could sit there until Steve showed up. The thought of having to deal with him made me change my mind, though. I decided to hitchhike back to Clarksburg. That Chas guy wouldn't be able to get his car out for a long time, so I wouldn't have to worry about him finding me out there alone on the highway.

Coming to the street that Steve had driven in on, I saw it was a straight shot back to Highway 13. The cars were whizzing by in the distance, so I took off in that direction. After a few minutes, I heard Kathy holler out, "Cos!"

Stopping, I turned around. She was standing under a streetlamp about two blocks back. When she started walking my way, I ran. Cutting across someone's yard into the shadows, I stumbled along between houses. I soon came to the concrete walk that ran alongside the highway. I started jogging and even though it was kind of clumsy, I still felt like I was making good time.

It wasn't long before I ran out of concrete and was soon walking along the gravel at the edge of road. Every time a car went by, I stuck out my thumb. But no one stopped. After what seemed like about a mile, headlights lit me up from behind for about the tenth time. Before I got the chance to stick out my thumb, tires crunched in the gravel as a car pulled off the asphalt. I turned around, but the headlamps were so bright, it was hard to see who it was. That was when the red lights came on. Throwing up my hands in surrender, I said to myself, "It's just not fair."

Chapter 17

<u>Smoke Gets In Your Eyes</u>

I heard the car door open and somebody said, "Come on back here, Cos, and get in this car." It was Deputy Jonny Herman. I was kind relieved it was him and not some other cop. He was the Clarksburg regular. So, he knew me. He always drove #126 and was the one who sat with the Marshal at the Standard station. They must have given him the Harvest Fair job. So, Marshal Tylor must have gotten stuck with handling Clarksburg all by himself.

"Get on back here! Now!"

Dropping my hands, I walked to the car as he opened the back door on the other side.

"In here! Get in here and hurry it up!"

"Hey, Jonny, what's happening."

"Just shut up and get in. I know you've been drinking, and… the highway is no place to be walking. Especially at night."

I fell into the back seat, landing right on my nose. Saying a few choice words, I lay sprawled out on the black vinyl as he closed the door. After climbing into his seat, he whipped the big Plymouth out onto the asphalt, the engine roaring. Squealing away up the highway, he turned off the red lights. It got quiet in the car except for the police radio and Jonny chewing gum.

"It's all about a girl, isn't it?"

"What?" I said, talking into a seat that smelled a lot like piss.

"It's because of a girl that you're like this, isn't it?"

"How'd you know?"

"Because, I'm really good at my job… you eejit! Going to make detective someday because I'm so good!"

He had just called me eejit. Something he heard me say one night when the guys and I were on the corner. He had walked over from his car at the gas station to check us out. We stood around talking, just like he was one of us. Now, he was teasing me. Which, was a good sign. But I wasn't in the mood. Turning my sore nose from the seat, I opened my eyes and said, "Just take me to that... to the hoosegow. Isn't that what you call it? The hoosegow?"

"You're not going there, you're going home."

"Take me to jail, Jonny. I might be better off there. Least ol' man Henton thinks so, anyway."

"Bullshit! And who cares what he thinks? He's an A-hole. You're better off at home, taking care of your mom."

So, he not only knew ol' man Henton, but he also knew about my ma. But I suppose him being a county guy, made that pretty easy. Seemed like there was a whole group of people looking out for me that I never thought much about. It made me feel better knowing this. It was just too bad there was nothing they could do about my Kathy situation. I figured that there had to be some things left up to me, though. Especially since everybody seemed to have this problem. The love problem.

Jonny turned the radio on and found the Platters singing, '*Smoke Gets In Your Eyes*' I knew that song, but I never really paid much attention to it. I guess, I couldn't sort what the guy was trying to tell us—least not until that moment. He was singing about me and Kathy. I covered my ears because I didn't want to hear it anymore.

Jonny drove me to Clarksburg and pulling into the alley, he stopped behind my place. Then getting out, he came around and opened my door. Grabbing the back of my shirt, he lifted me out, and set me on my feet.

"Careful, Jonny! This is Fiana's good shirt."

Looking into my face, he whispered, "Shut up, and listen. Now you go up those back stairs and go to bed... and don't wake your mom! Word is, you're doing a pretty good job taking care of her, so... keep up the good work. Now, I'm going to wait here until you get inside, so... get to it!"

He pointed me toward the back garden and gave me a little shove. I stumbled across the grass and went up the stairs, feeling more sad than drunk. It was like I'd lost all my energy. I mean, it was great to know I was doing a good job taking care of my ma, but I still felt crushed. It's like I'd been stepped on by a giant. I figured it would take me a while to get my normal shape back. Getting to the balcony, I raised a hand to signal Jonny, and he drove away.

I pushed opened the door, trying to be careful, but it smacked into my ma's bed frame anyway. She was snoring like a freight train and the bump only caused her to stop, snort, and start in again. After closing the door, I stood there for a while, just looking at her.

She was still my ma, but it was almost like I was the parent now. Feeling bad for her, I wondered what would happen when it came time for me to fly the coop. Somebody would have to come and look after her, or she'd end up back in the mental institution. I decided to worry about that later. The thing is, it made me feel sadder, which, in turn, made me hate my da even more. He had vowed to take care of her. He had lied. I thought about how hard he had tried to make me like him. I needed to tell him, someday, that he had failed.

Going through the curtain into my room, I kicked off my sandals as I went. After falling onto my bed, I lay there, staring up at the ceiling. The streetlamp made weird patterns over the cracked plaster and passing cars sent spots of light chasing each other across the walls. It was later than I thought. The clock said, 10:50 I'd lost track of time. The beer probably hadn't helped things. Drinking may have been a bad idea.

Laying there, memories of when we were a happy family ran through my head. Some good memories from my kid days. Times when I, Fiana, and Shauna, were together in Ireland. Orlin's face popped in there with that smile, showing her scary fangs and those troublemaker eyes. There were the moments from when we first came to America, and how excited we all were about it.

Then—Kathy. That day we first met and how happy I was. I kept seeing her face and the way she had looked at me with those sparkling green eyes. Then that first kiss. The way she'd clamp my head in her hands so she could look straight into my eyes and tell me what she loved about me. A picture suddenly popped in of her holding Chas's hands with their faces too close together. I actually winced at that one.

A feeling came over me that was a lot like the one from the sixth grade when I gave that girl, that poem. Except now, it was a thousand times worse. It was like someone had stabbed me in the heart, and not just with a knife, but something more like—a sharpened, fence post. It seemed there was a huge hole in me that you could push a football through.

I closed my eyes, hoping to block the picture. Then right out of the blue, the tears came. All the old tricks to stop them didn't work. Smoke got in my eyes. For the first time in years, I cried myself to sleep.

Chapter 18

Sunday Morning, Coming Down

Forcing my eyes open, I was nearly blinded by the sun shining in the window. I was still dressed in my street clothes and my pillow was wet. Flipping it over, I lay back down on my side to watch the second hand of the clock tick around. Static from the radio, told me Clyde Clifford had crashed in his own bed after a long night of spinning wax. There was a good chance he had a better time than I. It made me wish we could switch places. Because right now—I seriously wanted to be anybody but Cosantoir McDhai.

Sunday mornings, were always quiet mornings. But this one was a little different because the silence actually hurt. Why this day had to be so different from the other six was beyond me. I thought about that song by Kris Kristofferson. You know the one about a Sunday morning coming down? It was always hard to listen to and left me feeling lonely, no matter where I was. The song played in my head and I started to feel twice as bad as I normally did.

I thought of my ma and how there had been days when she never put her feet on the floor. She'd just lay in her bed, staring out the window. If I called out to her, she wouldn't answer me. It was like she was quitting. There was no way I was going to let that be me.

Jumping up and grabbing my sandals, I went to my doorway. Throwing open the curtain, I almost crashed into her. She was standing right there, her eyes big behind her glasses. I must have jumped a foot in the air, saying, "Jays ma! Whatcha thinking?"

Before I could say anymore, she said, "I heard ya last night in yer bed, Cos. But… don't ya worry, lad. It'll all work out for us."

She threw her arms around me and for the first time since I could remember, she hugged me. Two months earlier, I would have tried to get away. But I didn't this time. In fact, I hugged her back just like I did Kathy. When I let her go, I figured she'd say something wise or offer me advice. But no, all she said was, "Got to pish!" Then spinning away, she dashed into the kitchen and I heard the door to the toilet closet slam shut.

I suddenly got the urge to get out of there. With this new thing that happened, I had even more to sort out. I shouted, "I'm off, ma!" and didn't wait for her to answer.

Going out through the front door, I sat down on the stoop long enough to put on my sandals. Heading up to the corner afterwards, I noticed how dead the streets were. Since I usually stayed in bed until about noon, I'd forgotten how Sunday morning turned Clarksburg into a ghost town. That only made it worse.

Finding my place on the curb, I watched a big black dog run out in front of a line cars coming down Main Street from the east. The one in front slammed on its brakes and the rest followed. I thought it was funny how there was a whole string of little squeals that followed as each car tried to stop before hitting the other. I imagined the dog chuckling to itself as it ran away.

It was almost ten o'clock. So, I figured the church must have let out. In the time it took to light up a cigarette, the usual harassment started. People were staring and shaking their heads like I was some kind of fungus. When the fifth car passed, some guy with a back scat full of kids, leaned out of his window and yelled, "Get a job, freak!"

He turned to the kids, laughing, and I heard them laugh back. Well, all except for one girl about my age. She sat there at the window, looking at me like she wanted to be somewhere else. Slowly raising her hand, she gave me a wave. I didn't know her, but I gave her the piece sign as the big, tan Buick, rolled away. On the back was a bumper sticker that read, 'Jesus loves everyone–So… Love Jesus!'

"Yeah, right." I said, and jumping up, I shook my fist at him, hollering out, "Hypocrite!"

I really wanted to get out of this town. But I thought about what Jonny had said and there was no doubt that I couldn't just up and leave my ma. Not right now. Not like this. My stomach growled, and I cussed myself for not having eaten anything since yesterday. But I didn't want to go back home. So, after finishing my cigarette, I walked across the street. Going around the Standard Station, I walked to the backdoor of the Royal Blue.

The place was due to open about noon. The Sunday donut delivery had been right on time. The tall metal racks, waiting for the Schneider's to open up, were overflowing with pastry. I'm not sure what it was about donuts, but there never seemed to be enough of them.

I walked by and snatched up a box of the white, powdered kind and kept on going. Moving toward the alley, I figured I'd head down to the park.

"I saw that!" someone yelled, and I about pished myself.

The back of Slade's Auto Body was just across the small dirt lot from the Royal Blue. Brian broke through the horseweeds, grinned at me, and stuffed what looked like a cinnamon roll in his mouth, holding up the package for me to see.

"I'd check your shoes, if I were you."

He actually did, and I couldn't help but laugh. Walking over, I told him, "I think Steve might have taken a dump back there. So, you're going to have to watch where you put your feet."

He was still chewing, so he couldn't talk. I went by him, pushing my way through the weeds. Someone had flattened a big refrigerator box on the ground. Crates and buckets sat in a circle around it, something we'd never do. There an overturned in the center, and some playing cards scattered over it. I imagined other kids were coming in there, or Slade's workers had found a place to hide from ol' man Slade. Finding a crate to sit on, I opened the donuts.

I thought the fridge box was a good idea, like carpeting. It made things kind of cozy. On top of that, I felt relieved to see that there was no sign of Steve, anywhere. There was a worn-out comic book of the Fabulous Furry Freak Brothers lying on the crate next to mine. I figured Brian must have just been sitting there, reading, and eating rolls.

"So, what's happening, Cos?"

Sitting next down on an upside-down bucket, he turned his face to me and opened his mouth to show me all the mush inside. Making puking noises, he started doing that eyebrow raising thing.

"Shut your pie hole, you're grossing me out!"

"It's not a pie hole today! It's a roll hole," he said and grinned.

He swallowed and made a loud, smacking noise with his lips. I gave him a hard look, realizing that something was different.

"So… Brian, where have you been? Haven't seen you for, feking ever. Harry said you went to Paris?"

"Yeah. It was a long flight and you know those little Piper Cubs? They don't fly very fast… Geez, Cos! Did you think he meant France?"

"I did, why?"

"Iowa. Paris, Iowa. It's about four miles over that way," he said, pointing toward the river. He went to laughing so hard I thought he might choke.

"Ah! You guys suck! Do you know that?"

He couldn't talk, so he just threw his arm over my shoulder, causing me to laugh a wee bit too. When he calmed down, he said, "So, what are you doing up this early? I mean… besides, out stealing breakfast?"

I normally would have pushed his arm off, but this time, I didn't. He kept it there and honestly, it made me feel better. I didn't want to admit to myself that I liked it. Mostly because he was a boy. There was a good chance I needed for him to do that. The thing is—I was truly happy to see him.

It dawned on me why he seemed changed. He had gotten rid of that James Dean hairstyle. He had it parted in the middle now and had combed straight down like the rest of us. It was weird to see it so flat and thin. It didn't look the same without the spit. He'd also gotten rid of the red jacket and the boots and was now wearing a black tee shirt with 'The Doors' silk screened across the front, Levi's, and Ked sneakers.

"So, what happened to your hair?"

"I got tired of it… and quit changing the subject! Answer my question, shithead. I usually don't see you out until after noon on a Sunday. What's going on?"

Pulling his arm from my shoulders, he flicked my ear lobe.

"I had a bad night. Was feeling kind of crappy, and I couldn't stay in bed any longer."

"So, were you in town, or did you go partying somewhere?"

"I rode up to the Harvest Fair with Steve. You know… up in Coogan?"

"You were with Steve? No wonder you had a bad night! Oh… and yeah, fuckhead, I know where the Harvest Fair is. Did you see Kathy?"

"I did… but… ummm… she was with some creep."

He was quiet for a minute. I could tell he wanted to razz me and say crap like, "Ha! I knew it!" or "You can never trust a woman!" But he must have decided to go easy on me. All he said was, "Oh man, that sucks. I figured you guys would be getting married about now. So, it's kind of like the worst time to find your girlfriend cheating on you, huh? Especially after you've been dating practically all summer."

"I don't think she was cheating. I mean they weren't having sex or even kissing. She was only holding his hands, and maybe… she didn't really like it."

"Ah no, dude! Don't try to fool yourself. Sounds like there was something else going on."

Brian had called me dude. That was the new thing now, instead of: *'Hey, man.'* It was now, *'Hey, dude'* Surfer slang, something they say out in California. It had now worked its way out to us in Iowa. The kids at school were picking it up pretty fast.

"Maybe you're right… I don't know—dude," I said, and sneered at him.

"I'm right—dude!"

"Hey, Brian? Can we talk like grownups for a minute? You know what I mean, right?"

"Yeah, I got it. Like my mom's always trying to do, or Principal Trotman when I get in trouble at school."

"That's right. Kind of… I guess. I mean… listen, I'm sorry that we weren't getting along, but I couldn't help that Kathy showed up when she did."

"Don't worry about it. So, I get a little jealous, but… it was right after Bart got killed that things got really crazy for me. You know what I mean? Like with Kathy unexpectedly showing up. Man! You just don't know what it's like until it happens to you. I never thought Bart would go and get killed. I always believed we'd be together, forever. So, I reckon that's like you probably figured you'd be with Kathy til you kicked the bucket, right?"

"I imagine," I said, even though I didn't.

As much as I wanted to be with her, staying together forever was only dreaming. The chances of her meeting another guy were pretty good. It was probably going to happen while she was away in school. Brian had no idea Kathy was going off to college. He probably figured she'd just get a job here, then we'd get married and have a ton of kids.

"So, who was this guy? That she was with, I mean? Did you know him?"

"I didn't. Someone I've never seen around here before. I am pretty sure he drives a red Plymouth Roadrunner and…"

"You're shitting me? A red Roadrunner? That's Chas McCleary! He's a badass and almost twice our age. Man, I wouldn't mess with him. He came here from Oklahoma, and on top of that, he's a damn carny. He almost beat the hell out of me one night over at the dance hall in Prairieville. If it wasn't for Harry, I might be missing an eye or an ear, or—maybe even be in a wheelchair for the rest of my life. Harry held him back long enough for me to get out of there. I heard Harry got smacked a couple times for it. He never got over it. In fact, he kind of hates me for that. Probably because I never thanked him."

"You mean he stood up for you and you never thanked him? No wonder he doesn't like you."

"Well… it seems every time I get ready to tell him, he has to go and say something to piss me off. So, the hell with it. Now, it's been too long."

"You should try. It might make things better."

"Maybe…"

"So… do you suppose that Chas might be able to take Crazy Vaughn? I mean if he messed with Harry? I'm pretty sure Vaughn would tear him apart. It would be like a weasel taking on a bear."

"Hey, yeah! I heard about Chuck getting hammered… and not the way a guy wants to be. But I suppose Vaughn could kick Chas's ass, easy. But that doesn't mean Chas wouldn't be able to get to you first, and then just drop out of sight before Vaughn got to him."

"Well, I'm not going to stir shit up. I need some peace."

"So, what are you going to do then? I mean… about Kathy?"

"Nothing. I think it's over between us. My summer is over. My girlfriend is over and… I'm probably over. She's going off to college. I am going back to finish high school and get stuck spending the next two years with you and Steve."

"She's going to college? I didn't know that, and… hey! We're not so bad… are we? And there are other girls around here, you know? Mike T's been telling everybody that Shelagh Bennett has the hots for you. She's pretty good looking! Well, except for that bubble butt."

"Give it break, huh Brian. It's not that big. Besides, she's a nice girl."

"Oh crap, Cos. You're always saying that about girls. She's a nice girl… blah, blah, blah."

"Well, it's true."

"Okay, but she's kind waiting in line for you and… not me, even though I'm the coolest guy in this town. You know, Cos, I wouldn't pass up on that, bubble butt or not. I mean if she was hot for me…"

I punched him in the arm for saying that again, and he just laughed. Taking a bite of cinnamon roll, he spit it at me. I fished out a donut and slammed it into his back, turning his black tee shirt white with powder.

"Ahhh! You fucker."

"Not yet! But hope to be soon!"

He looked like he wanted to hit me, but only grinned.

"Hey! What's that?" he said, pointing.

I thought it was trick to get me to look away so he could pinch me, smack me, or pull my hair. That was when I noticed the blue condom package was sticking out of my shirt pocket. He snatched it before I got the chance to push it back inside.

"A rubber! So, you are doing it! You sneaky devil."

"No, Steve stuck that in there. He was expecting to get laid last night, so he gave me one of his."

"Steve? Who'd screw Steve? Man! He'd have a tough time finding a cave woman to have sex with."

I almost let it slip about Steve's cousin, but I realized that might be the end of Steve here in Clarksburg. I felt I had Steve's life in my hands. It would be easy to ruin everything for him by just opening my big mouth. I couldn't do that, though, it wasn't right.

"I believe I'm going to keep this. I might need it. Who knows?" Brian said.

"Me, that's who! You'll never use it, well… accept maybe in a water balloon fight."

"Hell! You're not going to use it either… not now."

"You're probably right there, as much as I hate to admit it."

"So, you're breaking it off with Kathy and you're back with the pack? The Rat Pack!"

"I suppose I am… and who the hell are you? Frank Sinatra? It was bad enough when you were James Dean."

Ignoring me and ripping open the condom package, he pulled it out. He surprised me by blowing it up and tying it off. I grabbed for it, but he pulled away. Then smacking me in the face with it, he got lubricant all over my nose. We tussled for it and the balloon got away. The breeze took it up into the sky with us just watching it disappear over the roof tops. Looking at each other like it was some kind of a sign, Brian grinned and said, "Oh man! That was weird!"

"Yeah, I suppose," I said.

"You suppose? There's no supposing…" he said as he ripped the bag of cinnamon rolls, down the side. Then pulling them out one at a time, he started flinging them against the side of Whitcomb's building, trying to make them stick. Then dropping the plastic bag on the ground, he surprised me by throwing his arm over my shoulder, again.

I figured this time he was trying to get close enough to put me in a headlock, but he only said, "Let's go do something fun. Hey, you know… Mike T has a brand new minibike. Let's go up there and ride the shit out of it! He won't mind."

"Sounds like fun… I guess. Hey! He has a sister. Kim, I think her name is. You might stand a chance with her."

"Naw, the hell with girls. Let's go have some fun that doesn't include somebody with boobs, alright?"

"Uhhh… okay," I said, even though I really didn't agree.

Brian seemed to be the happiest I had ever seen him. That was good for us both. I needed a friend, and he had mysteriously appeared at the right time. I started to worry that it was for all the wrong reasons, though. I was afraid my spat with Kathy was more like, '*My pain-his gain.*' I decided to just let it go, and that seemed a lot easier now than it did before.

I was right back to where I was in May. That was not what I wanted. I wanted a girlfriend. I wanted to spend time with girls, doing things that boy and girlfriends do together. Not riding mini bikes, or sneaking out to raid gardens, stealing pumpkins, or setting off fire crackers. I liked what I had with Kathy, and now that I had a taste of that—even going fishing seemed like a waste of time.

Brian stood up, saying, "Let's get our asses out of here."

Grabbing the comic book, he rolled it up and after smacking me on top of my head, he stuck it in his back pocket. Walking out into the lot, I followed him. As we made our way to the street, I thought it would be funny to leave a half-finished box of donuts on the rack. Closing the lid and putting it next to the others, I imagined Phil or Grandma Schneider's face when they came across it. That look would be priceless. Too bad I wasn't going to stick around to see it.

Brian and I crossed over to Nordon's just as Phil Schneider pulled his fancy black Mercedes into the lot. We took off running, laughing loud and crazy. Slipping in between the telephone office and the library, we headed up toward Mike T's place.

"Guess what? I heard some shit that you want to be a writer someday. True?"

"Ahhh crap! How did you find out?"

"Don't worry about it. You know, Bart wanted to be a writer. A newspaper guy, I think."

"Really?"

"Yeah. It's fine with me if you want to do that. Oh! And if anyone gives you crap about it, just tell me. I'll kick their ass! But right now… I going to kick yours."

Swinging his leg back from the knee, he kicked me in the backside with the heel of his foot. I returned the favor and jumped away when he tried to grab me. He finally caught me, though, but instead of giving me a snake-bite or a Dutch rub, he threw his arm over my shoulder for the third time. Throwing mine over his, I listened as he yakked on about his time over in Paris.

We rode the mini-bike all afternoon and then spent the rest of the evening at the Blue Front, playing pool. It was open until ten, and we both went straight home after. I was beat. It was the first time in a long time that I actually wanted to go to bed.

Brian and I seemed to be back to normal. That's what he wanted. And well, I guess—so did I. But I still had that feeling in my gut. Kind of like there was a beaver in there just gnawing away. I kept wishing that Kathy would come. If we had to end it, then it should be face to face. Even if it was like it was that one day in the cemetery. I'd try to see things her way, admitting to myself that it was partly my fault because I had run away from her last night. But I was drunk. I figured if she loved me like she said, then she wouldn't let it end this way. It was easier for her to come to me than I to her. I kept my fingers crossed, hoping that she would realize that, too.

Chapter 19

<u>Monday, Monday, Can't Trust That Day</u>

On Monday I went up to Eddy's place as planned, but the old Sachs wasn't ready yet. We sat around the shop, bugging his dad, and riding the Cushman around the yard. I was glad he was such a funny guy because there was never a dull moment. He could tell some amazing stories and he would act out every one of them. Being with Eddy was like going to a really good play. It helped take my mind off my Kathy problem. That was, until he brought her up.

We were sitting behind his da on upturned buckets in the shop. The Mama's and the Papa's were on the radio belting out 'Monday, Monday' and how you couldn't trust it. The way the day was stacking up, I believed it. Eddy's da was right in the middle of reinstalling the magneto on the faded blue Sachs, and he was having a tough time of it. We were handing him tools when he called out for them. That's when Eddy said, "So, how'd things go at the Harvest Fair?"

I sighed and said, "Not so great. I think it's safe to say, we broke up."

"Oh man! I just knew it. That was almost too good to be true."

"What do you mean?"

"Well, you're definitely no rockstar, or… some Robert Redford. I guess, neither are the rest of us. That girl was one serious babe."

"You really think that has something to do with it?"

"Well… yeah! I mean… you need to stick to your own kind, Cos. She was…"

"What? Too good for me. Too rich for me?"

"Uh-huh! You know damn well those people aren't like us. You need to find a biker chick."

"You think a biker chick is going to be any different? I don't think I want a biker chick."

"Why not? They'll stand by you and practically worship the ground you walk on."

"How do you know that? You've never had a girlfriend—ever. Least not since I've known you, anyway."

"Yeah, well… I've met a few biker babes and… that's what I see. My mom was a biker chick."

"Well, I think you're full of crap, Eddy Beltzer."

"Naw! Ask my dad! He'll tell you!"

Eddy's da was just finishing up and turning to us, he wiped a greasy hand across his sweaty forehead, saying, "If you two are going to keep carrying on like a bunch of imbeciles, you can just get the hell out of here."

"But dad… tell him!"

"Go!" he said and gave us look that would have stopped a charging bull.

Eddy didn't argue. Getting up, we went outside. He started up the Cushman and took off riding around the yard in big circles for the twentieth time. So, I sat on his little sister's swing set, watching.

What he had said, bothered me. Now, I agree with my sister, Fiana, on just about everything and not because I was afraid of making her mad. I mean, we've had some pretty serious fights. It was more because she just made sense. I knew she would have gotten royally pissed about what Eddy was telling me. If she had heard that stuff, she might try to kick his arse. I decided to just drop it. If I got up in his face any more than I already had, it would probably come to blows. If his ma was a biker chick, and his da felt the same, then I might get the crap beat out of me by the whole family.

An hour later, it was raining and we ended up in the house. Eddy went to telling me a story about the time he was doing jumps on his da's, Yamaha motocrosser down at the Pits. He was standing in the middle of his bedroom, acting out the more exciting parts, but I was getting tired at this point. I needed a change of scenery. His ma finally called us down for supper and I was glad for that.

I changed my mind about being glad ten minutes later. She was being a bear about everything. I, honestly, didn't know if that was the way she was all the time or just because I was there. She was being a real grouch, pushing everyone around, sometimes grabbing her younger kids by the fronts of their shirts and shaking her finger in their faces. It was making me uncomfortable. When she started coming after yours truly, I decided it was time to go.

Luckily for me, the rain had stopped. So, I asked Eddy if he wanted to go to the Dairy Dreem. He said no. His da wanted him to help out in the shop, holding stuff, and besides, the Sachs was almost done. I'd had enough of the Beltzer's. Leaving by the back door, I heard his ma mumble, "Good riddance." I wanted to tell her how much her meatloaf sucked, but she was washing knives and I wanted them to go in the drawer with the others, and not in my back. So, I decided to forget about sassing back and headed over to the Dairy Dreem.

I was going to give Shelagh a good teasing. It had been a while since I'd razzed her about anything. I knew she could take it, and would probably dish it right back. Least that was the plan, anyway, down deep, though, I think I just wanted to hang out with a girl. My sisters weren't available, and now with Kathy out of the picture, that left my ma. That would have made me too blue, I needed a little more sunshine and since it wasn't coming from the sky at the moment, it was going to have to come from somebody a wee bit more... optimistic, I think the word is.

With Shelagh close at hand and being somewhat of a captive audience, she would be the best choice. Besides, I was pretty sure she'd like the company. So, the good part about me walking in that door was that she was thrilled to see me. The bad part—every fifteen minutes she tried talking me into going out on a date. It was more of the same. After a while she tried coming at it from several different directions and I figured she thought she could fool me into saying yes. I never told her about Saturday night, but for some reason, she already knew.

"So, Cos… I heard you went to the Harvest Fair?"

"Ummm… yeah, who told you?"

"Oh… it doesn't matter. It's not like I'm spying on you or anything."

"So... tell me?"

"Why? So, you can have Crazy Vaughn go and hit them in the head with a hammer?" She laughed after she said that, and I gave her my Clint Eastwood squint from my booth across the room under the huge front windows. As I finished off my third free drink, she came over and sat down next. Sliding right up against me, she trapped me against the short wall. I had nowhere to go unless I slid down under the table and crawled out.

"So, tell me… how'd it go? The Harvest Fair, I mean. Did you have a good time? Rumor has it… NOT!"

"Yeah… well… it kind of sucked, because…"

"Because you broke up with, Miss Rich Girl?"

"What? Who told… Oh, forget it."

"Okay, if you must know, my boss… you know… Mr. Goldsberry? He was cleaning up in the backroom of the Creamy Cone and he saw you sit down on his bench. He said you were having a pretty tough time of it and that maybe you were drunk or… high?"

"High? I had a couple beers… that's all."

"Well, anyway… after you got up and walked away, he stuck his head out of the door and saw some guy coming after you. Then some tall girl was there… yelling at you. That was probably Kathy, right?"

"So, he saw the whole thing and now he's telling everybody?"

"I don't think he's telling everybody, but… he told me. He saw Kathy running after you and then he didn't see you anymore."

"So, what makes you think we broke up?"

"Well… don't be mad, okay? But your friend Brian was in here when I came to work. He stopped in with his mom to get burgers. So, I asked him how you were. I was a little worried. I worry about my friends… we are friends, right? I always felt like we were, anyway." Her look was serious and it made realize how important it was to her that we were. So, I said, "I suppose we are. So, what did Brian say?"

"Oh, nothing much really. He said, you weren't in good shape. When I asked why, he said you were pretty unhappy about your break up. So… did you? Break up, I mean?"

I didn't say anything and just stared out the window. She reached up and pushed the hair out of my face. It surprised me and I jumped. Looking back at her, I must have scared her a little, because her eyes got enormous. But then she smiled and went to playing with the hair on my arm, saying, "Well… did you?"

"If you must know—probably… I mean we haven't talked for a few days."

"Do you want to talk about it? I mean… to me? You might feel better if you told someone."

"No, I don't want to talk about it. I already talked with Brian and look what that got me."

"Well, don't be upset at him… or me, for that matter. We are your friends and we care about you. So… maybe we can hang out together, more often. You and me? Maybe, after you get over Kathy, we could go out sometime?"

"I don't want to make any promises. I don't know how I will feel in a week, or… even a month. Can we change the subject?"

"Sure," she said, in a dreamy voice. That was when a woman pulled up outside with a bunch of little kids. Leaning over toward me, she pushed her boobs against my arm and surprised me by kissing me on the cheek. Before I could say anything, she jumped up and dashed behind the counter to wait on her customers.

I should have taken that as my cue to leave. But like a fool, I stayed until closing time, helping her lock up. She didn't bring the dating subject up anymore. Instead, she talked about her future and how she was going to nursing school after she graduated. When she offered me a ride home, I turned her down. I will admit I was afraid to get in the car with her.

I didn't go inside the apartment when I got home. Instead, I crawled into Rowett's VW camper van that was parked way down at the end of the backyard on the grass. I had heard Rams Rowett loudly complaining, through our ceiling from their apartment upstairs, how he had blown its engine and it wasn't going anywhere. So, that made it a good place to crash.

I lay there on the mattress, in the dark, trying to sort out why I didn't want to give in to Shelagh. There were times when I wanted to hang out with her, but they were fewer than the times I didn't. It was like I thought she might be different when I saw her the next time. That made me wonder if I wasn't as smart as I thought I was. Soon, the memories of Saturday night rolled in and I just about drove myself nuts trying to sort out ways to fix this thing. It was going to take some time to get over it, that much I knew. Sadly, I had no idea how long.

Chapter 20

Tuesday rolled around hot and sticky. I crawled out of the VW camper, itching and aching, feeling a little crazy with worry. I simply wanted it all to end. I was as blue as the day I discovered my da had vanished and had taken my sisters with him. I thought about making a phone call to the Henton's, hoping I could convince whoever answered to let me talk with Kathy. Changing my mind, I just wandered around the town. I was in an out of the tavern, up and down the street, stopping sometimes to look at the phone booth. Finally, I sat down at the corner, to keep an eye peeled for that little green Pinto.

After an hour, I moved down to my stoop to worry in a different spot for a while. I saw Ernie come out of the front door of his shop and bracing himself up against the jam to keep from falling, he waved me down. I had never seen him stand on his feet before. The sight of him there made me glad I was still too young to have gone to Vietnam. I couldn't see myself wanting to live if I survived getting shot, being blown up by a grenade, or going around with parts of me missing.

As usual, he had work for me. I took it even though it would be hard to keep my mind on what I was doing. For some weird reason, it was he who switched the radio to 106.5. I wondered if he did it for me.

He wasn't a minute back to his project when 'Wildflower' came pouring out of the speaker. Part of me wanted to get up and shut it off, but another part of me wanted to listen to the whole song. The first part would have been the better of my two choices. Half way through, I couldn't take it anymore. There was no way I could stay. Dropping my wrench, I ran out with Ernie yelling, "Hey Cos! Where you going?"

I headed up to the corner but stopped in front of Carl's Dry Cleaner to wipe my eyes. Ever since Saturday, my tears came all too easily. It seemed I had a full tank, and the shut off valve wasn't working anymore. The song had caused me to lose control and even though Ernie B hollered at me to come back, I knew he wouldn't want me down there, sniveling away. I figured I'd go find Harry since Brian was out at Steve's helping bale hay. If I weren't able find him, I could always go up to Eddy's and see if the Sachs was ready to ride. Anything that would be different, fun, and not remind me of Kathy.

I realized I was missing Fiana something terrible. She was older and pretty smart for her age. We used to talk a lot. I figured if anyone could point me in the right direction, it would be her. Shauna was two years younger than me, so she wouldn't be of any help. Besides, we were always fighting. When I realized that Carl's wife and grown-up daughter, Eleanor, were standing at the window, watching me. I thought to flip them off but that whole 'trying to be a nicer guy experiment' must have helped. So, instead, I screwed up my face and stuck my tongue out at them. They laughed and I stomped away, deciding I should go someplace a wee bit more private.

When I got to the corner, there was a big surprise waiting for me. The Henton's car was out front of the Royal Blue. Seeing it gave me a kind of rush and my throat went dry. The bee's made a grand entrance and my face got hot.

There was a good chance that Kathy might be up there. It was SG night, but it was way too early. They had at least two hours before showtime. I figured it must be a special premier or something and they needed an early start to getting set up. Sitting down on the corner, I waited.

Not even two minutes later, Billy James came dancing up the sidewalk from the river bridge. Billy's was from the only black family that lived in Clarksburg. He lived next door to Willowbough Boyd at the south end of town where some really old cabins sat in a row along the railroad tracks. Willowbough was known to get a lot a crap for no reason other than she was an indian. But the James' got it twice as bad. I always stood up for Billy and sometimes I was the one who got the worst of it. The meanness went from being about black folks, to about being Irish. Of course, when I was getting the worst of it, if Brian, Steve, or Harry were hanging around, then they'd help me. Now, I'll admit that my friends didn't like Billy anymore than some of those other people—but they liked me. So, I decided I could use that to my advantage, and—I hoped, Billy's.

I watched him come my way. He was not only dancing, he was singing. His blue striped shirt was too big for him and because it was tucked into his trousers and his belt was cinched so tight, it looked like he was wearing a balloon. His clodhopper boots were untied, and the laces were flapping. When he got closer, I could hear the song he was singing. It was '*Stand!*' by Sly & The Family Stone and he wasn't so much dancing, as he was acting out the verses.

He'd stop and take up a stance and then pointing to the right with his arm as straight as he could get it, he brought his finger around until it got as far as it could go to the left. His eyes followed that finger all the way around. The song seemed to be meant for an audience he was imagining. Then he'd march forward, only to stop and raise a militant fist to the sky and stare proudly into the distance as if he too had taken a stand. It was a wee bit crazy, but I liked it. That kid was bold and he had some moves.

When he got up to where I was sitting, he didn't seem to care at all that I was watching. He kept right on singing and acting. Then he stopped and in what I would call a dramatic way, he pointed right at me and he sang out, "Stand!" this was followed by some words about me sitting too long and there being a crease in my right and wrong. I grinned at him and I felt myself blush.

He stopped for two seconds, winked at me, said, "Hey, Cos," and then spun away. He went right back into his routine, crossed the street, and continued on down the sidewalk past the Blue Front. When he got to the Davis' Café, some people came out, but he didn't stop. Those people acted like they were afraid of him and jumped back to give him room to get by. Some people just don't appreciate a good performance!

When Billy reached the next corner at Hale's Hardware, he took a right and was gone. Those people were still standing there, talking among themselves, and some old guy was scratching his head like he just couldn't sort it.

Now, I felt something that I don't normally feel. I think it's called inspiration. I didn't know for sure; I'd probably have to go look it up. But knowing the exact definition didn't matter as much as the feeling, even if I was wrong. It made me feel hope and that's a feeling I was quite familiar with. Billy had inspired me. It was unexpected, but it was just what I needed so I could move forward.

I heard the door at the top of the stairwell to the lodge slam shut, and I whipped my head around so hard I hurt my neck. I crossed my fingers, hoping it would be Kathy stomping down those stairs. But it was Averell. She was carrying a cardboard carton. Even at that distance she looked mad as hell. Stepping off the curb, she walked to the Cadillac and stuck the carton in the back seat. She then slammed that door and as she stood there staring in the window of the car, I heard, "Bullshit!"

She then looked up at the windows of the lodge and then around her like she wanted to make sure no one heard her. Our eyes met and she smiled big time. A window up on the second floor of the Royal Blue opened up and her ma poked her head out.

"Come on back up here, sweety, there's more."

"Okay, give me a minute," she yelled up and then looking back at me, she smiled even bigger than before and walked over. The window shut and that's when her da came down and stood on the sidewalk, watching her. I got ready to bolt.

"You come on back here, little lady, we've got work to do."

Then he stared right at me. If looks could kill, I would have been just a bleeding corpse on the sidewalk when Averell got to me. That's when Mrs. Henton came down, and taking Seymour by the arm, she led him back upstairs. She didn't have to say anything, he just went right along with her. He was still looking back over his shoulder, though, trying to kill me with his eyes.

Averell stopped to stand in front of me and said, "Hi."

"Averell… uhhh… what's happening."

She looked so much like a smaller version of Kathy that it kind of scared me. Her face was a little rounder, though, her boobs were bigger, and she had those pale blue eyes, instead of green. Averell had all the markings of a Henton, though. The freckles, the milky skin, and that big, second toe sticking out of her sandals.

Her short, pink Tee shirt said, 'FOXY!' in big, white letters across the front, and it showed her belly button. Her bell-bottom jeans were the new style—tight and low-riding. It was then I realized how gorgeous she was. I could smell her—all bubble bath and Tea Rose perfume. A brand Brian had sprayed on me one day when we were down at Nordon's. It was going to be tough talking to her.

"Can I sit down?"

"Sure," I said, "Free country."

She planted her backside on the curb and then had to go and slide right up against me. I got excited. My face got hotter, and I felt sweat come out on my forehead. There was something about her that turned me on. Why didn't I get like this with Tammy, or… Shelagh? Kathy and Averell seemed to have some kind of magic. Now, Averell's right hip was touching mine for the first time, and I was afraid I was going to melt.

The thing is, part of me didn't seem to mind, but another part said, '*No way! Don't be a fool.*' Then Fiana's voice in my head, "*Don't you sell out, little brother!*"

"You okay?" Averell asked. "You're not afraid of me, are you?"

"Uhhh… no. What about your folks? I bet they're not happy you're over here talking to me."

"Of course they're not, duh! At least my dad's not… but my mom's okay with it. She knows better. Well, anyway, they're probably watching me right now, and ummm… I don't give a damn. Besides, they know I'm not going anywhere. I've got to get ready for our skits soon, and I have to practice my lines. So, yeah… I'll have to get back up there in a couple minutes."

"So, why are you over here? Trying to get into trouble by being seen with me?"

"You were hoping it was Kathy coming down those stairs, right? That's who you were waiting for, I'll bet."

"You know, I was, and… so what?"

"Kathy's not coming. She decided to leave a week early. So, she packed up her stuff and left Sunday morning for Des Moines. She won't be back until Thanksgiving."

"What? But…"

"I'm sorry, Cos. She told me to tell you that she just couldn't face you. I think because she's ashamed—like she should be."

"She and I could've talked, you know. We could have sorted it. What the hell?"

"I don't know what to say. I'm still here, though. We get along okay. What about me?"

"You don't even have a car, how are you going to come down here, and what about your da, he hates me. Do you think he's going to be any easier on you? Besides, it not the same. I still love your sister."

She leaned back, looking at me like I was nuts. After a minute of that, she moved her eyes down to her hands lying in her lap. Scratching at the peeling red polish on one of her fingernails, she said without looking up, "Don't you think… you could love me? Don't you think you could fall in love with me? What's wrong with me, Cos? Aren't I pretty enough?"

Averell lifted her face just high enough to look at me out of the tops of her eyes. I felt like she was trying to make me feel guilty. I also didn't think she truly believed she wasn't pretty enough. She was casting her spell. She knew just what she wanted and she was going to try her damndest to get it.

"It's not like that, Averell. It's not that easy. I mean… your beautiful and all, but I hardly know you."

She smiled big like she was glad to hear the part about being beautiful. I got a feeling that she thought she'd hooked me. To finish me off, she leaned forward and brought her soft lips to where they were just touching my ear. A bolt of electricity shot through me and I shivered a little. I was pretty sure she felt it.

"You could… get to know me," she said in a sexy voice, reminding me of another I had heard that one day back in May.

I looked at her out of the corner of my eye as she added, "You know, Cos, I already have my driver's license. All I need to do is get that car you're so worried about."

She then slid away a wee bit, and broke contact. I felt relieved. The buzzing of the bees melted away and my head cleared. I realized there may be one way to get out of this. Get mad. If I got mad, I might not seem like such a nice guy, after all. So, I said in a loud, mean voice,

"I'm not worried about a car!" Turning my head, I faced her, giving her my squinty eyed look. She blinked a couple times like I'd surprised her. So, I pushed it a little harder.

"I don't think you understand. I love your sister. I love Kathy. It's not something that happened overnight."

"Sure it did."

"What?" I said, now doing some blinking of my own. She had called my bluff.

"Not something that happened overnight. More like… in a couple hours if I remember correctly. Least that's what Kathy said on the way home that day."

"She said that?"

"Listen, Cos. Couldn't we try? Couldn't you give me a chance? We are both sixteen now. I could come down and see you. I could get a ride or something. We could hang out together—all day, if you want."

That's when she crossed her left leg over her right. The Birkenstock sandal slipped off her foot and fell down to clack on the asphalt. The next thing I knew, her toes were moving up and down my leg. My plan wasn't going to work. Pretending to be mad seemed to make it more exciting for her. I kind of rotated to the right and put my legs out of reach. Then looking back over my shoulder, I said, "You're driving me nuts, Averell. Don't get me wrong, though, I like you, you're a great girl. It's just… I fell in love with your sister. That didn't simply end. And now, I find out she wasn't brave enough to come talk with me? Worst of all… she left me here. She just left me."

"I'm sorry, but it's not my fault. I tried to talk her out of it. The leaving… I mean. But she said, she'd had enough of this place. She had to get out of here. She didn't care, Cos. She really didn't care anymore. And so… she wanted you to see her with that creepy Chas guy. She decided it was time for it to be over and felt that was the only way she could convince you to forget about her. She didn't really like that guy. It was all for show."

"Well… seems like you Henton's are all about that."

"Cos! That's not fair. I'm not like that."

"Sorry, but…"

"Let me talk, please! Kathy told me in the beginning that because you were such a nice guy, she'd never have to worry about you cheating on her. She also said she tried to explain to you that it would be best if you two went your separate ways when it came time for her to go. My sister didn't feel like you gave her much choice. She knew you wouldn't like it if she was with some other guy. So, you'd get mad, and then want to break up. Kind of like, well… cruel to be kind, if you know what I mean?"

"I know about her plan. I heard you two talking that night at the fair."

"You should also know, I thought it was mean, and I told her so."

"Yes, I heard that, too."

She got quiet and looked relieved like there was a good chance she was changing my mind. But it was just that I didn't know what else to say. I stared into those pale blue eyes, wondering if I was making the right decision.

If I gave in, I'd be back to having a girlfriend. There was something about her that set me on fire, and I had to fight like hell to resist it. The Seymour issue came to mind, and I winced like someone had slapped me.

Averell's father wasn't going to let me into their life. I believed that, in his mind, I would be stealing his youngest girl. His princess. He would come down hard on me for that. I didn't want to be with someone whose family didn't like me because they thought I was trash. On top of that, it would be too weird if I dated Averell knowing sooner or later, I'd run into Kathy.

There was also something gnawing at me. Something about Averell that was obvious, but nobody ever talked about. She wanted whatever Kathy had. Like my little sister, Shauna, she wanted whatever Fiana and I got, and not so much one of her own—but more like she wanted to have ours, too.

Averell was looking at me real hard like she was waiting for me to say something. I felt like I needed to get away from her and break the spell. I gave her a look that was supposed to say, 'Sorry, not going to happen' But she didn't get it. Instead, she gave me a shy smile and flipped her reddish-blonde hair.

"Would you kiss me?" she said. Would you kiss me, like… you did my sister that day in the park? Right out in the open? Right… in front of my parents?"

My thoughts flew back to that moment when Billy had stopped and sang that line to me. It wasn't so much the words, but the look on his face, but he was right, I'd been sitting too long and I needed to get to my feet and take a stand. I got up and walked away without a word.

Chapter 21

<u>The Long And Winding Road</u>

After my talk with Averell, I began to feel like I needed a change. I started to avoid the corner, even if I saw the guys were up there. If I went out, I'd go straight to the tavern, calling them over to join me as I went through the door. I felt I needed to stay out of sight. A change of habit was instore, which meant doing something other than hang around. Mr. Ward had said one time that I needed to be more productive in order to create purpose. I had scoffed at him that day—but I wasn't scoffing now. He was right, it's just… he would never know, but he didn't need too. It was all on me.

It was about a week before school was to start that I saw Averell in town. She was driving a blue, '74 Camaro. I was sitting at the big window in the library, reading *Watership Down* when she idled by. She was looking around like she hoped to see somebody she knew. I stayed put, hoping she'd go away before the library closed.

Chuck and the other jocks had taken to avoiding me like I had leprosy. Even to go as far as to move to the opposite side of the hallway when I walked past. Mike T got brave enough to quit the football team; along with all the other sports. He grew his hair out and was spending more time with his car, plus, all the girls he was giving rides to. Sometimes Vaughn's pickup truck would rattle by the high school at lunch time. We'd toss the big roofer a wave when he laid on the horn. Chuck and his gang just melted away into the landscape, not to be seen until class time.

I started putting in a few more hours at Ernie B's, going straight down there almost every day after school, and all day on Saturday. There was something else that I got serious about: homework. I pushed my grade level up to all A's and of course, the guys had to give me a bunch of crap about that. But that didn't matter, we were going in different directions and I needed to be prepared. A few people took the time to convince me it was in my best interest to start taking my future into consideration. People I had come to trust. I quit smoking—and the drinking was put on hold. It was not like beer was going to disappear off the face of the earth anytime soon. It would be there when I went looking for it.

I was still spending a little time at the Dairy Dreem, and I did date Shelagh—once. We went to the dance at the county fair, but it didn't go well. She ended up with Mike T at the end of the night and they kind of fell out of my life forever. Harry did hookup with Saleena, and they seemed to get along quite well. But for me—I dated no one else from Coogan or Clarksburg, ever again.

It was in the spring of '75, when my ma ended up in the mental institution for her second time. I found myself back on the farm, but I would soon be off for college, come August. I'd won a government funded scholarship in Creative Writing with the help and prompting of ol' Wilhelmina Theobald.

I finally got my hair cut off, but I didn't let ol' Starkey do it. Margie, at Margie's Hair Salon, up on our corner, got that honor. It was kind of strange because she took 'before and after' photos and asked if she could keep the hair when she finished. I watched her gather it up and put it in a huge, plastic baggie as I looked back through the window in her front door. I figured she wanted to keep it for bragging rights. Somebody told me she braided it and had hung it on her bulletin board. They said she tacked the photos above it and wrote on a piece of tape, underneath, *'The only boy customer I ever had with hair as long as a girl's!'* Weird, huh?

The happiest day of that year was when I got an unexpected visit from Fiana and Shauna at the farm. Fiana had been off to UC Berkley and came back to Iowa for a visit at the end of her summer break. Shauna still lived with my da, but supposedly, she might move in with my ma when she got out of the institution. Fiana told me our da left that first woman he had run off with and married a second. Moving to a small town over by the Mississippi, he had taken up hauling corn to the barges.

He dropped my sisters off outside our uncle's place and took off without coming inside. When he returned to pick them up, he sat in the car down at the end of the lane, just honking his horn. He made them hoof it down there, which made me want to follow and give him some crap. Fiana told me not too. I gave in, figuring it was best for everyone.

It was about two weeks before I was off for my freshman year at college that I went with my aunt into Clarksburg for groceries. I thought I'd ride along and maybe say goodbye to everyone. I didn't see the guys around anywhere, so I headed for the Blue Front.

They weren't in there. Arnie was alone doing some spot cleaning. He was truly happy to see me and ruffled my hair. We talked for a wee bit and then I headed out. As I opened the door to leave, he called out, "Still have some cokes in the fridge in the back that have to go? If you stick around, you can have one on the house?" Laughing, he slapped his rag on the empty bar and then went to wiping it, grinning like a madman. I laughed and after giving him a thumbs up, I let the door close and did a fast walk down to Ernie B's

My time there was brief and somewhat bitter. When I told him why I was there, he grew quiet. Sitting on his mechanics creeper, he just stared down at the floor.

"I suppose you'd better get going or you might miss your ride."

When I didn't leave right away, his wrench slipped out of his hand and clanked on the floor. Not bothering to pick it up, he looked out the overhead door toward his little house and said, "See you, Cos."

I hesitated, and reaching out, I patted him on the shoulder. He sighed and dropped his eyes to the floor. I decided I'd better get out of there before something happened that he didn't want me to see. Walking out of the door, I headed up to meet my aunt, fearful she might have forgotten that I'd rode in with her and leave town without me. It would be a long walk back to the farm. Hoping the guys were at the corner by then, I found it empty. Our reign as the rockstars of the summer corner was over.

John and Stu were in their usual place with now about five other old guys sitting around them at the river's edge. I hollered their names and waved as we passed over the bridge. I'm sure they had no idea who was yelling at them.

I never came back.

Harry, Brian, and Steve all became ghosts in my past. I heard Brian joined the Navy straight out of high school. My uncle told me he'd run across Steve at auction, saying something about him taking over his father's farm. The newspaper told us that Harry got thrown in jail for thirty days. He had broken his own rule and went over to the Prairieville Ballroom. Some drunk guy made fun of Saleena for being an indian and Harry added him to the long list of people he'd sent to the hospital.

The curse of the quiet Sunday had not abandoned me. Without even the slightest warning, it snuck back, hitting me the hardest it ever had. It was the 3rd of August. I happened to be sitting at the table for breakfast with my uncle as he read the newspaper. My aunt had been in the kitchen, frying eggs and bacon. My uncle suddenly called out to her, "Darlin', I see dere's been anoder accident. Looks like a local lass, about twenty somedin' from up Coogan way. A Kaddy Henton? How about ya, Cos, know a Kaddy Henton? Got killed out on de motorway drivin' back from Des Moines, last evenin'."

"Such a shame," I barely heard my aunt say. "Always so sad when the young ones leave us before their time."

I knew he meant Kathy.

I stood up and walked around the table. He spread the paper open for me to have a look. The full color photo showed the Pinto smashed into an overpass abutment. The front end of another car was visible, seemingly fused into the back of the fire blackened Ford. The shock came as a wave of electricity rolling up from my feet to the top of my head. My guts turned cold as stone.

I would never see Kathy again.

Until this moment, there had been hope that maybe someday we'd cross paths. Then we could talk about all the things which never got talked about. Now—it would never be. And as my ma had put it once, "*Dere will be a lifetime of unfinished business.*" With her words running through my head, I now, without a doubt, understood what they meant. The pain of loss lay heavy like a cold, wet blanket across my shoulders.

I thought about Brian and his brother, Bart. Then, my granny, my mother's mother, and the moment we'd first learned of her suicide back in Ireland. The very thing that had driven my ma to try the same. Mae McDhai's ticket back to the mental institution. I felt that life was an ocean of tragedy with the waves constantly crashing into us, never allowing us to gain our feet.

I turned away from that all too confirming photo. Walking in a daze from that big farm house, a searing numbness filled my nose. A state of semi-paralysis took over my body, and I found it hard to move. It was like I was slogging through knee deep mud. Going to the barn, I climbed up into the hayloft and stumbled across the loose hay to the tire swing.

I don't remember climbing on, but I hung there for a long time, swinging slowly, my mind fast becoming a jumble of memories. One of them stuck and pushed itself to the front. A picture of Kathy down by the river. Her face came so very clear as she told me about that terrible day when she too rode a swing in the loft of a distant barn. The lyrics of 'Wildflower' flowed in, and I fell apart.

Tumbling backward into the deep piled hay, I curled up with my tears. My sobs echoed through the rafters, and I found I could not care less if anyone should hear. If my time with Kathy had taught me anything, it was how to cry. It was as if she'd broken through my fortification, and standing atop the pile of rubble, she had dared me to come out and face the world. Now, she was gone forever, and I wasn't sure I'd find happiness ever again.

Over a year would pass before that epiphanal moment would come. It showed up on a sunny, summer day as I sat at a table outside a place very much like the Dairy Dreem. I was sharing a banana split with my girlfriend, Marie. We were discussing our future together, listening to 'The Long And Winding Road' by the Beatles, as it flowed out of the speakers set high on the wall underneath the canopy.

A lime-colored Pinto, spotted with rust, came whipping into the parking lot and screeched to a halt. My heart leapt into my throat. Marie said, "Are you okay? You look like you've seen a ghost." Before I could confirm that I had, another car loaded with kids sped in. Pulling in beside the first, they piled out, laughing. With everyone talking at once, they gathered around the small Ford, waiting for the occupants to emerge. Soon, a long-haired teen boy and a very tall, dark-haired girl climbed out. Coming together at the front bumper, they kissed, the boy having to stand on his toes to reach the girl's lips. Then holding hands, they strolled inside, the others following in raucous banter.

I watched the young lovers through the huge windows as they interacted with the others. I took in all the signs of a budding romance and each kid's reaction to the couple. The harmless teasing, the innocent laughter, and the half-hearted disagreements. Looks were thrown, arms crossed in defense, and then hurt feelings were quenched with subtle touch and reassuring apology.

That heavy, wet blanket of misery that had lain across my shoulders for so long, seemed to melt away, becoming a mere, tell-tale ache. It was now just a feeling very much like tired muscles at the end of a satisfying workday. A discomfort that would soon to be extinguished by the reward of a well-deserved rest.

Out of the corner of my eye, I saw Marie throw me another questioning look as a ridiculously large grin spread across my face. The memories of life in a small Iowa town came flooding in and filled my head with reflection. I felt grateful for the lessons learned, and a time when I had such friends.

www.ingramcontent.com/pod-product-compliance
Lightning Source LLC
Chambersburg PA
CBHW071402100726
47908CB00004B/1068